"You."

Oh, no. Merryn's hear̶̶ ̶̶ ̶̶ ̶̶ ̶̶ ̶̶ ̶̶ buttoned boots because it was the man from the fair. Hearing the door close softly behind her, she realized the butler had retreated after doubtlessly taking in that short, damning greeting.

"My lord," she said at last. She made a formal curtsy; Liam, following her lead, gave a little bow. "This is a surprise to me also."

Her voice was calm and that amazed her, because inside she was so shaken that she felt sick. What kind of cruel joke had fate played on her this time?

"Please enlighten me," he said. His voice—every bit as rich and deep as she remembered—was etched with incredulity. "Is this some kind of blackmail, perhaps? Are you here to ask for money?"

"Of course not!" She clamped down on her anger while thinking, *Hateful, hateful man*. "I'm actually here on legitimate business, my lord."

"Really?" There was sheer disbelief in that one word.

"Yes! My name is Miss Merryn Hythe. This is my brother, Liam—and I'm here to claim Liam's inheritance."

You could have heard a pin drop. It was the earl who finally broke the silence. "Well." He spoke exceedingly softly. "You've been plotting hard since last night, haven't you?"

LUCY ASHFORD

—

Challenging the Brooding Earl

HARLEQUIN®
HISTORICAL™

Recycling programs
for this product may
not exist in your area.

ISBN-13: 978-1-335-72355-0

Challenging the Brooding Earl

Copyright © 2022 by Lucy Ashford

Harlequin Enterprises ULC
22 Adelaide St. West, 41st Floor
Toronto, Ontario M5H 4E3, Canada
www.Harlequin.com

Printed in U.S.A.

Lucy Ashford studied English and history at Nottingham University, and the Regency era is her favorite period. She lives with her husband in an old stone cottage in the Derbyshire Peak district, close to beautiful Chatsworth House, and she loves to walk in the surrounding hills while letting her imagination go to work on her latest story.

Books by Lucy Ashford

Harlequin Historical

Visit the Author Profile page at Harlequin.com for more titles.

Chapter One

Surrey, England—early spring 1802

It was past ten at night by the time Dominic, the Fifth Earl of Marchwood, glimpsed the travelling show camped on Weybridge Heath. It wasn't difficult to find even in the dark, since from almost half a mile away you could hear the infernal music and smell the strong odours of hot food. Grim-faced, the Earl guided his mare towards the assembly of caravans and canvas tents, all of them gaudily lit by lanterns.

In his opinion, gatherings such as these were the plague of the Surrey countryside, attracting riff-raff and troublemakers. It was as well for them they hadn't tried pitching up on his land, for he would have summoned the local yeomanry to clear them out, double quick. He was a proud man, the Earl of Marchwood, brought up from birth to know not only of his heritage, but of his obligation to society—which was precisely what he always tried to drum into the head of his young brother, Felix.

Unfortunately Felix was not inclined to listen, since the young fool believed he'd been put on God's earth purely to enjoy himself. Just over a week ago in London, Dominic had collared Felix sneaking into the family's Mayfair house at two o'clock in the morning, reeking of spirits and with his coat askew.

'You're coming with me,' Dominic had ordered him, 'to Castle Marchwood. Tomorrow.'

'Oh, for God's sake, Dom. Exile to the country—again! Do you want me to die of boredom?'

'I want you to learn some sense. I want you to show some awareness of responsibility towards our family name.' Dominic was quite sure by now that as well as brandy, Felix smelled of cheap perfume.

'But you're the one who sees to all that! Besides, you're nearly six years older than me and quite used to all those responsibilities you're so fond of preaching about!' Felix tried and failed to adjust his crumpled neckcloth. 'Dash it, Dom, I'll never be the Earl. At least, I most sincerely hope I won't.'

'At the moment, heaven help us, you are actually my heir.'

'Indeed.' Felix looked glum, then brightened. 'But you'll marry again. You're getting on a bit, of course, but any of London's debutantes would jump at the chance to grab an earl. Then you can have lots of bawling brats and leave me in peace!'

Dominic had reeled slightly at that. *Getting on a bit.* He was nearly thirty years old. He had once been married and… *Never again*, he'd vowed. But Felix was right; some day he would have to provide the estate with heirs. 'In the morning,' Dominic had repeated, 'we're going to Castle Marchwood, you and I. Where you won't find quite so many opportunities to throw your money around.'

But even in the depths of the Surrey countryside, it appeared that his brother had managed to seek out trouble. Earlier this evening the Marchwood estate's long-serving steward, John Galbraith, had come into Dominic's study. 'My lord! I've heard that your brother has gone with some friends to visit the fair on Weybridge Heath.'

'Good grief, Galbraith. Why?'

'There is—' Galbraith coughed '—a female there. She is a fortune teller, I believe, who has attracted a good deal of male interest.'

A fortune teller! Dominic had gritted his teeth. How low could Felix go?

He'd instantly ordered his horse to be saddled. Reaching his destination was easy, but finding his brother proved harder. He rode between the tents and stalls of the fair, soothing Meg as she fretted over the noise and bright lights. People turned to stare at him, exactly as he expected. By no means was he clad in finery, but he knew that everything about him—his upright bearing, his fine black mare—meant that he drew attention.

But he ignored them all and a moment later he spotted one of Felix's friends, Tom Brierley, who was trying his hand at the shooting stall, without success. 'Brierley!' Dominic called.

Tom Brierley blinked when he saw who it was. 'My lord. I didn't expect—'

'No,' grated Dominic, 'I imagine you didn't. Where is my brother?'

A young female had come to cling to Brierley's arm and her eyes widened on seeing Dominic. 'Saints above,' she whispered. 'Tom, who's this fine gent?'

Brierley ignored her. 'My lord,' he stuttered, 'your brother wanted to see the fortune teller. But there was a long queue at her caravan, so I left him to it. Then…'

'What, Brierley? Speak up!'

'A few moments ago Felix came to tell me he'd had his pocket picked and lost all his money. So he said he was going for his horse to ride home.'

On his arrival Dominic had noted that most visitors who'd come on horseback had left their mounts in a nearby field allocated to the purpose. Nodding curtly to Brierley, he turned Meg in that direction and soon saw his brother speaking to one of the lads whose job it was to watch over the horses. 'Felix!' he called out.

His brother, turning, let out an exclamation. 'Dom! How on earth did you know I was here?'

'Never mind that.' Dominic reined in his horse. 'Tom Brierley told me you were robbed. Is it true?'

'Oh, God, trust you to find out all about it.' Felix's face was a mixture of defiance and guilt. 'I wanted to see the fortune teller. There were dozens waiting, so I joined them. But a rogue in a shabby blue jacket picked my pocket—can you believe my bad luck? Naturally I chased after the fellow, but I was too late to catch him.

And my money's gone now, so I can't get my horse back!'

He gestured to the young lad who held the reins of Felix's chestnut mare. Grimly Dominic handed over the required coins and Felix, with some relief, said, 'Thanks, Dom.'

He was clearly eager to be on his way, but Dominic put out a hand to restrain him. 'Listen. Has it occurred to you that the pickpocket might have been in partnership with your fortune teller? She attracts the crowds, while he looks for likely targets—you, for example.' Felix was dressed as flashily as ever in a bottle-green riding coat with gilt buttons.

'No!' Felix was aghast. 'I've seen her, Dom. She actually came out of her caravan to apologise to us for the delay. She's really lovely and—'

'Felix, I've warned you before. If you keep getting into trouble like this, I'll cut off your allowance. Do you understand?'

Felix sighed. 'Yes. I do—but it's so damned boring in the country. You know?'

'You appear to find excitement wherever you go,' said Dominic grimly. 'Promise me you'll ride straight home?'

'I promise.' Felix swung himself into the saddle. 'Are you going to ride with me?'

'No. I'm going to take a look around. This fellow who robbed you—he wore a blue jacket, you say?'

'Indeed. And he had black hair and a bushy beard, but he looked dangerous. Be careful, won't you?'

'Aren't I always? You told me only last week I was the most cautious man in London. No sense of adventure and old before my time—I believe those were your precise words.'

Felix looked rather embarrassed and hastily rode off.

Leaving Meg in the care of the lad in charge, Dominic headed back to the fair on foot. The aisles between the stalls were more crowded than ever, but he shouldered his way through, looking in all directions. Where was this fortune teller? It was late, but he was damned if he would give up.

It was then that a nearby caravan caught his attention. Its door was shut, but a faint light glimmered in the window and a poster nailed to the door made him pull up sharply.

It said: *Have your cards read for a penny.*

This had to be Felix's fortune teller. There was no queue, but that could be because the woman had made quite enough money one way or another and had decided to shut up shop for the night. He felt like hammering on the door, but he paused, because below the writing was a drawing of a tarot card showing the figure of a man strolling headlong towards disaster. It was the card known as The Fool.

He gazed at it, suddenly cold as he remembered the craze for tarot cards at fashionable private parties a few years ago. He remembered his lovely young wife laughing over the cards with her friends, then laughing at him later that same night when he'd asked her if she was having an affair.

'Of course,' she'd said. 'And I'm leaving you, Dominic.'

He'd reeled. 'You can't mean it.'

'But I do. And I know that you'll accept the blame, noble as you are. Fool that you are.'

Though his fist had been raised to rap on the fortune teller's caravan door, he let it fall now and closed his eyes. Damn it. He couldn't face any more reminders, not tonight. Slowly he walked back to reclaim his horse, remembering how eagerly he'd walked into marriage. How blindly. As he rode from the lights of the fairground he tried to empty his mind of everything except the steady rhythm of Meg's hooves on a path still strewn with the dead leaves of winter.

Suddenly, he realised three men were charging out from a thicket brandishing cudgels. He tried to wheel round and gallop away, but they were striking at Meg's flanks with those cudgels until the terrified horse reared and pawed at the air. Dominic did his best to control her frantic kicks, but it was no good because Meg reared again and he flew to the ground, landing with such force that he was knocked senseless.

'Please pass me the cold water, Cassie. There, that's it.'

The voice was a woman's and it was gentle, almost musical—but Dominic registered that something was very wrong. He was lying flat on his back and his brain didn't appear to be working properly. He opened his eyes, then realised he couldn't see much either because some kind of bandage half covered his eyes and he was in… What the hell *was* he in? The roof above him was low and seemed to be made of painted wooden planks…

He was in a caravan, for God's sake. He was remembering now that he'd been attacked by fairground villains and they must have kidnapped him. Besides which, he must be losing his reason, for a young woman was leaning over him murmuring soft words just as Teresa had, causing him to feel the same weakness in his body and his brain, because he knew he couldn't resist her...

Teresa is dead, he reminded himself. My wife is dead.

He perhaps tried to say something to the woman in the caravan and must have made some kind of sound, because he heard her saying, 'I think he's coming round, Cassie.'

He could just about see the speaker now because the bandage above his eyes had slipped a little. She had chestnut-brown hair that tumbled past her shoulders and thick-lashed green eyes. She had to be Felix's fortune teller; he was sure of it. This woman's accomplices must have robbed Felix, then found themselves another target and attacked him, too. But why bring him here? Why hadn't they just stolen his horse and his money and left him lying in the woods?

He tried to sit up, but the startling colours of the woman's cheap dress made his head swim. He struggled to clear his dry throat, intending to say, 'I'll have you hauled before the magistrates for this', only it didn't quite come out like that, because his lip was split and he could taste blood.

He realised he was lying on a narrow wooden bed fixed to the caravan's wall and from here he could see a washstand, where another young woman with badly dyed blonde hair—Cassie, presumably—was rinsing out a cloth. Nearby were some shelves, on which sat several books and a piece or two of painted pottery, while at the far end of the caravan a pair of curtains divided off what he guessed must be space for sleeping.

Or for entertaining male customers.

Just then the fortune teller moved, allowing the light of the nearby lamp to shine more clearly over her features. He realised she was younger than Felix, easily. He saw also that her cheekbones were high, her nose was straight and her chin small but pointed. Around her neck hung a small gold-coloured locket set with fragments of green glass; the thing was probably made of cheap gilt, fake like her. And he needed to get back control quickly. He made another attempt to sit up, but failed.

'You'd best stay still,' the woman advised him. 'Does your head hurt? I'm not surprised. You've a fine bruise there.' She wiped his forehead carefully and as she drew the cloth away he saw that it was stained with spots of blood.

'I'll see you all in gaol for this,' he muttered.

She raised her eyebrows. 'I'm afraid you can't blame my friends for what happened. Those men who attacked you had nothing to do with our fair.'

He shook his head. 'Why should I believe you? I know for certain that a man had his pocket picked outside your caravan earlier!'

'I'm sorry to hear it.' Her voice was steady. 'But we fairground folk make our money from entertaining people, not from robbing them or knocking them over the head. You'll realise, I'm sure, that crime is not good for business.'

His head was reeling again because she was so very well spoken, so calm, as she regarded him with those amazing green eyes. 'Though I must say,' she went on, 'that most of our customers aren't foolish enough to come here looking so obviously rich. You might like to know that Mr Ashley Wilmot, the owner of the fair, spotted you riding away. He'd heard there might be thieves lurking, so he and two of his men followed you and rescued you, suffering more than a few blows themselves in the process. You owe them your thanks, sir.'

The *sir* was almost mocking. He gazed at her, knowing that whatever the truth of her story, he was still vulnerable here. At last he said, 'Those brutes struck my mare. Is she safe?'

'She's being checked over by our head groom, Jem. You may be sure that once Jem's convinced she's unharmed, you'll be able to ride home as soon as you feel ready. I trust you don't live far away?'

He shook his head. He was not going to let this woman learn anything about him. 'Not far.'

'Will there be someone to take care of you there?'

'Plenty,' he rapped out. 'I have staff.'

He instantly saw those green eyes widen in mockery. 'Staff,' she murmured. 'I can see we *are* honoured. Aren't we, Cassie?'

She turned to the female at her side, whose eyes twinkled. 'Indeed, we are, Miss Merryn,' she agreed.

Dominic closed his eyes again, briefly.

You're being an outright boor, he told himself, *if these people really are trying to help you.*

'You're from Ireland,' he said suddenly. He'd registered a strong lilt in the blonde woman's voice, though it was only faintly discernible in the fortune teller's.

She leaned forward to press her cloth against his forehead again. 'That is so. My grandfather was English, but he settled in County Kildare fifty years ago. My father and my mother were born in Ireland.'

'And what do they think of your chosen career?'

'Nothing,' she answered, 'since they are dead. Why? Do you think my occupation is something to be ashamed of?'

At first he didn't answer and instead swung his feet to the floor, intending to stand. But the effort made his head swim, so he remained seated and let his eyes roam until he spotted some cards laid out in three small piles on a low table. Tarot cards.

'Surely it's rather dishonest to make money out of people's dreams and vulnerabilities?' He pointed to the cards. 'Isn't that what you do?'

'Certainly,' she said, 'there are charlatans in the business.' She appeared to ponder for a moment. 'But then again, I've heard that rich merchants in the city of London are…shall we say, unscrupulous? I would also suggest that the mill owners who set children to work at their looms for fourteen hours a day are less than praiseworthy. At least, unlike those who are very rich, I work for my living and I bring people enjoyment.'

'Your skills haven't done much for your fortune, though, have they?' Her calm self-confidence was disturbing him ridiculously and he let his voice be tinged with scorn. 'Can't you predict something useful, like the next horse to win at Newmarket? Then you could maybe get yourself out of this truly pitiful lifestyle.'

He saw something blaze then in her extraordinary eyes, but she still managed a cool smile. 'I do have plans for my future, as it happens. But they don't involve vast sums of money, even though you and your kind think money is all that matters.'

She spoke over her shoulder to her companion. 'Cassie, go and ask Jem if the gentleman's horse is nearly ready for him, will you?' Once the caravan door was shut she turned back to Dominic. 'Do you wish to lie down again, sir, while you wait? I know you're eager to leave, but you really would be wise to rest a little longer after your ordeal.'

But Dominic didn't lie down. Instead he sat up even straighter, pointed to the tarot pack nearby and said, 'Humour me a moment, will you? I want to see exactly what you do with *those*.'

She looked surprised, almost as surprised as he was by the idiotic request that had sprung from his lips. She put her head on one side and said, 'Are you certain?'

'Yes.' It was a stupid thing to have said, that was for sure, but it was too late to back out now so he might as well get it over with. 'Tell me,' he went on, 'what you see in your cards for me. What do I have to do first? Cross your palm with silver—is that the way it goes?'

She shook her head. 'No need.'

She put a small table between them and lifted the pack of cards, which were clearly very old with a faded but distinctive marbling on the back. He thought again that this woman just wasn't what he expected. She was young—twenty-one, maybe twenty-two, but no more. Her clothes were cheap and bright, but she wore no rouge or powder. That small locket was her one adornment and the only perfume he could detect on her skin was the faint scent of rose petals.

He wondered—and now he was surely still suffering from that blow to the head—what it would be like to kiss her. Somehow he found himself doubting his early assumption that she made money from selling herself—indeed, he realised the notion disturbed him, which was quite ridiculous. Why should he care how she made her money?

She was looking at him again. 'Since you'll soon be on your way, I suggest I make a reading from three cards only. Will you pick them?'

She had already fanned the cards out, face down. He pointed to three and she eased them out. 'Do you see,' she said quietly, 'what you've chosen?'

'Yes.' His throat was still strangely dry as the images stared back at him. 'The Emperor,' he said. 'The Hermit. And...' his head throbbed '...The Fool.'

For a moment the silence hung heavily and Dominic was aware of the woman watching, waiting. He could almost hear his own heart thudding with—what? Anticipation? Dread?

She spoke at last. 'You have, I see, some familiarity with the cards,' she said. 'Tell me what you think they mean—though let me say that I never ask for personal secrets. Just explain to me what you guess their significance could be, to whoever draws them out.'

In the light of the lamp, Dominic gazed at the three cards again. He said, his voice still raw, 'I believe the Emperor represents power. The Hermit is a symbol of solitude. And the Fool...'

His voice faded. *The Fool*, he thought, *is me*.

There was a long silence. 'Your knowledge of the cards,' the fortune teller said at last, 'together with your cynicism, tell me that something happened to you once. Something that has damaged you badly.'

His heart had bumped to a stop. 'I thought your business was to predict the future. Not to drag up the past.'

She looked at him again with those vivid eyes of hers. 'All I will tell you is that you will not find true happiness until you rid yourself of your past and your pride—and believe me, sir, no cards are needed to inform me of that.' She was gathering up the cards again, indicating that their session was at an end. 'I'm sorry if you don't like what I said. But you did ask me, you know. Anyway, I imagine that you now feel considerably better, since there's nothing like a bit of self-righteous indignation to set a man back on his feet, that's what I always say.' She turned away from him. 'Don't I, Cassie?'

He realised that her friend had returned and was standing in the doorway. 'You do indeed.' The blonde woman bobbed a curtsy to Dominic. 'Jem says your horse is uninjured, sir, and you may depart whenever you wish.' She looked as though something about Dominic amused her hugely.

They were mocking him, he realised. Both of them.

He rose to his feet, thankful that his legs were steady now even though his head still ached like the blazes. The girl with the green eyes stood very straight, holding her head high; she had her own kind of pride, there was no doubt about that.

She wasn't pretty. She was more than that. 'Pretty' was insipid. 'Pretty' was a word he associated with the debutantes of London's *ton*, who were for ever being thrust in his direction and who were often the most boring creatures in creation. But he was aware of the desire rising in his blood even as she stared him out, and he guessed she was aware of it, too; he could tell it by the glint in her eye and the slightly scornful curl to her lush mouth.

'Well, sir?' she said. 'Jem will be waiting outside with your horse.'

Her friend Cassie added, 'Jem has also offered to escort you on your way, in case any more robbers are lurking.'

'I've no need of any escort.' Dominic fought off his lingering dizziness. 'I'll take my leave, ladies. I must express my gratitude for your aid, but I'm sure you'll understand my fervent wish that your cards do not predict a further meeting.'

'Likewise,' the fortune teller answered him softly.

And so the Earl of Marchwood rode home.

Cruel. Cold. Heartless. Those were a few of the words whispered about him when the news broke around six years ago that his young wife had fled the country rather than endure another month of living with him. A year later he'd learned that she'd died abroad in Brussels, penniless.

He'd thought himself in love with Teresa and believed that she loved him. He'd been wrong. A few months after their wedding she'd told him she had been forced into the marriage by her wealthy parents, who were eager, of course, to have an earl as their son-in-law. She also told him she'd hoped there might be compensations to being his wife—parties, adventures, fun—all of which, she said, he'd failed to provide.

'You have such a tedious sense of duty, Dominic,' she'd said with a sigh.

He'd been young then and naive. He'd hoped that she might want children and that they might make up for her lack of satisfaction with her new life. But as their intimacies lessened, he guessed there was little chance of that.

Then he learned that she was having an affair with an army officer. This was what she wanted, he realised. Fun. Excitement, no matter what the cost to others. She'd fled abroad with her lover, taking the jewels Dominic had given her. But that venture, too, had gone wrong, for her army officer turned out to be a gambler and when everything was gone the man left her. She died of a fever in Brussels soon afterwards.

Teresa had made sure to tell her friends that she left Dominic because living with him was unbearable. He let the rumours stand because you couldn't argue with the words of your dead wife. But he'd vowed that never, for the rest of his life, would he let his heart betray him so badly.

Chapter Two

By the time Dominic reached Castle Marchwood it was past midnight and no one, not even the dutiful butler, Inchberry, was around apart from the sleepy groom who took his horse. But candles still burned in the main hall and Felix was there, prowling up and down with a large glass of whisky in his hand.

'Dom!' he exclaimed. 'I ordered old Inchberry to go to bed and said I'd wait up for you.' He drew closer. 'By God, that's some bruise you've got on your forehead. You didn't get that at the fair, did you?'

'Yes.' Dominic's reply was flat. 'At the fair.'

Felix looked aghast. 'Was that because of me?'

'It was my own stupid fault. I was attacked by some ruffians as I rode across the heath.' Dominic pointed at Felix's glass. 'Do you know, I rather think I could do with some whisky, too. Shall we go to my study?'

Felix followed him and was all contrition as they both settled in leather armchairs there. 'I'm sorry, big brother. I didn't mean to get you into trouble. You must be cursing my very existence.'

Dominic sighed. With his boyish blond locks and slim build, Felix appeared—and often acted—even younger than his twenty-four years. Dominic rolled his whisky around in his own glass and said, 'Believe it or not, I'm actually quite fond of you. But for your own sake, Felix, I urge you to learn some common sense!'

'Where,' Felix pleaded mournfully, 'are you going to banish me to next? Not, please, to our home in Scotland, with all those ferocious mountains? Have pity on me!'

Dominic had to grin. 'Personally, I find Scotland a wonderful place. But, no, I wasn't thinking of sending you north, nor do I want to be preaching at you all the time. Though I do worry about all these females you keep falling for.'

'But when you married, you were even younger than I am now!' Felix clapped his hand to his mouth. 'I apologise. I should not have reminded you. Though what happened to Teresa was not your fault! She was abominable to you and you should have let everyone know it!'

Dominic shook his head. 'You know very well,' he said, 'that I never speak of her. But, Felix, tell me. You weren't seriously thinking of pursuing this fortune teller, were you?'

'She's really lovely, Dom! Tom Brierley and I spotted her this afternoon, when we rode out to investigate the fair. She smiled at us and my God, what a smile, what a face, what a figure! One of the men setting up the main tent told us she was the fortune teller, so we decided to go back there this evening, but...well, you know how that turned out.' He sighed. 'There was just something about her. You should see her!'

'I have seen her,' said Dominic flatly. 'In fact I've been far closer to her than I could ever have wanted.'

Felix's eyes widened. *'What?'*

'After I was knocked senseless, I came round in her caravan with a cold cloth pressed to my head.'

'Really?'

'Really.'

Felix grinned in that beguiling way he had. 'This is rather priceless, though, isn't it? There you were, trying to get me out of her so-called clutches—and you ended up being looked after by her! Wait till I tell my friends—'

'You'll tell your friends nothing,' interrupted Dominic. 'Because she's a charlatan.'

'Are you sure? Even though she looked after you?'

'I'm sure.' Dominic spoke with all the conviction of his age and rank, though actually he wasn't sure at all. Why was she with a travelling show? She was clearly well educated. She'd also responded to his sheer rudeness with a calmness that unsettled him mightily.

All of which reminded him exactly why he had to protect his brother from her wiles, for Felix was vulnerable and always had been. Dominic remembered him coming home from his first term at boarding school, afraid to tell their parents he was being bullied, but Dominic, studying at Oxford by then, had coaxed it out of him and spent the vacation giving him lessons in boxing. He still smiled at the memory of the gleeful letter Felix wrote to Dominic soon after the new term began. 'I planted the bully a facer, Dom. You should have heard how the other boys cheered me on!'

'Look, Felix,' Dominic said, drinking down the last of his whisky. 'Of course there's no harm in you having a few romantic adventures. But with a fortune teller?' He sighed. 'I realise it's dull here for you, though. So I promise we'll both go back to London, as soon as I've done all I need to do around the estate.'

'I'm certainly glad to hear it.' Felix finished his own drink, then pointed once more at the bruise on Dominic's forehead. 'Though country life does spring the occasional surprise. And—oh, drat.' He suddenly looked pained. 'I've just remembered. Of course, you know it's your birthday tomorrow? Your thirtieth?'

'You do keep reminding me.'

'Well, this evening when I got home from the fair, Inchberry told me a message had arrived from the Dragon.'

'Sarah?'

'Yes. Our dear sister, Sarah. Apparently she and her whole family are arriving tomorrow to help you celebrate your very special day.'

'Good God,' said Dominic.

On which note he headed up to his bedchamber, where his valet, Hinxton, a long-standing and dutiful retainer, awaited him. But Dominic dismissed him for the night and stood by the window, staring out into the blackness as he often did.

After her first few visits here, Teresa had told him she wasn't coming to Castle Marchwood ever again, telling him it was the dreariest building she'd ever had the misfortune to stay in. He'd tried to explain. 'It's my duty to visit often. This is the oldest part of the family estate and I'm responsible for the building and the staff.'

'You're proud of it, aren't you?' Teresa had exclaimed incredulously. 'This old, draughty place should have been left to fall into ruin years ago.'

Now he turned away from the window and imagined he heard the fortune teller's voice again. *'Something in your past has damaged you badly.'*

Merryn. That was her name. Merryn.

It had taken Merryn a good half hour to tidy the caravan, because the two men who'd carried the injured stranger inside had unwittingly left a trail of muddy footprints on the floor. Of course, Cassie had helped her clean up, but now she was outside and Merryn could hear her chatting to someone from a neighbouring caravan.

Merryn looked round to check that everything was restored to neatness, then she very quietly parted the curtains that divided off the area where her young brother lay sleeping.

Liam was eleven and small for his age. Thank goodness he slept so well, for the presence of their unwanted visitor would have made him anxious and kept him awake for hours. She closed the curtain again, then went to sit on a wooden stool to wait for Cassie. *That man.* As Cassie noted, he certainly made an impact for he was strong and fit, like most wealthy men with the time to indulge in pursuits like riding or boxing. And he might be considered handsome, but she couldn't forget the way his mouth looked as if it was for ever curled in scorn.

Although—and she felt a strange fluttering sensation at the memory—she had not failed to notice the flaring of lust in the stranger's eyes a moment later, though that hadn't lasted long and moments later he was looking at her as if she repelled him. Why? What had she done?

Of course, plenty of men thought that because she was with the fair, she must be easy prey. At least he'd not insulted her by offering her payment for more intimate services than card-reading, and he'd gone now, thank goodness, but somehow his scent had lingered and it was the scent of a rich man—pine and balsam soap, mingled with the aroma of fresh-laundered linen.

Just then Cassie came bustling back in at last and paused in front of the wall mirror to pat down her hair. 'That man!' she exclaimed in wonder. 'I was just telling old Mrs Oakes next door about him. Sakes above, Merryn, did you ever see such a fine specimen? Those shoulders and the muscles on him. Glory be, he'd be wondrous in bed, that's for sure.'

'He was detestable,' replied Merryn flatly, shaking out, then folding, the blanket on which he'd been lying. 'He was rude about us and rude about our friends. He didn't deserve our help, let alone our admiration.'

Cassie sighed. 'Well, as I always say, a girl's got to have her dreams. Whether you like it or not, the man was a handsome devil and I just loved that cleft in his chin. Didn't you notice it? Just imagine him kissing you and—'

'Cassie! Please. No more.'

Cassie studied her carefully. 'Yes. I'm sorry. Foolish of me.'

'No, not at all.' Merryn gave her a quick hug. 'And thank you, Cassie. For everything.'

'Heavens above, there's no need for tears!' Cassie hugged her back. 'Anyway, it's me who should be crying, because you're leaving us tomorrow, aren't you?'

Merryn nodded. 'I am. And you've been such a good friend.'

'Yes, well.' Cassie patted her shoulder. 'You've been good to me, too. Got me out of my silly ways with men, falling for every blessed one of them that made eyes at me. But that gentleman tonight—'

'Enough!' Merryn shook her head in mock despair. 'Now listen. I need to visit Ashley, to say goodbye. I won't be long, but will you stay here in case Liam wakes?'

'Of course.' Cassie's expression had changed. 'I'll miss you both, you know. We all will.'

Merryn nodded, a sudden lump in her throat. Then she set off across the now quiet fairground to Ashley Wilmot's caravan, which had enchanted her when she first saw it. Larger than most, it was beautifully adorned with scrolled paintwork both inside and out while Ashley himself, with his quaint attire and endless tales of fairs of old, was a suitably characterful occupant. How fond she'd grown of him during their journey. How safe she'd felt with him.

After knocking on his door, she entered and saw him sitting at a table studying his maps and plans. As ever, he wore a rather odd green suit and his thin, pale hair fell almost to his collar. No one knew his age and no one cared. He looked up at her and patted a nearby chair.

'Merryn! Come in. How is the unfortunate gentleman who was attacked?'

She thought, *You may call him a gentleman, but I would not.* Aloud she said, 'He has ridden off home, wherever that is, no doubt to take out his ill temper on his poor staff. I dealt with his wound, but I couldn't do much to deal with his arrogance.'

Ashley was indignant. 'The ungrateful fool! Never mind, we won't see him again, that's for sure.'

'No. But, Ashley—there's something else I must tell you.' She sat to face him. 'You knew, didn't you, that I would only be with you for a short while? That I needed to make this journey to fulfil an important promise?'

Ashley's face altered. 'I fear I know what's coming.'

'Indeed. You see, I've realised that I've almost reached my destination. I'm sorry.'

He reached out to press her hand. 'No,' he said cheerfully, 'don't apologise. You've always been honest with me and I've valued your company, Merryn. My dear, do you remember how we first met? You'd travelled to Dublin from your house in Kildare, hadn't you? Looking for a passage to England.'

She nodded. 'Though I'd almost given up all hope of making the journey, because either the fares were too expensive or...'

Ashley would know what she meant. Many a ship's captain had looked at her in a too-familiar way and told her she could travel for free, but she knew there would be a price.

'Then,' she went on, 'Liam spotted your fair, close to Dublin harbour. It was bitterly cold, you'll remember, and Liam wanted—no, he *longed* for—a toffee apple, only I knew I couldn't really afford it. But you came and gave him one. You explained that you came to Ireland every year and you knew a hungry boy when you saw one.' She smiled, though her eyes were bright with unshed tears of emotion.

'Then,' Ashley chuckled, 'your brother told me you were a fortune teller!'

'Yes, indeed.' Merryn smiled at the memory. 'He'd heard you suggesting we might like to come to England with your fair and he was afraid you might not take us if I had no suitable skills. So he came up with the story of the tarot pack I'd been given by an old lady my mother knew in Ireland. She was known locally as a wise woman and people used to come to her from far and wide for card readings.'

'But you told me she'd always insisted to you that there was no magic in it,' Ashley said. 'No trickery, which I was glad to hear.'

'Exactly. Instead, this woman used the cards as a way of prompting people to talk to her because often, she said, all that these people really wanted was someone to listen to their troubles.'

'They wanted a friend, in other words,' Ashley said, 'and you've certainly made many friends on our travels. Thank you, Merryn.' He pressed her hand. 'If you ever need me, I'll come to you wherever I am. Remember that, won't you?'

She rose. 'Of course I'll remember it.' Her words were heartfelt. 'And I'll always have very fond memories of my time with you and the show.'

He asked his next question carefully. 'Do you need money, my dear? A loan, maybe?'

'No. Oh, no.' She shook her head firmly. 'Thank you, but I have enough for Liam and myself for a while at least.'

'Then all I can do,' he said, 'is wish you luck with your quest—and I truly hope we'll meet again some day. Off you go, then. It sounds as though you'll have a busy day tomorrow, so you need a good night's sleep.'

Ashley. What a true friend he'd been. She walked slowly back to her caravan and stood a moment outside in the dark, breathing in the familiar night scents of the fair—the smoke from the torches, the savoury smells from the food stalls, the acrid odour of the fireworks that always provided the climax of the evening's entertainment.

Then she thought of the contrast between Ashley and the man who'd been such a reluctant visitor to her caravan. Ashley was kind and gentle. The dark-haired intruder had been rude and hateful.

He'd dismissed her as a fairground fraud. She'd tried to explain to him that there was no magic in reading the cards and her only skill lay in judging people's reaction to them; indeed, almost always you could work out their hopes, their disappointments and even their worst fears by listening carefully to their questions. She'd summed up the arrogant stranger swiftly. She guessed there was some deep-seated grief rooted somewhere in his past—not only grief, but an immense burden of guilt also. Something had happened for which he could never forgive himself.

So be it. She would not forgive him for the contempt he'd shown to her friends who had rescued him from the robbers. The trouble was, he'd shaken her badly. Something about his husky voice and the way his dark eyes searched hers—for what?—had stirred up feelings inside her that she wanted neither to accept nor even admit to herself.

Yes. He'd been hateful, but of one thing she could be sure. Even if for some strange reason he came back to the show, she would be gone.

Cassie was waiting for her in the caravan and to Merryn's surprise she'd brewed a pot of tea and was pointing to one of the stools. 'Sit,' she said. 'Because I've got something to say.'

Merryn sat and waited, not quite sure what was coming next. Cassie was only a year or so older than Merryn, but she'd endured years of poverty and worse, for she'd been orphaned and found herself on the streets of Dublin at far too young an age. But Ashley, on one of his trips to Ireland four years ago, had met her and had been her saviour, too, welcoming her into his travelling community as a seamstress and cook.

'Now,' said Cassie, settling down on a stool herself, 'you thought that you'd seen the last of me, didn't you? But I'm telling you, Merryn, that I've made up my mind. Wherever you're going, whatever you're up to, I'm coming with you. You've made this journey for Liam's sake, haven't you? You're going to claim the inheritance your father told you about. And you're going to be a lady of leisure—so I can be your maid! What do you think about *that*?'

Laughing, Merryn shook her head. 'It's true. There is a small property Liam is entitled to and we're almost there, which is why it's time for us to say goodbye to our friends here. But, Cassie, I don't think for one moment that Liam will be inheriting a great fortune. Though I'm hoping there is a cottage and some farmland—so most likely I'll be spending my days mending the roof and ploughing the fields!'

Cassie clapped her hands. 'A farm? That's just grand. I am definitely coming with you.'

'Are you sure? Won't you miss everyone here?'

'Of course I will.' Cassie took her hand and squeezed it. 'But how could I leave you and Liam?'

Gladness filled Merryn's heart, for Cassie had been her close friend since she joined the show. 'Cassie. You are an absolute dear.'

'Not just a brassy tart, then, eh? As His Lordship earlier as good as said?'

'You,' Merryn said, 'are a lovely person. And I'm so glad you're coming with us!'

Suddenly she was aware that the curtains concealing the sleeping area had been pushed open and Liam stood there in his nightshirt.

'Merryn,' he said. 'I wanted to make sure you were still here.'

Her brother always knew, somehow, when something was happening and he was terrified of change of any kind. Merryn was already hurrying towards him. 'Oh, sweetheart. Were you having bad dreams again?'

He nodded, wordless.

'Everything's fine,' Merryn emphasised. 'Listen. Tomorrow we're going on an adventure, Cassie and me and you. We'll be saying goodbye to our friends here, which is sad, but we're going to a new home, a home of our own, where we'll make lots of new friends. Do you understand?'

Liam looked only slightly reassured. She guided him back to his bed, but paused before returning to Cassie, because often she had bad dreams, too. Dreams of betrayal, by those who told her they cared.

What if she failed her brother? What if she failed in her promise to their father? She wanted to add, *Liam, all this is for you. We've come this far for you. It will be worth it, in the end.*

But—a happy ending? No one could safely predict that, ever.

Chapter Three

It was just after nine when Dominic went down to breakfast the next morning and he was taken by surprise to see Felix already there, cheerfully tucking into eggs and fried ham.

'Morning, Dom,' said Felix cheerfully. 'Happy birthday.' He waited until Inchberry had left the room for fresh coffee and leaned closer. 'How's your head?'

After helping himself to a selection from the hot dishes on the sideboard, Dominic sat down also. 'My head,' he said, 'since you ask, is not half as sore as yours this morning, I would guess.' Dominic nodded towards the butler, who'd just returned with the coffee pot. 'You may leave us, Inchberry. We'll see to ourselves from now on.'

Inchberry looked somewhat crestfallen. 'Your Lordship. It really is no trouble—'

'That will be all.' Dominic quickly added, 'Thank you.'

Poor Inchberry. He'd been the family butler ever since

Dominic could remember and Felix was always joking that he'd not bought himself new clothes for decades—which was quite likely, since his black coat and breeches had faded with age and his wig, an old-fashioned peruke, was for ever slipping to one side. He was a devoted butler, but the family spent so little time at Castle Marchwood that the fellow's undoubted skills were wasted.

Dominic reached over to pour himself and his brother some coffee, waiting for what he knew would come next—an apology.

'Look, Dom,' Felix began, 'I need to tell you again how sorry I am about last night, dragging you out to that fair and getting you into a nasty spot of bother.'

Dominic raised his eyebrows. 'Lesson learned?'

'I should jolly well think so!' Felix nodded heartily. He peered closer. 'And do you know, I can hardly see that bruise on your forehead. But all the same, that fortune teller really was dashed pretty and I'm sure she didn't have anything to do with those rogues we both encountered!'

Felix was right, Dominic silently acknowledged. He, too, accepted now that the woman wasn't in collusion with his attackers, but he was determined all the same to dismiss her from his mind. 'It's over and done with,' he replied. 'And I think we've said enough about the fortune teller, don't you?' He glanced out of the window. 'I wonder—do you fancy a ride this morning? There's an acre or two of woodland over by the lake that the estate manager tells me needs coppicing. I'd like your opinion.'

Felix swallowed his last piece of butter-laden toast. 'Yes,' he said eagerly. 'Yes, I do fancy a ride. But Sarah—'

'With luck, she won't arrive till noon. Shall we set off in, say, half an hour?'

'Definitely.' Felix jumped to his feet. 'I'll go and tell the grooms to get our horses ready.'

But their morning ride was doomed, because only moments later Dominic heard the sound of a carriage arriving. Looking out into the courtyard, he almost groaned aloud. It was his sister and her family. He drank the last of his coffee like a soldier downing his rum ration before battle, then glanced out of the window again to observe that an unsuspecting Felix had just emerged jauntily from the stables, only to pull up in horror on seeing the coach and its occupants.

Felix looked for a moment as though he was going to run back into the stables, but he didn't get the chance, because immediately he was being quizzed by Sarah and tugged at by Sarah's boys, Marcus, aged ten, and Luke, eight. Sir Wilfred Challoner, Sarah's unfortunate husband, stood in the background looking uncomfortable and no doubt wishing himself far, far away.

Right. Dominic calculated he had about five minutes before his peace was shattered. Inchberry would already have gone to dutifully welcome the family into the castle and indeed, five minutes later, the door to the breakfast room burst open.

'There you are, Dominic!' His sister's voice scalded his ears and he winced also at her clothes, which were horribly expensive, no doubt, but dreary in style and colour. 'Now,' Sarah went on, 'what have you been up to? I gather you got involved in a brawl last night!'

She didn't even wish him a happy birthday. 'Did Felix tell you that?' Dominic couldn't believe his brother could be so stupid.

'Well, actually,' his sister declared, 'I overheard two of your grooms muttering out in the yard that you arrived home very late last night with a sore head and might not be up to a visit. A visit from your own family—what nonsense! So is it true, about this brawl?'

That fried ham on the hotplate called silently to Dominic as his older sister's sharp eyes continued to bore into him. 'I was set on by a couple of chancers,' he said. 'They got nothing from me. No real harm was done.'

She still regarded him suspiciously. 'I am most disappointed to hear of the risks you take. I assume you've not forgotten that if anything happens to you, Felix will inherit the entire Marchwood estate?'

This time Dominic met his sister's piercing gaze with a good stare of his own. 'Tell me, Sarah. Have I shown signs lately of losing my wits?'

She looked huffy. 'All I'm trying to say is that for the sake of the estate and for your own good, you really ought to get married again.'

'Right. You're recommending the situation from personal experience, then?'

His sister's rather pinched face tightened a little more. 'Well, of course! And dear Wilfred would tell you he couldn't be happier!'

Wilfred wouldn't dare say otherwise, thought Dominic. *Poor creature.*

'After all,' Lady Challoner went on remorselessly, 'today you are thirty years old. And how can I describe the joy of having children? Our two little darlings brighten up our lives!'

Hmm. 'Would you like some coffee, Sarah?'

'No, I would not.'

Dominic glanced out of the window and realised Felix had vanished—ridden off at full speed, if he was wise. Meanwhile Sarah's two little darlings were hurling clumps of hay at some frightened hens and whooping like savages. One of the grooms was doing his best to rescue the hens, but Sarah's boys started throwing hay at him instead, until the poor groom resembled a scarecrow with its stuffing falling out.

Dominic opened the window. 'Marcus! Luke!' he roared. 'Stop that behaviour *now*. Do you hear me?'

The boys turned instantly at the sound of his voice. Marcus looked surly and Luke began to cry—no, that was the wrong word, he began to *wail*. Sarah hastened to Dominic's side as he stood at the open window. 'Dominic, how could you? They're only young!'

Dominic closed the window again and turned to his sister. 'They're old enough to know a good deal better, in my opinion.'

'Really, though, you've made poor Luke cry!' Sarah shook her head. 'Well, what a welcome this is. You knew we were arriving today. It's your birthday, after all, and we always get together to show that we're a loving and united family. I'm going out there to comfort my boys, though they'll be so upset that they probably won't want any lunch!'

Dominic doubted that exceedingly, for he'd noticed how they always gobbled up everything presented by the castle's cook, Mrs Butterworth. He mentally resolved to be a good distance from Castle Marchwood when his next birthday arrived.

Pouring himself more coffee, he sat down again and looked round the dark-panelled room. Every time he came here, he silently regretted the fact that he'd inherited this sombre old building, put up by the Normans and fortified by various English kings against invasions and civil revolts that never actually materialised. The castle was constantly in need of repairs. Every room was crammed with Jacobean furniture and tapestries and the atmosphere was in no way lightened by the grim-looking medieval weapons hung on various walls.

It was his duty, of course, to leave his Mayfair town house at least once in a while and check that the edifice was still standing but unfortunately his sister lived only four miles away and was always guaranteed to turn up and remind him, in no uncertain terms, that it was time he married and produced heirs.

Luckily for her, she did at least have the sense never to remind him of his first marriage. What had that fortune teller said last night? *'You will not find true happiness until you rid yourself of your past and your pride.'* Good grief, she'd disturbed him—it was as if she'd seen right through him. He realised that his head was aching again and it wasn't from the bruise on his temple. Just then the door opened once more and Sarah marched in, this time holding each of her sulky-looking boys by the hand.

'Say sorry, boys, to Uncle Dominic,' she was urging them. 'You know very well that he doesn't like the sound of children playing!'

Dominic almost growled. 'Sarah, let us be precise. I do *not* like the sound of hens being frightened half to death, nor do I like to see a hard-working groom being pelted with straw.'

'Sorry, Uncle Dominic,' muttered Marcus.

Luke began to whimper and Sarah tutted. 'Oh, Dominic. Do you have to be so harsh? I told you, they'll be unable to eat their lunch!'

Dominic said nothing as she ushered them out of the room, but his hackles rose again when he heard Sarah saying, rather loudly, 'There, there, my darling boys. Uncle Dominic doesn't mean to be cruel. It's just that he is not used to children.'

'Why doesn't he have any, Mama?' Luke's petulant voice echoed along the corridor.

'Well, dear, it would be rather difficult for him since he doesn't have a wife.'

'Why not, Mama?' Marcus spoke up now. 'Is it because he shouts all the time?'

Dominic didn't hear any more because he'd shut the door. Sarah and her family usually stayed for just two nights, so it wouldn't be long before they returned to their own home. But it would seem like an eternity.

He sought refuge in his study with the news sheets that Inchberry had laid on his desk in perfect order. Poor Inchberry—he never lost the chance to show how delighted he was to have him here. Dominic leaned back to enjoy some peace, but after twenty minutes or so there was a cautious knock on the door and Sir Wilfred entered.

'Sarah's been having a word with me…' he began.

A word? Poor Wilfred, an insipid nonentity of a fellow, looked as if he'd just faced the full battery of one of his wife's tirades. Dominic set aside the news sheet. 'Is that so?'

'Yes. And I'm afraid she's a bit upset. Frankly, Dominic, she thinks you're sometimes a bit hard on our children. She feels you don't like them very much.'

Dominic said nothing, which unsettled Wilfred even more. 'So we've decided,' Wilfred went on, 'that perhaps we ought to leave tomorrow morning, instead of staying for our usual two nights. I hope you're not offended?'

'I'll cope,' said Dominic politely.

'Yes. Well.' Wilfred drew an enormous breath. 'She also asked me to remind you that unless…' His voice faded.

Dominic leaned forward and supplied the missing words. 'Unless I marry again and have children, Felix will be my heir. Sarah has already spoken to me on this matter.'

'Already?'

'Indeed. In fact, it was virtually her first topic of conversation.' Dominic looked at his brother-in-law steadily. 'You know, you really need to be a bit firmer with her. And with your two boys.'

'Yes. Yes, of course.' With that Wilfred beat a hasty retreat, leaving Dominic shaking his head. Wilfred was basically a decent sort and rich enough to keep Sarah and his family in some style, but the man had been a fool to marry a woman so much stronger-willed than himself.

He had just returned to his news sheet when he had yet another visitor—Felix. Dominic eyed him from behind his desk. 'I take it you went for a ride on your own?'

Felix blurted, 'Yes, but not far. I just rode as far as the summer pavilion and sat there for a while—anything to get away from the Dragon and her ghastly boys. And, Dom, I'm sorry she found out about that attack on you at the fair last night! She heard the grooms talking, you see, and apparently quizzed them mercilessly.'

Dominic raised his hand to silence him. 'I've been trying to hide from her, too, but with little success.' He rose from behind his desk. 'Look, Felix. Do you still fancy that ride we talked about? I could do with some fresh air. I'll tell Sarah it's estate business and a matter of necessity. Agreed?'

'Most definitely.' Felix gave a sigh of relief before adding hopefully, 'Will we be out for long?'

Dominic was already heading for the door. 'We are going to be absolutely as long as possible,' he replied. 'You can be sure of it.'

Chapter Four

Later that morning

'I regret, madam,' said the very elderly man who'd opened the castle's huge doors, 'that His Lordship is not at home.'

The ominous creak as those doors opened should have warned Merryn there was trouble ahead. And this man had to be the butler—no mere footman could wear such a haughty expression or wear such a peculiar wig, which looked even older than he did. The sun might be bright, but the atmosphere was frosty. Merryn touched Liam's shoulder to reassure him and said, 'Not at home? That's strange, because a groom has just told me that the Earl went for a ride earlier but most definitely returned here over half an hour ago.'

The butler looked taken aback by her temerity, but quickly recovered. 'I think,' he said, 'that you don't quite understand my meaning. His Lordship is not at home to casual visitors.'

'But I'm not a casual visitor! That is, the Earl and I haven't met, but I'm sure he will know of my family. Please tell him that I am Miss Merryn Hythe and my brother is the heir to the nearby estate of Hythe Farm.'

The butler looked astonished. 'But Hythe Farm is looked after by the Earl's steward. It is part of the Marchwood demesne.'

'No,' she said politely but firmly. 'I have to correct you there. I believe the Earl's forebears wrongly assumed ownership of it many years ago and I have come to claim it back.'

She noticed that the aged butler's mouth had thinned so much that it was scarcely visible. 'How did you get here?' he said at last, straightening his wig and looking around suspiciously.

'Oh,' Merryn replied cheerfully, 'we managed to find transport in Weybridge.' No need to tell him it was a turnip cart. The butler still looked as if he was considering calling someone to bodily evict her, so she added, 'I rather fear that if you don't tell the Earl of my arrival, he might be annoyed. And anyway, I'm not leaving until I've seen him.'

For a long moment they stared at one another until, very slowly, the butler nodded. 'You will please wait in the hallway while I inform His Lordship of your arrival.'

'I shall indeed wait.' Merryn smiled sweetly, then touched Liam's shoulder and they both followed him inside. 'I told you—I'm going nowhere.'

The butler adjusted his wig one final time and set off along the hall. This place was enormous, she realised, with a huge, vaulted ceiling soaring overhead and a vast staircase climbing upwards in the distance. Merryn glanced down at her brother. 'Everything's going to be all right, Liam,' she whispered.

If only, she added to herself. Even her whisper seemed to reverberate mockingly around the lofty building.

After bidding farewell to her fairground friends this morning, she had walked with Cassie and Liam to the market in Weybridge and enquired if anyone could give her a lift in the direction of Castle Marchwood. A local farmer had obliged, quite refusing her offer of money— the drawback being that his three passengers had to balance themselves on several great sacks of turnips, whose odour was all-pervasive.

The farmer had dropped them off at the entrance to a long drive. 'There are quite a few ways to reach the castle,' he explained. 'This one isn't often used, but it's not far for you to walk, whatever your business may be.' He'd looked at them curiously. 'The Earl's expecting you, is he?'

'Well, yes and no,' said Merryn as all three of them had climbed down from the cart. 'That is, he's probably been expecting to hear from me for quite some time now.'

And that was enough to tell their kindly driver, she'd decided, even though he was clearly avid for gossip. He'd driven on and Merryn had looked all around, seeing a vast wooded park with swathes of green lawn and magnificent old oaks about to burst into leaf. Then she'd been suddenly transfixed, because beyond the trees she'd spotted the towers of a castle—a real English castle.

Forbidding wasn't a strong enough word.

Cassie had already settled herself comfortably on a fallen tree cushioned with moss. 'I'll tell you what, Merryn,' she'd said. 'You and Liam go to the castle and tell the Earl what it is you want, while I wait here with our bags. And don't you fret about His Lordship. You've got that letter as proof and he can't argue with that, now, can he?'

It should be simple, as Cassie had said. A matter of justice, that was all. But now, as she stood in the castle's vast entrance hall waiting for the butler to return, she glanced at her brother anxiously. She'd done her utmost to tidy him up for this meeting, but his suit looked threadbare and he was white with tiredness.

Merryn's heart ached for him, but she'd not come all this way to fail at the last hurdle. Unfortunately, the sheer size of the Earl's ancestral home had shaken her rather more than she'd expected and now two footmen had appeared in the distance and were eyeing her suspiciously. She guessed the butler had ordered them there to ensure that she didn't steal anything. Liam, meanwhile, was gazing up at a display of ancient weaponry hung from beams overhead, central to which was a pair of ferocious-looking swords with their blades crossed as if to say: *Enter here if you dare*.

Quite a warning.

Merryn smoothed her cloak and tried to pat down her ever-rebellious brown curls. This morning, Cassie had helped her pin her hair tightly back at the nape of her neck, but some pins had come loose and she feared the wayward locks falling around her shoulders would do nothing to impress His Lordship.

'The Earl and his family will be cold, proud people,' her father had warned her when his final sickness was claiming him. 'But this letter from London confirms that Lord Marchwood is under a legal obligation to restore Hythe Farm to Liam. Keep it with you and remember always that your brother is heir to the Hythe estate.'

Realising the butler was coming back, she touched the letter in her cloak pocket and waited.

'His Lordship,' the butler announced, 'has graciously agreed to grant you some moments of his time. But remember, it is quite unheard of for anyone to arrive without an appointment.'

'I shall be sure,' Merryn replied, 'to express my heartfelt gratitude.'

She held her head high. But her heart was thumping as the butler led her past the watchful footmen, then through one room after another filled with gloomy furniture and more dark oil paintings of aristocrats who gazed sternly down at her. Liam followed, no doubt as oppressed as she was by this soulless display of wealth.

At last the butler opened the door to a large study. Long velvet curtains blocked much of the light from the windows and the resulting gloom was only slightly relieved by a lamp placed on a huge mahogany desk. Merryn blinked and realised that a man stood behind that desk, watching her.

He was tall and wore a sombre coat that seemed moulded to his powerful shoulders and chest. His hair was as dark as the expression in his eyes, which had narrowed at the sight of her. His face was angular, almost harsh in fact, and his mouth was set in a thin line that epitomised disdain.

He said but a single word. *'You.'*

And Merryn's heart sank to the soles of her buttoned boots because it was the man from the fair. Oh, no. How could this be possible? Hearing the door close softly behind her, she realised the butler had retreated, after doubtless taking in that short, damning greeting.

'My lord,' she said at last. She made a formal curtsy while Liam, following her lead, gave a little bow. 'This is a surprise to me also.'

Her voice was calm and that amazed her, because inside she was so shaken that she felt sick. What kind of cruel joke had Fate played on her this time?

'Please enlighten me,' he said. His voice was every bit as sonorous and deep as she remembered, though this time it was also etched with incredulity. 'Is this some kind of blackmail, perhaps? Are you here to ask for money?'

'Blackmail? Of course not!' She clamped down on her anger while thinking, *Hateful, hateful man.* 'I'm actually here on legitimate business, my lord.'

'Really?' There was sheer disbelief in that one word.

'Yes! My name is Miss Merryn Hythe. This is my brother, Liam—and I'm here to claim Liam's inheritance.'

You could have heard a pin drop. It was the Earl who finally broke the silence. 'Well.' He spoke exceedingly softly. 'You've been plotting hard since last night, haven't you? What, exactly, is this so-called inheritance you're after?'

It so happened that Merryn, though still fighting to control her dismay at the situation she found herself in, had spotted a large, framed map hanging on the wall of the Earl's study. She walked over to it, her heart thumping at her own presumption, but saw that, yes, she was right. It was a map of the Earl's estate and the area that surrounded it, just like the ones she'd studied when she began to plan her journey to Surrey many months ago.

She pointed to the lower corner of the map. 'There is a small estate here, my lord, that is named on the map as Hythe Farm. It adjoins your own property. I believe it to be my brother's inheritance, which your ancestors took over illegally.'

He laughed and it wasn't a kind sound. 'Well,' he said at last. 'This is certainly different. I imagine this interview will take a little longer than I thought. It would be best, don't you agree, if your brother were not present?'

Merryn felt Liam move closer to her. She declared, 'We will not be separated!'

The Earl drawled, 'Madam. Do you think we are monsters here?'

She shook her head. 'No. No, of course not.'

He glanced at Liam. 'Your brother looks tired and hungry. The castle's cook always keeps tasty treats in her kitchen and I imagine the boy might be content to spend just a short time there while you and I talk.'

Reluctant as she was to admit it, the Earl was probably right. And if this hateful man was going to insult her, she would certainly prefer her brother not to be present. She bent to whisper to Liam, 'Darling, do as the Earl says. I promise you I won't be far away.'

During that brief time His Lordship must have rung a bell, because within moments a footman had appeared. The Earl murmured some instruction and Liam, casting one last look at Merryn, set off with him, a small and vulnerable figure.

The door closed after them and the Earl pointed to a chair. 'Sit,' he said. He was already lowering his domineering frame into the leather chair behind his vast desk.

She didn't sit. She wanted to say, *I am not one of your minions*, but he was speaking again before she could get the words out of her mouth. He demanded, 'How old is your brother?'

'He's eleven, my lord.'

'He looks younger.'

'He was ill for some time after our mother died six years ago. But he has recovered well.'

He nodded curtly. 'So you're claiming that you—or rather, your brother—has a right to the Hythe estate?'

Merryn sat and faced him squarely. 'I have legal proof.'

He raised his black eyebrows. 'Legal proof,' he echoed. 'And I'm meant to accept this proof as genuine, from a woman who earns her living as a fortune teller?'

Merryn found herself shaking inside. 'I have a lawyer's letter,' she said.

'How impressive.' He settled back in his chair and folded his arms across his chest. 'This was concocted, I assume, by one of your fairground friends?'

Somehow his rich voice filled the room without any sign of effort, and as he continued to scrutinise her from behind his desk, Merryn felt as if she were on trial just before the sentence was pronounced.

She also felt all kinds of other things. She was absolutely furious that he'd assumed without question that she was a fraud. She was deeply anxious, too, about Liam, who would feel lost and alone in this place no matter how tempting the cook's treats. And worst of all, she was afraid of this man's almost overpowering masculinity.

As she'd insisted to herself last night, he wasn't handsome, oh, no. His nose was too long and his chin, which Cassie had so admired, was far too square, his hooded eyes too forbiddingly inscrutable. But goodness, he had such a *strong* face, with every plane and hollow emphasised by the subtle light and shadows cast by that solitary lamp. Her heart pounded as she remembered the way he'd gazed at her last night in her caravan; the way that just for a few seconds, he'd looked as though he was driven by some devil inside him to take her in his arms and kiss her.

As if she would have let him, she thought scornfully. As if she would have allowed him to get anywhere near her if he'd tried. And now, it was time to proceed with the purpose of her visit. Reaching into her cloak pocket for the precious letter her father had given her, she handed it over defiantly, then watched as he unfolded and read it.

At last he put the letter down on his desk. 'You are clearly an enterprising young woman,' he said. 'But I guess you and your friends at the fair are well used to seizing opportunities for trickery.' He tapped the letter, but never took his eyes off her. 'I doubt you have any connection to the Hythe estate whatsoever. This letter must be a forgery.'

She was truly grateful now that Liam wasn't here to witness all this. 'My lord,' she declared, 'I grew up in Ireland totally unaware of this inheritance. But shortly before he died a year ago my father, Jonathan Hythe, told me about the estate. He handed me this letter— which he'd only recently received—and made me promise to come here for Liam's sake. I had no idea until I set foot in this room that our paths had crossed at the fair last night. I regret the nature of our first meeting every bit as much as you, probably far more.'

'Right,' he mocked softly. 'So you say you didn't know last night that I was the Earl of Marchwood?'

'I do not claim magical powers, as I've told you. Of *course* I didn't know who you were last night! I've come here to claim my brother's inheritance. I trust there will be no problem?'

He glanced at the letter again as if it contaminated the air. 'I think I told you,' he said, 'during our unfortunate encounter last night, that I've been accustomed all of my life to tricksters. Any clever craftsman could have forged this.'

'But look!' Merryn pointed. 'There is the address and signature of a London lawyer!'

'I've not heard of this lawyer, ever,' he calmly replied. 'And even if he and his firm actually exist, the entire matter needs very careful investigation.'

Merryn gazed in silence at that map hanging on the wall. Compared to the Marchwood lands, the Hythe estate was insignificant. The man must be worth a fortune. But her father had warned her about the English aristocracy. 'No matter how rich they are, they always want more,' he'd told her. 'I warn you, it can be easier to get water from a stone than to ask them for anything.'

She reached out to take the letter back, but he put his hand on it. It was a big hand, strong with blunt fingers, and since it brushed hers only for a fraction of a second he probably didn't even notice the contact. But she shivered.

He said, 'I will require this if the matter is to proceed any further.'

Now she felt a little faint. 'Very well, my lord. But I must inform you that I, too, will seek legal assistance with my claim.'

Damn the man, his aristocratic lip actually curled at that. 'Are you threatening to take me to court? You will find it extremely expensive. And tell me, if you can—why didn't your father claim the estate long ago? Hythe Farm has been under Marchwood governance for many years because it was, quite simply, abandoned. Why this sudden interest in it?'

'My lord, there is a reason. May I explain?'

He shrugged. 'Go ahead,' he said.

But his tone implied, *Say whatever you like, because I shan't believe you.*

'Very well. In his final sickness, my father explained that his own father—Hugo Hythe, my grandfather—grew up at Hythe Farm, but Hugo's older brother,

Charles, inherited the estate. So Hugo left to travel abroad and married a Frenchwoman, then eventually they moved to Ireland, where they had one child, my father, Jonathan. What neither my grandfather nor father knew was that Charles Hythe had died unmarried and with no offspring. My father was the heir to Hythe Farm, but never realised it.'

The Earl's lip curled. 'I find it extremely hard to believe that any family could ignore inherited land for so long.'

She hated the scepticism in his voice. 'Then let me explain further. My grandfather had, as I said, lost contact with his brother, Charles, but he assumed Charles had had children. My father would have supposed the same. Besides, he was not looking for an inheritance. He was very happy in Ireland and was devoted to my Irish mother. As I've told you, she died six years ago when Liam was only five, but my father had no thought of leaving the place where the two of them had been so happy.'

The Earl was silent a moment. 'Then why,' he said, 'did he decide to stir all this Hythe business up on his deathbed? Why, if you'd all been happy in Ireland, did he send you off on an errand that could well be in vain?'

Merryn heard the words that couldn't be spoken whirling in her brain.

Because he was on the verge of bankruptcy. Because he realised that Hythe Farm was Liam's last hope of a decent future.

But all she said was, 'Perhaps my father's illness made him remember matters of the past that he'd always pushed aside. As I explained, it was only recently that he explored the business of the inheritance and in response he received the letter I've handed to you.' She found she was clenching her hands into fists. 'Let me emphasise that I'm doing this for Liam, not for me. And tell me, my lord—if you were informed that something belonged to you, wouldn't you claim it?'

'Most certainly I would,' he drawled. 'If my claim was justified.'

She felt herself flush. 'Are you saying I'm a liar?'

He rested his hands on the desk in front of him. 'Given the highly questionable story you've just told me, yes, I do have my doubts. The fact remains that the estate was as good as abandoned long ago and my own grandfather was forced to take responsibility for it, since the neglected fields and boundaries were becoming a problem for his own lands. Such a process is known in law as "adverse possession".'

He rose from his seat. 'You will understand, I'm sure, that I need time to look into all this. But I must warn you that English law imposes a time limit on claims such as yours and it's highly possible that even if all you say is true, your claim to the property is no longer valid.'

Merryn suddenly realised she was exhausted. For so long she'd been anticipating this crucial moment and now she found that the Earl was exactly what she'd most feared—an aristocrat, every inch of him, icily self-contained and judgemental.

But what shook her most was that she'd been disturbed by him in a way she'd never felt before. She felt shaken by the power of him and the challenge in his dark eyes. She had the feeling that if he were to touch her, she would…

What, exactly?

She felt a curious swooping sensation low in her stomach and realised her pulse was unsteady. Dear God, that look in his eyes made it easy to remind herself that a man like him would feel nothing but scorn for her. The thought strengthened her. She tilted her chin and said, 'I wish to see the farm for myself.'

He shook his head. 'Never. Not without further proof of your claim.'

They stared at one another. The impasse was only broken when a middle-aged woman in a white apron and cap came bustling in, followed by Liam. She looked flustered. 'Your Lordship. I do apologise for interrupting!'

'It's all right, Mrs Butterworth. We'd almost finished here.'

Merryn realised this must be the cook. Liam looked very pale.

'I swear,' Mrs Butterworth was saying, 'that down in my kitchen I turned my back just for one blessed minute to go to the pantry for some flour, when somehow young Master Marcus and Master Luke arrived. They started tormenting this lad, trying to pinch him and the like. I would have given them what for! But then I saw that the boy was standing up to them like a proper little soldier. He's a silent one all right, but he's brave. And there was something else.' Mrs Butterworth was looking puzzled. 'I thought it best to bring him back here, but on our way he spotted something and wouldn't move on. My lord, you know those old paintings in the hall? The ones of all the neighbouring farms?'

Merryn saw the Earl nod. 'I know them. Go on.'

'Well, this boy stopped dead in front of one of those pictures. He just couldn't take his eyes off the thing, and though I asked him, he wouldn't tell me why.'

Merryn looked straight at her brother. 'What was it about the picture, Liam?'

Liam hesitated. Then he said, 'It was a painting. A painting of an old house, with three big yew trees to one side. And, Merryn, it looked exactly like that painting hanging over the fireplace in our house in Ireland!'

Chapter Five

Throughout this unexpected and entirely unwanted interview, Dominic had decided that the woman who called herself Miss Hythe had rather cleverly done a substantial amount of research about her brother's so-called inheritance. But Dominic was still puzzled—which was unusual and he didn't like it.

When he inherited the Marchwood lands he'd asked his steward, Galbraith, to find a tenant for the farmhouse, with no success; the truth was that no one wanted to live there, since it was such an old and slightly dilapidated building. As a youngster, Dominic had heard vague tales about the deserted estate and knew that his grandfather had taken over the management of it only to stop it being a nuisance to the well-tended Marchwood lands.

He'd accepted he would have to do the same. He'd also always been aware that somewhere there could be a genuine claimant. But this woman?

She had to be lying. The boy's statement about the

painting was mildly troubling, but he brushed it aside. After all, the sister had lived with a travelling fair and the reputation of such folk was questionable, to put it mildly. She was bold, she was determined and she was the sort of brazen female who caused trouble everywhere. Just look at Felix, who'd made himself a fool over her already. As for himself, she had as much chance of getting him on her side as she had of making a fortune from her tarot cards.

He said at last, 'Thank you, Cook. You may go.' Then he turned to the woman who called herself Merryn Hythe and said, 'Madam. As I told you before, I'll begin making preliminary enquiries into your claim. In the meantime, you had better tell me where you're staying.'

She raised her eyebrows in mock surprise. 'I thought it would be obvious. Liam and I plan, naturally, on living at Hythe Farm.'

Damn it, no. He drawled, 'Aren't you being rather presumptuous?'

'Certainly not. I know it belongs to my brother and I've shown you the proof.'

'I'm afraid I dispute your proof.' He walked to the door and opened it. 'I suggest you return to your friends at the fair and I'll be in touch with you as soon as my lawyers have researched the legality of your claim. I would certainly advise you not to raise your own or your brother's expectations.'

All the while the boy was watching him in silence. At last she said, 'You say the farmhouse is in poor condition. Is it actually derelict?'

'My steward has maintained its structure,' he replied crisply, 'and I believe that the shepherd who looks after the Hythe flocks lives nearby and keeps an eye on it. But of course it's barely furnished and is probably cold and damp.'

'How long is it since you've actually seen it?'

He was still holding the door wide open. 'I've not visited the place for a while. I have many demands on my time. And that's really all I can tell you, until I've spoken to my London solicitors about your claim.'

'But that could take months!' Her dismay was clear. 'And how can you get in touch with me if I'm with the fair?'

'You know where I am,' he answered. 'I suggest you write to me here in, shall we say, two months? Now if you'll excuse me, I have a good deal of other business to attend to.' He gestured to the door. 'I'll arrange for one of my grooms to drive you to Maybury. That's the nearest village and from there you can make arrangements to re-join your travelling friends.'

He gave the appropriate orders for a carriage to be brought to the courtyard immediately. After that he stood in front of the castle's main doors, arms folded, and watched as the young woman followed her brother into the carriage after brushing aside the groom's offer of assistance. He waited till the vehicle rolled off down the drive, then turned to go back inside.

Her visit had been an unwanted intrusion into the meticulous order of his routine, nothing more. This, he informed himself, was positively the last time he would see her. He would let his London solicitor, Winslade, deal with her should she have the temerity to try her tricks again. If he felt in any way disturbed by her, it was because her brazen attitude had taken him aback. That was all.

As he walked back to the house he realised that Sarah was waiting in the hallway for him.

'Dominic,' Sarah began, 'I heard that the woman who's just left has been trying to claim part of the Marchwood estate. I'm extremely glad you sent her packing. The impertinence!'

Now, how the devil had she learned the content of their conversation? It must have been her maid—quite probably she'd had her ear glued to the door of his study. Dominic suddenly felt very tired.

'Sarah,' he said, 'I'm afraid you've received inaccurate information. My recent visitor has most definitely not laid claim to any part of the Marchwood estate. But she does believe her brother has a right to Hythe Farm, which you may recall was left without heirs long ago. I've told her the matter will go to my lawyers. Will you excuse me? I need to write a letter to them.'

Dominic went to seclude himself in his study once more, where he picked up a freshly sharpened quill pen and started composing a letter to his lawyer. But at that moment Felix rushed in. 'Dom. Was that who I think it was, leaving the castle in your carriage?' He sat down, his eyes alight. 'What on earth was the lovely fortune teller doing here?'

Dominic put down his pen. 'Your fortune teller, Felix, has revealed her true colours. She's an out-and-out charlatan. She's trying to lay claim to Hythe Farm for her young brother.'

Felix's eyes widened. 'That run-down old place on the edge of your property? But I thought she was with the fair!'

'So she was.' Dominic settled back in his chair and folded his arms. 'But my guess is that she'd somehow heard there were no heirs to Hythe Farm and concocted a somewhat far-fetched way to get her hands on it. She even produced a lawyer's letter. It's fake, of course.'

'How do you know?'

'Let's call it a fairly accurate guess, shall we?'

Felix was still frowning. 'So what have you done with her? Where was she off to just now?'

'I've sent her to Maybury and from there she can go about re-joining her fairground friends. I said I'd investigate her brother's claim, but she has to be a fraud.'

His brother stared at him. 'Does she? But there just might be a distant heir somewhere. You told me so yourself once.'

Dominic sighed. 'Somewhere, I agree, there may be an heir to Hythe Farm, but it will not be that woman's brother.'

Felix rose to his feet, looking slightly flushed. 'Don't you think it might be time for you to stop condemning every woman who happens to have an ounce of spirit in her? Just because she reminds you of—'

Dominic rose also. 'Enough,' he said.

Felix turned and marched out of the room. Dominic sank back in his chair and closed his eyes—then opened them again, because he'd suddenly realised that his study still bore the faint scent of rose petals.

He flung open a window to let in some fresh air. That audacious young fortune teller was not worth a minute more of his attention, but she had disturbed him, by God, she had—which meant he'd been completely right to get her out of his life as swiftly as possible.

Cassie was still sitting on the tree trunk with their baggage, but she rose as the Earl's carriage pulled to a halt beside her and her face lit up with excitement.

'Oh, my,' she whispered to Merryn. She climbed in happily as the driver lifted their two bags in after her. 'Now, this is grand. Better than putting up with the reek of turnips, isn't it, Liam love?' She patted Liam's hand. 'So, how did you get on with His Lordship? Is everything sorted? Are we on our way to Hythe Farm?'

Merryn didn't say a word until the carriage was rattling along at full speed through Marchwood parkland. Then she said, 'Do you know, I'd rather put up with that turnip cart—I really would—than endure another minute of the Earl's company.'

Cassie's face fell. 'Oh, no. Was he horrible?'

'He was utterly detestable. And the castle is like a...' She hesitated a moment. 'Like a morgue.' Yes, that was the word. As if it was filled with bad, bad memories that the Earl couldn't bring himself to banish. She still felt oppressed by the dark panelling and the sombre relics of the castle's ancient past.

'Oh, dear.' Cassie sighed. 'What about the Earl himself? Wasn't he even earl-like? Handsome, perhaps?'

Merryn tensed as she remembered the cursed man's imposing frame and stark features. 'Cassie,' she pronounced at last, 'the fact is, we've already met him.'

'*What?*'

'It's true. He's the man who was carried to our caravan last night, after those robbers attacked him.'

For once, even the ever-talkative Cassie was lost for words. Then her eyes widened with hope. 'So is he going to help us? Are we going to the place you told me about? This farm?'

'His Lordship,' declared Merryn, 'took great pleasure in refusing his permission. And that, as far as he's concerned, is that.'

Cassie sank into silent melancholy. But Merryn was watching their surroundings very carefully as the carriage rolled onwards and the minute they were out of sight of Castle Marchwood she leaned out of the window and called to the groom. 'You may drop us off here, if you please. We shall walk the rest of the way to Maybury, since it's such a lovely morning.'

The groom pulled up his horses and turned round on his bench to address her sternly. 'Maybury is a good distance away yet. You have bags to carry. And the Earl said—'

'We shall be perfectly fine,' she said blithely. And before he could say another word, she jumped out and Liam followed. Cassie, too, although she gave Merryn an expressive look that said, *Lord's sake, Merryn. What are you up to now?*

The groom still looked grumpy as Merryn reached for their bags. 'Just you be sure, now,' he said, 'to tell

His Lordship that this was not of my doing. That you insisted I let you down here.'

'Of course,' Merryn said cheerfully. 'I won't let you take any blame whatsoever. We happen to be fond of walking. That's all.'

Cassie watched the carriage set off back to Castle Marchwood and sighed. 'Oh, Merryn. Why did you do that?'

'Because we're not going to Maybury. We're going to Hythe Farm.'

'What?'

'You heard me. The very arrogant Earl said I was to re-join the fair and wait for his further communication, but I've decided differently.' Merryn bent to pick up the heavier of the bags. 'We'll walk and we'll find Hythe Farm easily because I know from a map on the Earl's wall that it's just beyond the copse of oaks on the far ridge—you see? It's less than a mile away.'

'Darling, the Earl will be furious when he finds out!'

'That's too bad. Liam, do you think you can manage the walk, my love?'

Her brother had been listening intently. 'Are we going to the place my father told you about, Merryn?'

'That's exactly right.'

Liam's face was determined. 'Then let's go.'

It took them longer than she'd expected to climb the hill to the oak wood. Cassie chattered happily most of the time and Liam plodded manfully along, but Merryn was having second thoughts. What would the Earl do when he found out? Was she out of her mind to flout such a powerful man?

After her friends had carried the unconscious Earl into her caravan last night, she'd felt a sense of wild relief when he'd opened his eyes. She'd been praying aloud almost, *Don't die. Please don't die,* partly because he was clearly a man of wealth who could maybe do great harm to her kind friend Ashley and his show. But also because...

She'd lied to Cassie earlier. She'd said he wasn't handsome and in a way she meant it, for his looks were too raw, too elemental. When he'd regained consciousness and opened his dark eyes, she'd had the bizarre feeling that she was no longer quite in control of herself; in fact, her skin had tingled and her heart had thumped against her ribs in a most peculiar way.

Of course, she'd pulled herself together pretty quickly. He'd been hateful, treating her as if she'd leapt out of one of the fair's sideshows. But worse was to come, because who could have guessed that last night's injured stranger was the very man she'd travelled all this way to see?

As they trudged along that path she remembered how she'd begun planning her journey in the days after her father had died, for she'd realised they would have to leave their rural home in Ireland for good.

She'd always vaguely understood that it was on some kind of long lease. What she hadn't known was that the lease had in fact expired months ago, though the first she knew of it was when the debt collectors began visiting, the day after the funeral. She already knew by then that her father was bankrupt and when someone she'd thought was a friend called and offered to help she'd been both relieved and thankful for his kindness.

He came several times over the next few days, promising to do his utmost to enable her to save her home. But her gratitude had turned to terror when suddenly his pleasantries vanished and he made it brutally clear to her what he expected in return. The hateful scene that followed had since played itself out in her mind over and over again: both in her dreams and even in her waking hours.

After that, quite frantic with fear, Merryn had found Liam and packed a bag of clothes for them both, with the lawyer's letter about Hythe Farm and the small locket of her mother's hidden at the bottom. Then they'd gone to Dublin, where they'd met Ashley.

She had trusted Ashley implicitly. He was kind and gentle. But she knew far better now than to trust a man of power like the Earl. With a little shiver, she wondered again why he wasn't married. No doubt he didn't go short of female companionship, but a man of his age and his station in life needed a wife and heirs. Surely he must be for ever presented with young women of suitable wealth and breeding and most of them, she guessed, would have an arrogance that matched his.

Her thoughts were abruptly halted when Cassie stopped and cried out suddenly, 'Merryn. I hear horses.' She had put down the bag she carried and was looking all around. Merryn halted, too, and turned to gaze back down the hill—only to realise she could see a smart gig drawn by two splendid bays, coming fast in their direction.

Her first thought was: *It's the Earl. He's guessed where we're heading and he's coming after us in person.*

She tried to prepare herself for that steely gaze and daunting physique but it wasn't the Earl, neither was it the groom who'd dropped them off earlier. No—it was a smartly dressed young man with curly fair hair and a pleasant face, who pulled up close and called out, 'Hello there. Do you need a lift anywhere?'

Cassie gazed open-mouthed at this vision, while Liam was absorbed by the sight of his beautiful horses. Merryn made up her mind. Whoever he was, he looked decidedly less obnoxious than the Earl and he was offering them a lift. Liam was tired and their bags were heavy so she was not going to refuse his offer.

'Indeed, sir,' she replied, 'if it's not too much trouble. We are heading…' she took a deep breath '…for Hythe Farm.'

If he was surprised, he didn't show it. 'Very well,' he said. 'Climb on up.'

Within minutes, they were all cosily seated with their bags stowed, then the young man drove them onwards with an air of relish. He didn't ask them any questions, neither did he offer information about himself, which surprised her rather. But once they were over the crest of the hill, he pulled the gig to a halt, then pointed. 'There it is,' he said. 'Hythe Farm.'

They all gazed. The farmhouse was solidly built with high chimneys and mullioned windows, but there were clear signs it was unoccupied. Weeds grew around the courtyard and the outlying barns, while the sadly ne-glected garden was nothing more than a huge bramble patch. But Merryn felt her spirits rise, for it was a house that had been built to last centuries and those three huge old yew trees stood beside it like ancient guardians. It felt like home already. A forever home, for Liam.

'Oh, my,' said Cassie softly.

Once more their obliging driver set off and a few minutes later the gig was rattling into the courtyard. The young man pulled up his horses and turned round to them. 'No one's lived here for as long as I can re-member,' he said. 'The only person you're likely to en-counter is a pleasant fellow called Gabe, who looks after the sheep that graze the fields around here. He lives in a cottage along the lane and he'll help you out if you need him. Oh, and you'll find the key to the door under that stone trough by the nearest barn.'

Merryn was growing more and more astounded. 'Sir, why are you helping us like this, when you've surely no idea who we are?'

He grinned openly. 'I guessed that you needed a lift. That's all.'

'Yes,' she said. 'Yes, thank you.' She pulled her-self together. 'My name is Merryn. This is my brother, Liam, and Cassie here is my very good friend.' She hesitated a moment. 'You've not asked yet why we're here. But I believe that Liam is the rightful heir to Hythe Farm, so I called at Castle Marchwood, hoping to get some assistance from the Earl. But there was none to be had there.' She tried not to let bitterness creep into her voice.

'I could have told you that,' the young man said cheerfully. 'The Earl is a grumpy fellow at the best of times.'

'Then you know him?' she tried to ask, but by then he was already turning to climb back into his gig.

'I'll maybe call by later,' he said as he took up the reins. 'To see if you need anything.' Then off he set at an extremely lively pace while they all watched.

At last Cassie said, 'Well. I never. Is this entire county populated with delectable men?'

'I've no idea,' replied Merryn. 'But at least that one's proved himself a friend. And I feel we're going to need all the friends we can find.'

Because no one—not even the grim Earl—was going to take Liam's inheritance away. Her heart stopped a moment at the thought of the Earl because he was a bad enemy to have made, no doubt of it. But...

'You're strong, Merryn,' her father had told her when he lay ill. *'Take Liam to where he belongs.'*

Just then a dozen or so sheep came trotting into the yard, their little hooves clattering on the cobbles. They were followed by a black-and-white collie dog and a bearded young man who wore a leather waistcoat over his shirt, together with corduroy breeches and stout boots. He was obviously startled to see the two young women and the boy, but he lifted his cap and said, in a voice that was polite but shy, 'Good day to you all. Can I be of any help?'

He must be the local shepherd. This was a piece of luck. Merryn quickly said, 'I'm Miss Merryn Hythe. This is my brother, Liam, and here is my friend Cassie.

This property was once owned by my great-uncle and Liam is his heir, which is why we're here. I have informed the Earl,' she quickly added.

He looked slightly startled, but gave a little bow. 'My name is Gabe Barton and I'm pleased to meet you, Miss Hythe, I'm sure.' Merryn felt a twinge of guilt, knowing he wouldn't be nearly so welcoming if he'd heard the Earl's reaction to her claim. But before she could add anything further he was turning away, because some sheep were starting to wander back the way they had come. 'Nell, girl!' he called to the dog. 'Fetch 'em…fetch 'em!'

Cassie was looking at Gabe Barton, full of curiosity. Liam said nothing, but Merryn noted how raptly her brother watched the dog, Nell, skilfully round up the sheep in a corner of the yard.

'Yes,' Gabe said to them at last. 'The land here is rather underused and we're a little behind the times, I fear. As for the farmhouse, as you can see, it's very old.'

'How many acres are there, Shepherd?' asked Merryn.

'Forty altogether, miss. And there are around two hundred ewes in the flock,' replied Gabe swiftly. 'I believe there were far more in the old days. My grandfather once tended the sheep, then my father, and now I'm doing my best to take care of them.'

Merryn chose her next words carefully. 'I hope you make a reasonable living from your work?'

'I do. The Earl's steward, Mr Galbraith, sees that I'm fairly paid.' He hesitated a moment. 'If you don't mind

me saying, Miss Hythe, you sound as if you've come
here to stay. Is that correct?'

'It is,' she said very steadily.

He looked anxious. 'But the house hasn't been lived
in for years. There's a good deal to be done.'

'And I shall do it,' Merryn replied. 'Shepherd Gabe,
would you be kind enough to show us around?'

They followed their guide eagerly from room to
room. First there was a large oak-beamed kitchen with
a big table, where she guessed all the workers would
once have dined with their master. Then Gabe led them
through to a parlour for entertaining guests, with a huge
inglenook fireplace and diamond-paned windows. Several smaller rooms on the ground floor included a laundry room and a larder, while on the first floor were four
large bedrooms, with a further two up another flight of
stairs. Both of these had sloping ceilings and box-beds
that Merryn guessed were as old as the house itself.

The furniture, what there was of it, was carved from
oak and all of the ground-floor rooms were stone-
flagged. In the kitchen was an old-fashioned spit for
roasting meat over the fire, while a multitude of cooking pots hung in glorious disarray above the iron stove.

There were also spiders' webs everywhere and in the
corners were heaps of crisp brown leaves that must have
somehow blown in during the last winter's storms. But
there was no doubt about it—the house could be lovely.

Though with that thought, Merryn felt her anger
building up. Why hadn't the Earl and his predecessors
looked after it better?

'Well,' said Cassie, who'd been exploring the kitchen.

'After giving everywhere a good clean-up, I could be right at home here, baking cakes and griddle scones.' She cast a playful look at their guide. 'You'd like my griddle scones, Shepherd Gabe, I assure you!'

Merryn realised Liam was at her side.

'I saw some lambs out there,' he whispered. 'May I go and look at them?'

Shepherd Gabe heard and smiled at Liam. 'I'll show you them, lad. Those ones out there in the courtyard are several weeks old now, but you can see some newborns, too—they're in the hay barn where it's nice and warm.' He looked at Merryn. 'Soon, miss, you'll meet my young brother. His name's Dickon and he's out in the fields with George.'

'George? Is he another brother?'

'Oh, no. George is a horse, a faithful old creature who pulls the wagon we use to carry hay. The wagon's useful, too, for bringing the ewes from the further fields into the barns here for lambing. Dickon and I have done our best to look after everything, although I'm truly sorry that the house isn't in a better state.'

'It's not your fault in the slightest!' Merryn declared. 'The house isn't your responsibility and it sounds as if you've kept up with the farm work admirably.'

Gabe looked pleased. 'I've done my best, miss. I'll take your young brother out to see the lambs in the yard, shall I? Then I'll have to be on my way since there's a fence needs fixing over by the far field. But I'll be here several times a day to check on the lambs, so let me know if there's anything else I can help with.'

After he'd led an eager Liam outside, Merryn sat

down, absorbing all that she'd learned. This house really could be beautiful. But surely the Earl must realise it needed someone to care for it—in other words, someone who lived in it!

Cassie had been eagerly exploring the kitchen cupboards and pantry, but now she was gazing out of the window to where the shepherd was showing Liam the lambs. She turned back to Merryn with a gleam in her eyes.

'Lovely,' she said.

'The house? Yes, even though it's been neglected for so long.'

'I'm not talking about the building.' Cassie's eyes positively twinkled. 'I'm talking about the shepherd. He's a grand figure of a man, wouldn't you say?'

Merryn hesitated. 'Oh, Cassie, darling. Yes, he does seem nice, but—' She broke off at the sound of clattering hooves, which meant that someone was riding into the yard, at speed. With a sinking heart, Merryn quickly joined Cassie at the window.

'Oh, my goodness. It's the Earl,' said Cassie.

Merryn braced herself, knowing their brief idyll was over.

Chapter Six

When Dominic learned that his brother had actually driven his unwanted visitor to Hythe Farm, he had been incredulous. He already knew that the woman had dismissed his carriage and led her little group away on foot—his groom had told him the story rather sheepishly—but he had no idea where she was heading.

He said to Felix, 'You actually went after the fortune teller and her companions and gave them a lift to Hythe Farm?'

Felix was forced to confess after Dominic caught him driving his gig back into the yard with a rather foolish grin on his face. 'Yes,' Felix said defiantly. 'She was going to walk there anyway.'

Dominic heaved in a deep breath. 'Right. Now I know where she's gone, I'm going there myself, to make her situation quite clear to her.'

He had Meg saddled up and rode there straight away. There was no sign of her outside the house, but by one of the barns he saw the boy with Gabe Barton, who looked somewhat startled by the Earl's arrival. Dominic nodded to him, looped his horse's reins around the iron post by the front door and headed straight in.

Miss Hythe was in the big kitchen with her friend Cassie. Cassie looked nervous, but the fortune teller met his gaze with more than a hint of defiance.

'My lord,' she said, 'you should have let me know you were coming. I would have liked to prepare for your visit.'

Her damned impudence was staggering. 'You had no right,' he said icily, 'to dismiss my driver and come here. You are wrong to talk and act as if your claim is settled.'

'But it is!' she responded with mild surprise. 'May I remind you that you have that lawyer's letter to prove it?'

Dominic gritted his teeth. 'As I explained, even if your claim is a valid one it needs to be proved in a court of law. And I do not admire your tactics in taking advantage of a rather gullible young man to bring you here.'

She looked up sharply at that. 'So he's a friend of yours, then?'

'In a manner of speaking, yes. He's my brother.'

For the first time she looked shaken, but a moment later she was back on form. 'Then your brother,' she said, 'is wiser than you are. He accepts that my claim is valid and so should you.'

Dominic saw her friend, the one with the dyed blonde hair, edging a little nervously towards the door. 'I think,' Cassie said, 'that I'll go outside and find Liam. Just to see what he's up to.'

She exited the room with a sense of relief, he guessed. He waited till the door was shut again before declaring, 'Miss Hythe.' He had to call her something, whether it was really her name or not. 'Let me repeat that you cannot take possession of this property until your claim is validated. Anyway, I imagine you must be extremely disappointed by what you've seen of the house and its lands. I expect your hopes ran considerably higher.'

He was both angry and frustrated. Normally he dealt with any problems calmly and coldly, but this woman threw him at every turn. She was years younger than him, younger than Felix even, but those unusual green eyes of hers seemed to see and understand far too much.

They were also sparking fire again. 'Unlike many people,' she declared, 'I don't judge everything by its monetary value. I'm not used to wealth and I don't desire it; indeed, for Liam to have this kind of life is all I could ever want for him. Also, I am astonished that you have the gall to claim you are responsible for this property. Is that an example of your care?' She indicated a pile of leaves in the corner of the room.

Damn it, he knew she was right. He'd not visited the farmhouse for years. Of course, he'd instructed Galbraith to see that the structure was maintained, but an inevitable air of neglect hung around the building and its barns. However, he was unused to anyone at all, let alone a young woman from a travelling show, speaking to him in such a manner.

He should have been enraged. He should have dealt her one of the icy put-downs for which he was famed.

Instead he had a most odd feeling, as if something was stirring his blood and challenging his frozen inner self into some sort of reluctant life.

Nonsense. He would enjoy the forthcoming battle, nothing more.

She said softly, 'You're not used to people arguing with you, are you, my lord? Not used to them pointing out the truth.'

Now, *that* brought the iron gates clanging down on any slight softening of his opposition to her. It was perhaps as well that, before he could make a suitably crushing reply, her excitable friend appeared at the door. 'Merryn. I can't see Liam, anywhere!'

Miss Hythe—Merryn—was already heading for the door and Dominic realised he'd been instantly forgotten. 'He'll be close by,' he heard Merryn saying, as if trying to reassure herself as much as Cassie. 'Perhaps he's gone round the back of the house. Will you check there, Cassie? I'll go to look for him in the outbuildings.' Briefly she turned to Dominic. 'I hope you'll forgive me for cutting short our conversation, my lord, but I'm sure we can continue it some other time.'

She loved her brother, he realised. Really loved him. He made no reply, but followed her outside, seeing that she was hastening from one barn to the next, pulling open the great doors, then coming out again, her face pale with anxiety. On realising he was still there she shook her head and said, 'My lord, there is no need at all for you to stay. He'll not have gone far, but I'm afraid Liam may have heard our difference of opinions just now. He sometimes wanders away when he's upset, to find somewhere quiet—'

She broke off and he guessed it was because she, like him, could hear a feeble bleating sound coming from a wooden shed over by the furthest barn.

She was already on her way there and he followed. They both stopped at the open door and he saw that inside the shed, a tiny lamb nestled close to its mother on a bed of loose straw. The boy was kneeling there gazing at the lamb, his face alight with wonder.

Dominic suddenly remembered how he and Felix, many years ago, had loved to come to Hythe Farm when it was lambing time, to watch the old shepherd—Gabe's father—at his work and to see the miracle of tiny lambs taking their first, tottering steps.

He realised that Merryn Hythe was speaking to him again, in a different tone this time. 'I told you he wouldn't go far,' she said quietly.

He nodded. 'The mother must have somehow escaped Gabe's eagle eye and brought her lamb in here.'

'Do you think they'll both be all right?'

'I do,' he answered. 'Gabe will be back soon and he'll move them safely back into the barn with the others.'

He saw that some straw had stuck to the hem of her skirt and her thick brown hair was dishevelled, but he guessed that she just didn't care. She had absolutely no vanity, but he felt the challenge of her settling warningly in his spine, the stirring of desire even, and he clamped down hard to rid himself of it.

He prepared to speak to the boy, but she made a gesture to stop him. 'Don't disturb him yet. Please.' She moved away into the sunlight and he followed.

At that moment the boy came out. 'Merryn!' he said. Dominic could see he was almost bursting with excitement. 'The shepherd showed me all the other lambs in the barn. But after he'd gone, I found this one and its mother, on their own. Will they be all right? Oh!'

The moment he saw the Earl his chattering ceased. He stood close to his sister, looking young and anxious. With their parents both dead, Dominic realised his sister must be a vital figure in the boy's life.

'They'll both be fine,' Dominic said to him. 'Fortunately, they have an excellent shepherd, who should be here soon to put them back where they belong.'

He heard footsteps behind them—not Gabe, but Miss Hythe's blonde-haired friend again.

'Liam. You're here!' She rushed to the boy and hugged him. 'You gave us a fright, child.'

'He's fine, Cassie,' Merryn said. 'Take him back inside, will you?'

'Of course.'

Dominic watched as Cassie and Liam set off together to the farmhouse, then he turned back to Miss Hythe. Merryn. 'Tell me. Is the boy usually so silent with strangers?'

She didn't answer him straight away, but at last she looked at him again with those vivid eyes and said, 'He's shy, certainly. But if you'll permit me, I'll tell you of his other qualities. He is warm and loving. He is intelligent. But as I've said, when our mother died that was a great blow to him, followed a year ago by the loss of our father. He finds meeting new people difficult, though you've maybe noticed that he loves animals—perhaps because they don't waste their time in talking.'

Another reluctant feeling stirred inside Dominic's chest, of unexpected admiration. But before he could think what to reply, she was speaking again.

'So you see, my lord, that Liam will never have an abundance of natural confidence or ambition. He would find it difficult to cope with great wealth and I have never wished it for him. For Liam to have this kind of life—' she spread out her hands to indicate their surroundings '—is all I could ever want for him.'

She looked different here, thought Dominic. The strange thing was, it was almost as if the soft light of the old house suited her. As if she and the boy truly belonged here. Though she was clever, that was all too evident, and he must not allow himself to be weakened by sentiment. Also, he was suddenly wondering if Miss Hythe had realised she might have a chance of collecting a far more valuable prize. His brother was clearly infatuated with her—dangerously so.

When he spoke next, it was in a tone that held no kindness. 'Tomorrow,' he said, 'I must go to London, where every iota of your claim must be thoroughly checked. You, in turn, must make no further attempt to assume ownership of Hythe Farm until this matter is settled one way or the other.'

Her answer was swift. 'Stop talking down to me, please.' Those words were softly spoken, but her eyes glittered like chips of ice. 'And do not treat me like one of your minions.'

Dominic allowed his mouth to curl. 'Very well,' he said. 'And you resent being treated like a minion? An interesting point, that, because I have another proposition for you.'

'You do?'

That had thrown her. He guessed she would receive varied propositions from men wherever she went. 'I do indeed,' he answered. 'I think it might be a good idea if you come to dine with me tonight. Then we can go over everything properly before I travel to London tomorrow to visit my lawyers.'

'Dine with you?' She sounded incredulous. 'At Castle Marchwood?'

Dominic pressed on ruthlessly. 'That's exactly what I said. I shall send a carriage for you at seven. We dine early in the country.'

She still looked slightly dazed. 'Will it be a formal dinner?'

'My meals are always formal.'

'So you intend to test my manners in front of your household. What could be more amusing for you?' Her eyes were glittering with defiance again. 'No doubt you'll enjoy telling everyone that I earned my living telling fortunes with a travelling show?'

He retaliated immediately. 'Most definitely not. After all, my staff would immediately realise that your fortune-telling skills have let you down vastly if you came here hoping for great wealth.'

'But I wasn't, you see,' she breathed. 'I wasn't.'

The absolute simplicity of that statement knocked him sideways, so much so that it took him a moment to recover his breath and head for his horse. She was still standing there as Dominic rode off and he spent a large part of his journey trying to obliterate the memory of those defiant, dark-lashed eyes set in a picture-perfect face. Trying also to dismiss the impression he'd formed of the absolute bravery of a young female who was ready to do battle with anyone, even him, for her brother's sake.

He brushed away the warning signs of sympathy. Utter coldness had, after all, become a habit since Teresa left him and he knew he was known by some as the Earl with the heart of stone. Some of his enemies would also say he was losing his mind inviting Merryn Hythe to dine with him, but there was method in his madness. She hadn't realised that all his family would be there as well.

Felix, for a start. Dominic would be able to let his brother see this young woman for what she was—a fairground hussy, who would no doubt make an absolute spectacle of herself in such a formal setting. Of course, Sarah and Wilfred would be there, too, and Sarah's horror at the sight of Dominic's unexpected guest would be something to behold. Indeed, he found himself rather hoping Miss Hythe would give Sarah a taste of the acid wit she'd shown to him earlier…

No. He reminded himself he was swerving to the wrong side of the battle lines there. He wanted Merryn Hythe, with her challenging eyes and bold demeanour, to retreat from the conflict and leave the district as swiftly as possible.

He should have been delighted with his plan. But somehow he wasn't. Not in the least.

As the hoofbeats of the Earl's horse faded into the distance, Merryn stood there unable for a while to move. She had no idea at all how she was going to deal with this man.

It should be simple, since she had right on her side and he was wrong. He was haughty and disdainful; in fact, he was clearly someone who found it burdensome to show even basic good manners. As for his hard-featured face and those hooded eyes, they killed off any illusion that he was in any way physically attractive.

She was well armed against a man like him, against any man for that matter. So she simply didn't understand why she felt so thoroughly confused by him. Why some truly ridiculous thoughts flickered through her mind whenever she looked at him, making her slightly dizzy and considerably dismayed.

She drew a deep breath and pulled herself together. At least he was honest. At least he wasn't trying to trick her with false words and fake promises; on the contrary, he could barely disguise his contempt. Yes, he'd made his feelings towards her quite clear—and she was ready to prepare herself for battle.

On going back into the big kitchen, she saw that Liam was setting some plates on the table while Cassie prepared a platter of bread and cheese. 'For our supper,' Cassie pointed out. 'Gabe sent his young brother, Dickon, with food for us—he popped by while you were out there talking with His Lordship. My, the man is extraordinarily good-looking. Clearly that's why you didn't even notice Dickon arrive.'

'Cassie! The Earl is not—'

'Dickon,' went on Cassie, slapping butter on to the bread with a knife, 'also said to tell you that Gabe gets his supplies from Weybridge market every week and he'll pick up whatever we want next time he goes.'

'How very kind. But I won't be needing any supper. You see, the Earl has invited me to dinner at the castle tonight.'

Cassie dropped her knife. 'Dinner? With His Lordship? My, oh, my.' Then she grinned. 'He must like you. I'm sure of it.'

Merryn glanced to make sure Liam wasn't listening. 'The Earl of Marchwood,' she said in a low voice, 'is detestable.'

Cassie raised her eyebrows. 'If you say so.' She began slicing more cheese energetically. 'Now for myself, I'd be quite happy to make friends with a man like Shepherd Gabe.'

'Yes, Gabe does seem very pleasant and we're lucky to have him around. But, Cassie, will you mind keeping Liam company tonight while I deal with the Earl?'

'Of course not.' Cassie turned to face her, bread knife in hand again. 'And you stand firm, my girl. You've shown him that lawyer's letter proving it's Liam's, haven't you? You tell him you won't take no for an answer!'

Merryn nodded. 'Cassie,' she said suddenly. 'When you unpacked those clothes for me, where did you put that green gown that once belonged to my mother?'

Cassie's eyes widened. 'Merryn, no. Really?'

'Yes,' Merryn replied. She took a piece of cheese and ate it with relish. 'Really.'

On reaching the castle, Dominic had barely had time to hand over his coat to Inchberry when he realised Sarah was fast approaching. 'Is it true,' his sister demanded, 'that you've been to Hythe Farm to see *that woman*?'

Not one to mince her words, Sarah. 'If you mean our recent visitor,' Dominic calmly replied, 'then, yes, I've been to visit her at Hythe Farm.'

'Are you saying—' Sarah looked incredulous '—that she's staying there? That you've actually accepted her story?'

'I haven't.' He said to the butler, 'Thank you, Inchberry. That will be all.' Then he turned back to his sister. 'She's at Hythe Farm, Sarah, because our young brother took matters into his own hands and drove her there.'

'Then you must have her evicted!'

Dominic felt a peculiarly strong desire to tell his sister it was no business whatsoever of hers. Instead he merely said, 'There is a possibility that her claim is true. And she will be our neighbour for a while, so I've invited Miss Hythe to dine here tonight.'

This time Sarah was lost for words. At last she said, 'Then Wilfred and I will be able to demonstrate to you what a cunning schemer this woman must be!'

'Fair enough,' he said equably. 'You'll enjoy that, won't you?'

His sister stormed off.

After that Dominic went in search of Felix. His brother was in the billiards room intent on a tricky shot, but when Dominic entered, he glanced up apprehensively. Clearly he guessed exactly what was coming.

'Listen,' Felix began, putting down his cue, 'I didn't realise Miss Hythe was going to stay there, I truly didn't. And anyway, I do not understand why you're in such a lather about an insignificant piece of land that was never really ours anyway. Besides, the house is a mess!'

'To someone used to living in a caravan,' said Dominic, resting one hand on the corner of the billiard table, 'Hythe Farm must resemble a palace.'

'But you always guessed someone might turn up to claim it some day. Why should you care who it is?'

'Perhaps because I happen to dislike fraudsters.'

Felix swept aside the billiard balls in an angry gesture. 'Have you,' he demanded, 'any actual proof that Merryn is a fraudster? You are such a cynic as far as women are concerned! There's no need to condemn them *all* just because your marriage turned out to be a disaster—'

'Careful, Felix.'

Dominic's gravelly tone made Felix hold up his hand in a gesture of appeasement. 'All right, Dom. I'm sorry. But I think Merryn's really lovely—and she's brave, to have travelled all this way and to stand up to you, of all people.'

'I sincerely hope you're not falling for her.'

'I wouldn't be alone if I did!'

'No doubt. But I expect higher standards from you.'

Felix stared at him. 'I know that. I also know that I've been a bitter disappointment to you from the day I was born.'

Dominic reached out a hand. 'Felix. I didn't mean...'

But his brother was already marching out of the room.

Dominic sighed, then he picked up the cue Felix had abandoned, examined the table briefly and cannoned the black into the furthest pocket. Tonight, in the formal setting of the castle's dining room, he hoped Merryn Hythe would prove herself to be a complete fraud—and that the ridiculous urge he'd felt this afternoon to take her in his arms and kiss her would be utterly dispelled.

The Earl with the heart of stone, they called him. So be it.

Chapter Seven

By the time the Earl's carriage arrived to collect her, Merryn had noticed that leaden clouds were gathering on the horizon. Her fairground friends would have warned that a stormy evening lay ahead and she was not encouraged by the realisation that the Earl had sent the same driver as last time, who as he opened the vehicle's door for her muttered something like, 'No hopping out of my carriage this time!'

Once they were on their way Merryn settled back on the leather seat and wrapped her old cloak around her. Cassie had braided her thick hair and coiled it at the nape of her neck, but already some rebellious strands had come loose.

'You look wonderful!' Cassie had assured her, but Merryn wasn't at all sure of that. What a day she'd endured. Yes, she had reached Hythe Farm after months of travelling, but then—then, she'd met the Earl.

What awful luck, for him to be the man she'd clashed with at the fair. It meant, of course, that he immediately despised her. Well, so be it. Her spine stiffened in fresh resolve as the carriage jolted along the track. She'd always tried to brush her fears aside by making plans and she decided that in the days ahead she and Cassie would clean the farmhouse from top to bottom, polishing the ancient furniture and opening all the windows to air it. Maybe they'd even clear those brambles from the garden to plant some herbs and flowers, and these daydreams gradually soothed her—until she saw the turrets of Castle Marchwood looming near.

She would never admit it to Cassie, but she was very afraid tonight would be a fresh disaster. All too soon they were coming to a halt in the castle's courtyard and she realised the elderly butler with the strange wig was standing at the door. As she climbed the steps he gave her a stern bow, disappeared for a moment and then the Earl himself arrived.

'Miss Hythe,' the Earl said, in a far from engaging manner.

'My lord.' Somehow Merryn managed a brief curtsy, noting that this time he was dressed in formal attire—a dark grey coat, silk breeches and a crisp white cravat. Once more she felt an unsettling pulse of alarm because he looked staggeringly...what was the word?

'Whether you like it or not,' Cassie had said, *'the man's a handsome devil.'*

No. He wasn't handsome. She would never admit that this man was handsome. He was proud, he was intimidating and he was her enemy—it was as simple as that. She shrugged off her shabby cloak and handed it to the hovering butler. He took it and as his eyes flickered over what she wore beneath, his features altered not one jot.

But the Earl's did.

His dark eyebrows lifted in total surprise and she was glad to see him lost for words. *Touché, my lord*, she thought to herself, for she could see he was rapidly adjusting to the fact that she was wearing a summery gown of pale green organza—not all-revealing in the way of modern gowns and no doubt the style was completely out of date. But it had been her mother's and Merryn, not normally a creature of vanity, had been determined to bring the gown with her. It was the one luxury she'd allowed herself.

But was the Earl going to say anything? No. Of course not. Instead he led her along that vast hall hung with shields and finally pointed the way into the candle-lit drawing room. She entered, her confidence rising a little, only to realise that—oh, goodness, on a sofa over by the window sat a stern-looking woman wearing a severe grey gown that would almost have marked her as a servant were it not for her stupendous diamond necklace. Behind her stood an anxious-looking man.

'Miss Hythe,' the Earl said, 'allow me to introduce my sister, Lady Challoner, and her husband, Sir Wilfred.'

Merryn cursed herself for a fool. She'd assumed she and the Earl would be dining alone. She'd never dreamed he would wish to introduce someone he judged an impostor to his sister—who must, she realised, be the mother of the two boys who had tormented Liam earlier.

It was Sir Wilfred who offered the first nervous greeting. 'Miss Hythe! We hear you are related to a family that once lived in the neighbourhood.'

'So she says,' cut in Lady Challoner. Merryn noticed that she had the Earl's aristocratic nose, although on her it looked almost venomous.

'Indeed, Lady Challoner,' Merryn replied cheerfully. 'And this is proving to be a positively delightful return for me!'

No one replied. Then suddenly, the door opened to admit a familiar figure and Merryn froze as the Earl announced, 'Here is my brother, Felix. I believe you and he have already met.'

Felix bowed over her hand and gave her a secret grin. 'Delighted to meet you again,' he said.

Oh, heavens. This was all extremely embarrassing. Why hadn't the Earl warned her that she was to be paraded in front of his entire family?

Matters did not improve. Shortly afterwards they moved into the huge, gloomy dining room and it wasn't long before Merryn was wondering if her ordeal would ever end. The Earl was at the head of the table to her left; Felix was on her right and opposite her sat Lady Challoner, whose glare was constant. There were so many courses that Merryn's appetite, never large at the best of times, vanished completely and she lapsed into a futile longing for the cosy kitchen at Hythe Farm.

Lady Challoner was telling them all about the difficulty of choosing a suitable school for her talented sons. Eventually Felix murmured softly to Merryn, 'I feel sorry for whichever school gets landed with those spoiled brats. In the meantime, Miss Hythe, do have some more of this ragout. It's absolutely delicious!'

Sarah picked up on that. 'My brother the Earl,' she

told Merryn loftily, 'prides himself on keeping a fine table and his cook is exceptionally skilled in preparing French dishes. You'll have realised, of course, that the fish course was salmon *à la Genevoise*, which is perfectly delicious. But this ragout *à la Périgueux* is Cook's speciality—accompanied, always, by petit pois and another treat of hers, purée *de marrons*.'

Affecting a puzzled look, Merryn pointed to the meat dish. 'Why, do you know, that's exactly what my mother used to make. It's lamb stew, surely! And as for the dish of...*marrons*, I think you called them? They're chestnuts! We used to gather them in the woods then roast them over the kitchen fire and eat them with salt when we were children.'

Felix was choking back laughter. 'Admirable, Miss Hythe! That's exactly what my friends and I used to do whenever we were here at Marchwood in the autumn. We'd hunt for chestnuts in the woods, make an outdoor fire and roast them to perfection. Calling them by some fancy French name doesn't make them one jot tastier!'

Silence ensued for several moments until, at last, Sir Wilfred attempted to engage the Earl in a conversation about a bill going through Parliament. But the Earl, though making the occasional reply, appeared to be mostly watching Merryn and waiting for her to make a fool of herself, no doubt.

So she obliged. She beamed round at them all and took a large sip of her white wine. 'Goodness,' she said to the footman who had just poured it. 'This is delicious. Thank you. Tell me, do you prefer white wine or red? I'm sorry, I don't know your name.'

The young footman turned pink. 'My name is Peter, miss. I—I actually prefer ale, to be honest.'

'Peter, I find your honesty most refreshing! Do you know, I'm rather partial to a glass of home brew myself.'

Once more, silence enveloped all seated at the table. Of course, she knew she'd broken one of the first rules of the nobility. *Apart from giving instructions, never acknowledge that the staff are even in the room.* But then Felix grinned and said to the footman, 'Quite right, Peter. When you've a real thirst on you, there's nothing to beat good English ale.'

Lady Challoner had a look of frozen horror on her face. Sir Wilfred was fumbling nervously with his napkin. The Earl… Well, Merryn didn't quite like to look at the Earl. But she did smile back at Felix. 'How delightful it is,' she sighed happily, 'on my first night in this neighbourhood, to receive such a warm welcome from you all.'

Dominic just could not make up his mind about Miss Hythe. Was she clever, or was she very, very naive? She'd certainly been shaken on realising she would be dining with his family, although she'd quickly squashed whatever nerves she was feeling and was acting hideously brashly, on purpose, he was sure. She knew full well what she was doing. She was baiting Sarah—he couldn't blame her for *that*—and deliberately taunting him by flirting with his idiotic brother. She intended to make it clear to him that she didn't give a fig for his opinion of her. All in all she was most infuriating.

And yet. And yet…

It was quite an ordeal that he'd thrown her into, but she'd not sought refuge in cowed silence, far from it. In fact, he couldn't help but be amused by the way she ruffled Sarah's feathers and, by God, no one could deny she looked tempting in that pretty dress of hers, old-fashioned though it was. The green flattered her colouring immensely and no red-blooded man could fail to be intrigued by her dark-lashed eyes and the way her thick brown hair glittered almost golden in the candlelight. All in all, he experienced a variety of feelings that he knew he needed to extinguish. Very firmly.

As for Felix, the young fool had hardly taken his eyes off the woman and was obviously enjoying her often startling comments. But Sarah was gunning for her and each question was like a sugar-coated poison dart.

'So, Miss Hythe,' Sarah purred. 'When did it first occur to you to travel all the way from Ireland to England? I suppose it coincided with the moment you realised there might be some property to be claimed?'

'Oh, indeed,' Merryn replied, after setting down her wine glass with a sigh of pleasure. 'That's all I've dreamed of. Reaching England and laying my hands on the land my father told me our family was entitled to. Our very own estate! How we have moved up in the world!'

Dominic saw Sarah's jaw drop. Felix was grinning. Merryn reached for more butter for her bread roll and spread it lavishly.

'Of course,' she went on, 'I know that such a small estate wouldn't be seen as luxury by nobility such as yourselves. But it's perfect for my brother, as I told the Earl. I'm used to hard work, so Hythe Farm will be a great adventure. And how exciting to find that I have such distinguished neighbours! No doubt you have coachfuls of rich and elegant people visiting here all the time, although of course—' and she fluttered her eyelashes '—I wouldn't presume to be introduced to your grand friends. But I will be able to watch them from our fields should they go out for rides around your estate and maybe I could even exchange the time of day with them.' She put her hand to her heart and sighed in pleasure.

Sarah looked ready to explode while Dominic watched Miss Merryn Hythe assessingly. Those amazing eyes of hers were dancing with mischief, he would swear. She was clever, he decided. *Very* clever.

Sarah, meanwhile, was saying glacially, 'I understand your brother's claim to the Hythe property is far from settled, so I trust you appreciate my brother's generosity in acknowledging you as his *very* temporary neighbour?'

Dominic thought he saw a quick flash of anger darken Merryn's expression. But she sounded unperturbed as she replied, 'Goodness, you are perfectly right to remind me that I must remember my place. I realise that I'm extremely honoured to be allowed to dine with my superiors like this.'

Felix lifted his glass in a salute. 'It's a pleasure, Miss Hythe. A real pleasure.'

Sarah pushed aside her plate. 'Maybe for you, Felix. You, after all, are used to mingling with the lower ranks of society. Wilfred and I are not.'

'I don't imagine, though, Lady Challoner,' said Merryn, 'that this will be a regular occurrence. Do you?'

There was that spark of fire again, Dominic registered. But then she was beaming round at them all once more and saying, 'This pudding, by the way, is utterly delicious. In Ireland, we had nothing like it. What did you say it was?'

'Gateau *à la Polonaise*,' said Dominic.

'Well, at home we usually finished our meals with bread and the raspberry jam our mother had made. That was quite delicious, too.' Merryn continued to demolish her gateau with a hearty appetite.

'Ridiculous,' muttered Sarah. 'The woman's claim to Hythe Farm is intolerable.'

'Now, Sarah…' began Wilfred in his conciliatory way. 'As your brother says, Miss Hythe's case needs to be taken through the due process of the law.' Miss Hythe appeared to be listening politely to all this. 'And,' went on Wilfred, 'until a decision is made, Dominic is very generously welcoming his new neighbour to the district.'

'Hear, hear.' Felix raised his wine glass again. 'Welcome indeed, Miss Hythe.'

And—good God—Dominic realised that Felix wasn't Miss Hythe's only admirer, for he saw now that Wilfred was really rather fascinated by the coy smiles she kept throwing in his direction. As for that dress of hers, it might be modestly cut, but it was still far too easy for a young fool like Felix—and an older fool like Wilfred—to visualise the tempting figure beneath it.

Not him, though. Not him.

'Would you tell us a little more about your upbringing in Ireland, Miss Hythe?' said Wilfred—rather daringly, since his wife was already glaring at him.

But Merryn positively beamed. 'Where to begin? I think I've told you that Liam and I grew up far from any town. The nearest one was three days away on horseback.'

'Goodness,' said Sarah rather faintly. 'But I assume you had a carriage, or at least a gig, for your mother and yourself?'

'Oh, I preferred to ride everywhere!' said Merryn cheerfully. 'I loved horses and for that reason I wore breeches a good deal of the time. I assure you, no garment could be more useful for country life. Hoeing cabbages, planting turnips—who wears a frock for such tasks?'

Sarah gasped in shock, but Dominic caught the hint of rebellion in Miss Hythe's eyes and realised she was doing her very best to provoke his exasperating sister. He found the corners of his mouth lifting in something that was almost a smile, then told himself very quickly that it wasn't because he admired Miss Hythe, oh, no.

But he did rather appreciate her way of responding to Sarah's attempted put-downs, though unfortunately so did Felix, who said, as the next course was served, 'It sounds as if you'll be entirely suited to looking after your estate, Miss Hythe.'

'It's Liam's,' she said swiftly. This time her expression was deadly earnest. 'It's for Liam. Not me.'

Wilfred was nodding earnestly. 'Of course,' he said. 'We completely understand how much you want your brother to be properly provided for.'

Sarah gave him such a look that Dominic felt compelled to create a diversion. 'I've never been to Dublin,' he said. 'Why don't you tell us a little about it? I understand you sailed from there to England.'

He saw that expressive face of hers altering once more. She said at last, more quietly than before, 'It was crowded with people. The docks were full of sailors and tradesmen shouting to one other. There were also many poor families who had come from the countryside and were desperate to reach England. In many ways, I found it all rather distressing.'

There was a moment of silence, broken inevitably by Sarah, who brusquely said, 'It's their own fault, surely? To leave their homes and travel to England for no good reason, except to look for an easy life?'

Dominic saw that Merryn's whole body had become tense, but she spoke calmly enough as she answered, 'Many of those men had lost their jobs in their home towns and villages and were hoping to find work in England so they could feed their families.' She looked directly at Sarah. 'But I shouldn't think you can even imagine what that feels like. Can you?'

'By Jove,' said Felix heartily, 'I can't imagine it for a moment. But good for you, Miss Hythe, for reminding us. Tell us, will you, about your voyage? And your journey here, with that fair?'

'I made some good friends,' she said.

And that was all. Dominic found he had been cynically waiting for some glib boast about the travelling fair and the fun she had as a fortune teller, but there was nothing.

Just at that moment the door to the dining room burst open and in rushed young Marcus, followed by a hassled-looking maid. Marcus ran straight to his mother and flung himself into her arms. 'Mama. Mama!' Then he spotted the bread roll on her plate and grabbed it, knocking over her glass of red wine in the process. A footman rushed forward with a napkin to try to mop up the mess on the pristine white tablecloth.

'My lady,' began the flustered maid, 'I'm truly sorry, but Master Marcus wouldn't go to sleep. He's frightened of ghosts in his bedroom, you see. He says he dreamed of a headless knight.'

Felix and Dominic exchanged meaningful looks. Sarah was already on her feet, holding Marcus by the hand. 'Oh, my poor darling.' She turned to her brother. 'These dreams, Dominic, are thanks to the unpleasant relics around the castle. Swords, suits of armour and those great axes hanging on the wall—haven't I told you such sights are quite unsuitable for young children? Marcus, my sweet, I'll come upstairs with you and make sure you're not scared any more.'

In fact Marcus had stopped his sobs and was staring at Merryn. 'Mama, what is that strange lady doing here? Why is she wearing such a funny dress?'

Dominic was on his feet before he realised what he was doing. 'Sarah, I do believe it's time you taught your sons some manners. Marcus, apologise to my guest this instant.'

Marcus looked rebellious, but Dominic's stern glance quelled him. 'I apologise,' the boy muttered. Sarah grabbed him by the hand again and marched out.

Wilfred had risen, too, and was glancing ruefully at Dominic. 'I'd better follow my wife and son to calm things down, or there'll be even more trouble. Miss Hythe, it's been delightful to make your acquaintance. I hope to visit Hythe Farm and meet your brother very soon.'

Dominic began, 'The claim is far from settled yet—' But Wilfred was already heading for the door.

And Felix?

Felix was giving Merryn Hythe a conspiratorial wink and Dominic clenched his teeth. He consoled himself with the thought that Felix would come to his senses sooner or later—after all, his sudden infatuations usually lasted a week or two at most. All the same, Dominic felt a tingle of unease. What if Miss Hythe encouraged Felix to suggest some kind of paid liaison? Besides being damnably pretty, Miss Hythe was strong-willed and clever, too. She would drive a hard bargain.

He said, 'Felix. I think you told me earlier that you needed to speak with the grooms about the loose shoe on your bay mare.'

'What? Oh, that. It'll wait till tomorrow morning, surely!'

'I rather think,' replied Dominic testily, 'that the sooner you see to it, the better. Don't you?'

Felix got the message. Sighing, he left, but not before bowing to their guest and saying gallantly, 'Your servant, Miss Hythe. Don't let Dominic bully you, now, will you?'

Which left the two of them together—and Miss Hythe was suddenly showing slight signs of nerves,

Dominic realised. Yes, despite her bright and sometimes outrageous comments, she was nervous. Of him? Surely not. It was quite clear that she thought very little of *him*.

She was pointing to the gilded clock on the mantelpiece. 'Oh, dear, is that truly the time? I really must be returning to Hythe Farm. Cassie is there, of course, but I doubt that Liam will be able to sleep until I return.'

She'd risen, but he gestured her back to her chair and poured her more wine. Clearly she wanted to escape. Maybe Miss Merryn Hythe was not quite as tough as she pretended to be.

'Before you go,' he said, sitting down again himself and resting his forearms on the big table, 'indulge me by answering a question or two. Firstly, why did you feel the need to make up those quite ridiculous stories about wearing breeches all the time and hoeing cabbages?'

She hesitated. 'It wasn't all a lie.'

'But…hoeing *cabbages*?'

She shrugged, her defiance returning. 'Maybe that was a lie, but I found it amusing. Besides, I quite enjoyed fulfilling your sister's obvious expectations. She wanted to see me as a country bumpkin, so I obliged.'

'You've made an enemy of her.'

Her eyes were flashing sparks again. 'Could I have expected anything else from your family? I don't know why you invited me to this gathering, but I strongly suspect it was to make a fool of me. Am I right?'

Dominic was struck by a pang of absolute guilt because she'd hit upon the exact reason why he'd invited her here tonight. And Miss Hythe hadn't finished with him yet.

'You can reassure your sister,' she continued, 'that she will see little enough of me in future. I never expected Liam and I to be accepted as your equals, of course I didn't. Nor do I wish to be condescended to like this. I hope you believe me?'

Before Dominic could even start to think of a reply, his butler entered. 'My lord. Your steward has just arrived and wishes to have a word with you.'

'I'll be back, Miss Hythe,' Dominic told her as he headed for the door. 'Be sure of it.'

Chapter Eight

The minute he'd left the room Merryn sat back, closed her eyes and felt her heart sinking to the soles of her shoes.

Her father had warned her about the English aristocracy. 'They cling fiercely to their inherited privileges,' he'd said. 'They can be overbearing, particularly in their attitude to women not of their own rank.'

Overbearing indeed. She felt absolutely furious with the Earl for his assumption that she would tell lies to get her hands on what, to him, was merely a small and inconvenient parcel of land and a crumbling old house.

Yet it was just her luck that he should be so disturbingly...*masculine.*

As a young girl, Merryn had dreamed of one day falling in love. She'd imagined it would be something magical, maybe like a fairy tale when the lonely princess suddenly caught sight through her window of the prince of her dreams.

She'd been cured of such fancies by the man who'd

preyed on her after her father's death. He'd been a bailiff, sent to evict her and Liam by the owner of the now-expired lease, but he'd told her he might be able to make some arrangement with the owner that would allow her to stay.

He'd caught her upstairs in a bedroom when she was sorting through her mother's few possessions and attacked her. He'd forced his hot tongue down her mouth and grasped at her breasts, then pulled her against him so she could feel the hateful, threatening hardness of his arousal. He'd had a knife, but she'd fought and scratched and kicked until he finally gave up. After calling her a teasing whore, he'd said he would be back the next day and if she and her brother weren't gone, she would regret it to the end of her life.

Once he'd gone, she had been physically sick.

Never again. Never would she let any man get close to her.

At that very moment the Earl strode back in. She lifted her head proudly.

'I've just been speaking to my steward, John Galbraith,' the Earl announced.

Right. He'd likely decided to throw her out of Hythe Farm. Tomorrow, probably. She rose, the better to meet his steady gaze. At least there was no danger of his words or actions melting her resolve, since he'd done nothing but insult her.

'I've told him,' he went on, 'about your claim to Hythe Farm. As I've explained to you, the whole matter has to be investigated by my lawyers. In the meantime, however, I've informed Galbraith that I will permit you and your brother to stay on there temporarily.'

'My goodness,' Merryn said softly, 'that's mighty generous of you. But do you still believe that I've invented my claim?'

His mouth thinned. 'You'll understand, I'm sure, that someone in my position is frequently plagued by people concocting all kinds of falsehoods. I really cannot be too careful.'

'Indeed. Your rank must make life exceedingly difficult for you, my lord!'

'Sometimes it does, yes.' He gave her a quick, sharp glance. 'I have responsibilities to my family as well as the estate.'

'Ah,' she exclaimed, letting a hint of amusement lighten her voice. 'I know what it is! You're worried about Felix.'

He stepped closer, towering over her in a way that was almost menacing. 'Do not use my brother as a pawn against me, Miss Hythe. I'm sure you realise that Felix needs to lead a lifestyle that is suited to his rank.'

From that exact moment, Merryn resolved that she would do everything she could to make this obnoxious man squirm with discomfort whenever she was near. 'Your brother,' she replied, 'must surely realise he has to emulate your own concern for the reputation of your illustrious family. Though don't you, my lord, need to embark on an even more crucial task and find yourself a wife? I do find myself wondering why it hasn't happened yet. For a man in your position, surely it's a necessity?'

She saw him visibly gritting his teeth. 'Tomorrow,' he said, 'I warn you, I shall be setting off for London at first light to see my lawyer and I'll be in touch to let you know how matters develop. You've already met Gabriel Barton, the shepherd, so I recommend you let him get on with his usual routine. As regards the Hythe estate in general, my manager, Galbraith, will continue to oversee its maintenance. He has always felt a keen responsibility for it, even though its acreage is extremely small in comparison to the Marchwood lands.'

'Scarcely worth bothering with, I imagine,' she murmured.

His mouth thinned. 'I don't pay Galbraith to keep an eye on the Hythe estate out of generosity, I assure you. My own concern in it is one of pure self-interest, since its lands, being close to mine, could present problems were they not properly kept. I believe I've already explained that. Oh, and until we know more about the legalities, please do not take advantage of your occupation of the farm.'

'Really? In what way?'

He shrugged. 'By having guests there, perhaps. By entertaining...*friends* of yours. If you do so, I will take prompt action to remove you.'

'Really? I assume,' she said, 'you're afraid I might invite my fairground companions to stay? I really don't think the idea would appeal to them, so you may settle your mind on that score.' She spoke calmly, although inside she was trembling with rage. 'Well, delightful though this evening has been—so charming to meet your sister, especially!—I really feel it's time for me to return to Hythe Farm. Oh, and I must remember to be up at the crack of dawn, to check if perhaps a torrential flood has overrun the lower fields, or maybe a plague of locusts has descended and is endangering our eminent neighbour's property.'

She waited for some glacial put-down. Instead, he said, after a moment of silence, 'I'll drive you home in my carriage. I could do with some fresh air.'

Alone with him in a carriage? No. A thousand times, no. 'Escort me home?' she exclaimed. 'Oh, dear me. And put your reputation at risk by being seen out at night with a woman of my lowly status? I'm already aware that being of such inferior birth, I've been honoured indeed to be permitted to dine with you all this evening! No, I shall manage perfectly well, if you'll be so kind as to ask your groom to drive me. Unless you're afraid that I might try to seduce him with my wicked fairground ways?'

She felt a certain satisfaction as she watched him cope with *that*. His voice, when it came, was a little strained. 'If you're thinking of trying to ensnare any of my staff,' he said, 'then I warn you you're doomed to failure.'

'That's quite a prediction.' She gazed up at him. 'I think I told you in my lowly caravan how I don't believe that clever tricks with cards or with anything else can accurately foretell the future. But I also reminded you that a study of the tarot cards can lead to a period of profitable self-examination.'

He frowned. 'Meaning?'

'Meaning, my lord, that a serene contemplation of

one's own character can be enlightening, particularly for anyone who finds life—and people—difficult.'

His dark eyebrows snapped upwards. 'I do not, in general, find life and people difficult,' he said cuttingly. 'And I see no way in which anything you say, madam, could be enlightening. My butler is waiting in the hall with your cloak.' He gave a stiff little bow. 'He will see you out to the carriage. I bid you goodnight, Miss Hythe.'

Actually Merryn would rather have walked—no, stomped her way home, kicking at pebbles all the way like a furious child. As the carriage rattled along, her thoughts bounced in time to the rhythm—*Hateful, hateful man. Hateful, hateful man.*

At least she'd discovered that the best way to deal with him was to laugh at him.

He represented every masculine characteristic that she detested and perhaps she should be grateful to him for that, since it meant there was no danger of her resolve being weakened. She could easily fight away the memory of that cleft in his strong chin and the fierce slash of his eyebrows; she had already forgotten, surely, the faint but enticing scent that clung to him of pine and balsam soap. She'd pushed aside the way his deep voice caused her to shiver in a most unsettling manner.

But how very foolish she'd been to talk, however briefly, to those proud people about her childhood home, because her memories of it and her family were precious. That was partly why she'd made a joke of it

all, about hoeing cabbages and turnips, because she'd
had such a happy time growing up there.

Of course, they'd not been rich by Marchwood standards, but her father had a reasonable income from investments and they'd lived in a pleasant country house.
Like the Hythe estate, it was basically a small farm; her
father had employed two labourers to help with the land,
while her mother cooked and cleaned for them all and
grew vegetables in the sunny garden.

Merryn had loved those days, but they'd vanished
swiftly: first with her mother's death when Merryn was
fifteen, then with the news that their long lease was
drawing to an end and their landlord was refusing to
renew it.

She gazed out of the coach window and allowed
the sight of the moonlit countryside, damp and earth-
scented after the heavy rain, to soothe her because, after
all, she had her future ahead of her. A tear or two still
sparkled on her eyelashes, but whatever battle she faced
with the Earl, it was worth it—because she was fighting
for a new home, a perfect home, for Liam.

The Earl of Marchwood often sought refuge in his
library when he felt particularly disturbed. All his servants knew it; they also knew better than to intrude. But
tonight there was no respite from his troubled thoughts
as he sank into his favourite chair because he couldn't
stop thinking about Miss Merryn Hythe.

'She is a fraud,' he muttered to the shelves of leather-
bound books. Somehow she must have got hold of the

story of the unclaimed estate, then decided to use it to concoct the tale of her family's chequered past.

It was at that precise moment that Felix burst into the library, the draught from the opening door making all the candles quiver. He sprawled in a nearby chair so he was facing his brother. 'Dom! I guessed you'd be in here. Isn't Miss Hythe marvellous? I thought the way she handled the Dragon's put-downs was quite something, didn't you?'

'She is a conniving temptress,' said Dominic, 'and I've every intention of fighting her claim to Hythe Farm all the way to the High Court if necessary.'

Felix looked crushed. 'A conniving temptress? But I say, Dom…'

'I think I've heard quite enough on the subject of Miss Hythe for one evening. So unless you've anything else to say, Felix, I'll bid you goodnight.'

Felix rose, then hesitated. 'Look. I know you'll hate me saying this, but you must stop thinking all women are only out to get what they can. If Merryn was merely after a life of comfort, she could find herself a far better target than Hythe Farm.'

'Meaning?'

'She's beautiful. She's clever. She could make a really good marriage, I'm sure of it!'

'Marriage? Oh, Felix. Certainly she could entrap a wealthy man. But never, surely, as his wife!'

Felix had gone a little red. 'Well, I think that's a malicious thing to say. In fact, I believe you've misunderstood her completely!'

Damn. Felix had the look of a truly infatuated young

man. Dominic guessed that if he sent Merryn Hythe packing, Felix would quite likely follow her in hot pursuit. At least Dominic hoped he'd made the best of an appalling situation by allowing her to stay on for a while, so Felix could appreciate what she was really like.

He said, as calmly as he could, 'Maybe you're correct. Maybe she genuinely believes in her brother's right to the estate. But as I've said, I'm going to London tomorrow to look into the business properly. Do you want to come with me for a couple of days or so? I know you must be missing town life.'

Felix paused with his hand on the door and a sudden look of calculation in his eyes. 'Do you know,' he said at last, 'I've been thinking over what you said, about the country air being good for me and all that.'

'*Really?*'

'Yes. Really. So I think I'll turn you down on your offer of the trip to town and stay here. Keep an eye on things for you. You know?'

With that, Felix departed jauntily, while Dominic's suspicions darkened.

His mood wasn't improved when he realised that Sarah's boys were still awake—at this hour!—and squabbling somewhere upstairs. He ran his hand tiredly through his hair, thinking that some day he would have to have children of his own. Hopefully he'd enjoy a few more years of peace first, but there was little chance of that at the moment, because Sarah and her husband were next to enter.

'That woman…' began Sarah, flapping her fan. 'You

surely don't believe her story, do you?' She turned to her husband. 'Go on, Wilfred. Speak up!'

Wilfred, looking embarrassed, said nothing. Sarah gave a huff of exasperation. 'There's no getting around it, Dominic. We think she's a liar.'

'I'm inclined to agree,' Dominic said.

Sarah looked astonished. 'What? But you invited her to dinner. And you're actually letting her stay at Hythe Farm! Do you know who she reminds me of?'

Wilfred murmured, 'Steady on, Sarah.'

But Sarah carried on regardless. 'Dominic, she reminds me of your wife. Not in her looks especially and, of course, Teresa was a lady. But Teresa had the same bold way with men that entrapped them all. And we all know what a disaster your marriage was!'

Dominic was silent a moment. Then he said, 'I believe you're leaving tomorrow, Sarah? As it happens, so am I. I'm heading for London in the morning, so I'll wish you both goodnight and please accept my apologies if I set off before daybreak.'

He headed for the stairs and his bedroom, leaving Sarah gaping after him.

Hinxton helped him remove his coat and boots without saying a word. As usual his valet always guessed when polite conversation with his master was definitely not required, but for once Dominic might have welcomed some light chatter about the weather, for example. Instead, his mind wandered back to the inevitable—the sudden upheaval to his life with the arrival of Miss Hythe and her brother. As Hinxton poured hot water into the basin for him to wash, he considered it was a damned good job that he'd seen the fortune teller for what she was from the start. There was absolutely no danger of her rather seductive face and figure appealing to him in the slightest, of that he could be sure.

'Hinxton,' he said, 'I'm off to London tomorrow, so I'll rise early. Be so good as to pack my portmanteau, will you?'

'Certainly, my lord.'

Hinxton attended to him assiduously, as always. His vast bedchamber was warmed by a coal fire, his bed linen was crisp and fresh, indeed everything was exactly as it should be. Normally, he slept almost as soon as his head hit the pillow. But tonight he couldn't sleep at all, and when he did, it was to dream of a woman with lush brown hair and haunting green eyes, who wore a dress that was years out of fashion but still made her look absolutely breathtaking. A woman who was murmuring to him, *'Your rank must make life exceedingly difficult for you, my lord!'*

Worst of all, damn it, he dreamed, too, that his pillow was scented with rose petals.

'I met Gabe out in the yard just now,' announced Cassie the next morning as she heaved in a pail of water from the outside pump. She and Merryn had been mopping the floor of the big kitchen. 'He asked if Liam would help him load hay on to the wagon and Liam's happy as can be.' She paused, setting down the pail. 'Gabe told me that His Lordship set off early for London this morning. Did you know?'

'He mentioned it last night.' Merryn decided to feign

indifference to the news about the Earl. After all, there really was no point in spoiling a lovely sunny morning by thinking about *him*. Earlier she and Cassie had polished all the windows so the sunlight could pour in and suddenly the idea of a refreshing drink seemed more than tempting. She rinsed her mop in the pail of water and pointed to the kettle. 'Let's make tea for everyone, shall we?'

Soon she was carrying the tray of mugs outside, but she stood and watched for a moment while Liam heaved up a half-bale of hay and placed it carefully on the wagon. 'Is that right?' he asked Gabe anxiously.

'Exactly right.' Gabe nodded. 'We'll make a shepherd of you yet, young man.'

Her brother had the biggest smile on his face that she'd ever seen.

Just then Liam saw Merryn. 'I'm going to help Gabe take this hay out to the sheep in the higher fields,' he told her proudly. 'Gabe said they need it because the spring grass up there is slower to grow. I like learning from Gabe. We don't have to leave here, Merryn, do we?'

'We are staying,' she said.

She repeated silently, *We're staying, whether the Earl likes it or not.*

She walked over to offer Gabe a mug of tea. 'Tell me, Gabe. Where does the Earl spend most of his time? In London, or here?'

The shepherd, with his dog, Nell, close to his side as ever, took the mug with a nod of thanks. 'It depends on the time of year,' he said in his slow, careful voice. 'London's mostly his choice, especially during spring and early summer when all the gentry are in town. But he does his duty by the Marchwood estate even when he's not here. Keeps an honest steward and treats his workers decently, not like some grand lords I've heard of. Though I'll give you a word of advice, miss, if I may.'

'Please do,' Merryn encouraged.

'I understand that you and young master Liam intend to live here for good?'

'That's perfectly correct, Gabe.'

'Yes, miss. What I wanted to say was this. You see, His Lordship is accustomed to having a lot of influence in the district, so if I were you, I'd keep on the right side of him always. That way, I reckon you'll find him a fair man.'

After a final nod Gabe went to check on old George's harness and Merryn was left alone. She saw now that Dickon, Gabe's young brother, was there, too, fetching out more hay from the barn and Cassie had gone back inside. Sighing, Merryn finished her tea and went to pick up some clumps of fallen hay. Maybe, she thought, the Earl could be fair to some, but a woman from a travelling show was not the kind of neighbour he wanted.

That was His Lordship's ill luck. He would have a fight on his hands because she was not giving up. But— and she felt a sudden chill as the sun slipped behind a cloud—the Earl would have some of the best lawyers in London, while she had no knowledge of the law whatsoever and no tame attorney to come to her aid.

She was about to take the hay to the wagon when

suddenly Gabe called out to her, 'Miss Hythe. I believe you have visitors.'

An open chaise was rattling along the track and as it drew closer, Merryn could see that in it sat Sir Wilfred and Lady Challoner, with their two boys. Oh, no. The chaise entered the courtyard and stopped. It had been quite clear at the meal last night that Lady Challoner thoroughly loathed her, so what on earth was she doing, bringing her family here?

The groom had climbed down from the driver's seat and was already helping his passengers descend. Gabe moved silently to hold the bridles of the two fine horses harnessed to the vehicle and soon Lady Challoner was standing in the middle of the courtyard. Merryn greeted her. 'My lady. Good day to you and your family.'

Lady Challoner, who wore a huge hat laden with pretend fruit, didn't even look at her, but addressed Gabe instead. 'My business is with you, Shepherd. We are actually on our way home, but our two boys heard there are some new lambs here and they badly wanted to see them. I trust you will oblige?'

Sir Wilfred hovered behind his wife, looking uncomfortable. The boys appeared bored; in fact, Marcus was slyly pinching Luke to entertain himself. Only then did Lady Challoner suddenly seem to notice Merryn. 'Good gracious me. Is that you, Miss Hythe? I know you've had an unusual life, but I hardly expected to see you carting hay around like a menial! What would the Earl have to say to that, I wonder?'

'It's hardly his concern, my lady,' answered Merryn, 'since Hythe Farm is not his property.'

Sir Wilfred murmured to his wife, 'Sarah. I warned you we should have sent word before just landing on them like this—' He broke off as a squeal of indignation came from the corner of the farmyard.

Marcus was lying sprawled on the cobbles. Luke was pointing accusingly at Liam, who was standing with his fists raised in front of two lambs that were cowering behind the water trough.

Marcus struggled to his feet, his clothes mired with mud. 'He hit me, Mama!' declared Marcus. 'This farm boy hit me and knocked me down!'

He came running to his mother, his brother Luke at his heels, and Merryn went quickly over to Liam, who stood very still. 'Liam, tell me. What exactly happened?'

'They were chasing them,' he said. He was pointing at the lambs behind the trough. 'They were frightening them and I needed to make them stop.'

'Of *course*. But did you hit Marcus?'

Liam said nothing, but Gabe had come up behind her. 'I saw it all, miss,' Gabe said to her quietly. 'Lady Challoner's boys began tormenting those lambs and your brother shoved them away. I'd have done exactly the same.' He put a reassuring hand on Liam's shoulder. 'Good for you, lad. Lambs can easily stumble if they're chased, and if they break a leg, they're done for.' Gabe aimed a frown at the little family group, where Marcus was being comforted by his mother. Sir Wilfred appeared more uncomfortable than ever.

Gabe approached the family, doffing his hat. 'My lord. My lady. Perhaps if you intend to call here in future, you'd send warning first, so we can pen the livestock away safely.'

Merryn guessed he would rather pen up the two boys, in which case she would be at his side, giving him a hand.

Lady Challoner said, 'We shall, of course, be leaving immediately. But I did have something to say to you personally, Miss Hythe. I hope you know that you did yourself no favours by presuming to dine with us last night? You must have realised that you were quite out of your depth amid such company.'

Merryn observed with wicked pleasure that a crowd of flies was buzzing around Lady Challoner's enormous bonnet. 'Dinner with you all was certainly an experience, Lady Challoner. But don't worry, I have no intention of ever repeating it.'

With a snort of disgust, Lady Challoner allowed her husband to help her into their carriage and Merryn held her head high as she watched them depart, but she felt a tear or two of indignation pricking at her eyelids. Hateful, hateful woman! She was conceited and cruel. And she—Merryn—would be a fool to think that the Earl was any different to his sister.

I will not be beaten by them, she vowed. *I will not.*

Gabe's calming voice interrupted her turbulent thoughts. 'I've been meaning to mention, miss,' he said, 'that round about this time of year, a group of travelling actors always arrive in these parts and put on one of their plays for us. The local farmers take it in turns to host and since you have a fine big courtyard, they're wondering if you'd maybe like to have them here. There's usually dancing and music after the play's finished and it's a grand way to celebrate the end of the lambing season.'

She guessed that he'd recognised her anger with Sarah and was doing his best to raise her spirits. 'I think,' she said, 'that it is a brilliant idea, Gabe. When does this actually take place?'

'At the full moon,' he said, 'which is in three nights' time. Are you sure you won't mind, miss, them all gathering here?'

She suddenly thought of the Earl, who would surely hate her hosting such an event. But it was an old custom—and besides, the Earl had gone to London. 'I don't mind in the least,' she declared. It certainly sounded far more fun than a dinner party at the castle.

Gabe grinned. 'Thank you. That'll be a mighty popular decision. Well, I'd best be off with old George and the hay cart and I'll spread the word around. It'll be like a "welcome home" for you and young Liam.'

Merryn sighed. 'I'm not sure the Earl would think so.'

'Oh, he's not likely to be back by then.' Gabe tilted his hat. 'There's plenty to keep him busy in London. Lots of pretty women dangling after him, for a start.'

He was about to leave, but Merryn stopped him on impulse. 'Gabe. Why is he not married?'

He was giving her a look she didn't understand before answering at last, 'I don't think that's for me to tell, miss. Like I've said, what goes on at Castle Marchwood is none of my business.'

They'd both heard old George shifting his big hooves

on the cobbles and Gabe walked over to him. 'Come on, then, old fellow.' He took George's halter and spoke to Liam. 'Are you going to ride up on the driver's seat, young man?'

'Yes, please!' Liam was already scrambling up eagerly, helping Nell to climb aboard, too, and soon the wagon was moving away down the lane. Merryn went slowly back inside. Liam could be so happy here. She had loved her father dearly, but if only he'd acted earlier to claim the estate!

Inside Cassie, bless her, was taking down all the china from the kitchen shelves, giving every piece a wash and polish. 'Who were they?' she asked Merryn. 'That woman had a hat like a giant fruit bowl.'

Merryn had to smile. 'That was the Earl's sister. I think she came to warn me not to seduce His Lordship.'

Cassie put her hands on her hips. 'Then if I were you, I'd do my very best to let her think you're doing just that.'

'*Seduce* him? Never,' said Merryn. 'Never!'

Cassie looked slightly startled by her vehemence and Merryn rushed to fill the silence. 'Listen, Cassie, here's some good news. In a few days we're going to have a troupe of actors here and all the neighbours will be coming to enjoy themselves!'

Her friend looked a little anxious. 'What will His Lordship say to that?'

'I don't know and I don't care.' Merryn had picked up one of the washed plates and was polishing it vigorously. 'And anyway, it doesn't matter, since he'll still be in London.' She smiled suddenly. 'It should be fun. As well as the play, there'll be music. And dancing!'

Cassie did a little dance of her own around the kitchen. 'Oh, Merryn,' she exclaimed. 'It's grand here, absolutely grand. And if the Earl should happen to turn up, I shall ask him to dance with me. Or even better, he might dance with *you*!'

Merryn put the plate down then. She'd had the sudden feeling she might drop it, because she'd had a vision of the Earl dancing with her outside under the moonlight, with his strong arms around her and his husky voice melting her to her bones…

'Don't be ridiculous, Cassie,' she said lightly. 'And pass me another plate, will you?'

Chapter Nine

London, the next afternoon

Dominic tapped the document lying on his solicitor's big mahogany desk. 'I sincerely hope, Winslade,' he said, 'that you can assure me you'll act swiftly to prove that this letter is an utter fake.'

He'd come to Chancery Lane to visit the legal firm of Winslade and Trott, where the rooms were dark even in daytime and were filled with air that was musty with the odours of parchment and ancient law books.

Winslade, a middle-aged man rather dwarfed by his enormous desk, adjusted his spectacles and said earnestly, 'My lord, I will certainly do my utmost to check if this letter is indeed falsified, as you suspect. My clerk has already attempted to contact the solicitor who composed it, but unfortunately he died a short while ago. Since he was a sole practitioner, it could take some time to sort through his files, though I must warn you that the letter does look genuine.'

Dominic shifted restlessly in his chair. 'But it's impossible that this woman should simply turn up out of nowhere and claim Hythe Farm for her brother! The estate was left without an occupant when old Charles Hythe died and it would have all run wild if my family hadn't taken responsibility for it—with, I might add, no financial advantage whatsoever for themselves.'

Winslade cleared his throat a little nervously. 'My lord, I did warn your father many years ago that it was always possible someone from a distant branch of the family might one day appear. Your esteemed grandfather, the Third Earl, was only able to take over the farmhouse and its lands by virtue of the fact that no heir could be found and thus the rules of adverse possession came into effect. Certainly your family did nothing wrong in assuming responsibility for the Hythe estate. But this woman's claim needs to be investigated and unfortunately the situation is complicated by the fact that you have allowed Miss Hythe and her brother to occupy the farmhouse.' He eyed Dominic over his spectacles. 'Is that correct?'

'I warned her she could live there on a temporary basis only.'

'Of course.' Winslade heaved a sigh. 'But I'm afraid that if she and her brother insist on staying and her claim proves harder than I think to dispute, then it could actually be rather difficult for you to remove them.'

Dominic was suddenly beset by the memory of Miss Merryn Hythe's startling behaviour at the dinner party. All by herself, she'd defied an earl and his family—and damn it, he'd almost enjoyed it, though she'd nearly driven Sarah into a state of apoplexy. But he absolutely could not let her claim Hythe Farm and be his neighbour. It was impossible, especially with Felix so vulnerable to her wiles. He said coldly to Winslade, 'Please do everything you can to speed up the process.'

'I will, of course, do my utmost to discover if there is any way of relieving you of this problematic situation, my lord. But I'm afraid the due process of the law has to be followed and—'

Dominic said abruptly, 'I don't want any of your lawyerly faradiddle, Winslade. I want this whole operation conducted swiftly, do you understand?'

'Yes, my lord. Of course, you probably have at your disposal other methods—shall we say?—of quietly dissuading this woman from pursuing the claim even further—'

'Bailiffs, you mean? *Force?* Damn it, man. I will not stoop to that!'

'Indeed, my lord. I quite understand.'

Winslade began making notes again rather nervously, while Dominic tried to imagine the triumph he would feel in telling Merryn Hythe the estate was not her brother's, no matter what kind of struggle she put up. But suddenly, out of nowhere, there came a vision of her standing in the decidedly humble courtyard of Hythe Farm, looking all around and saying to him, 'For Liam to have this kind of life is all I could ever want.'

For a moment, he'd felt his secure world rock to its foundations.

'You're behaving like an idiot,' he muttered to himself as he strode out of Winslade's office. *You cannot let one woman throw your life into chaos.*

Miss Hythe was clearly playing some kind of game with him and he would resist her with all the force of his position and the law.

His town carriage awaited him in Chancery Lane, but instead of heading straight home to Grosvenor Square he told his driver that he wished to make a detour to a street in a far less respectable area behind the Strand.

Once there, he alighted and entered the shabby basement office of a firm that specialised in making delicate enquiries for gentlemen.

'There's a travelling show,' Dominic told the proprietor of this business, whose name was Frank Nugent. 'It's run by a fellow called Ashley Wilmot and was recently camped near Weybridge. A fortune teller travelled with them whose name, she claims, is Miss Merryn Hythe.' He handed over a fistful of coins. 'I want you to find out everything you can about Miss Hythe. Do you understand?'

Frank Nugent understood all right. As a former boxer and one of the great Jackson's friends, he had mingled often with the gentry and knew how to keep silent about their sometimes mysterious requests. 'I understand, my lord. I'll be in touch, you may be sure.'

Dominic returned at last to Grosvenor Square, where he was reminded by Hinxton, who'd travelled here with him, that he'd agreed to attend Lady Somersby's party tonight and perhaps he ought to consider what he would wear. Dominic groaned inwardly. The Season had not officially started, but several rich families had already moved to London after wintering at their country houses and invitations were being sent out for private soirées. He knew what was in store for him— another evening to be spent with the gossip-hungry *ton*, all asking the same question: When—*when*—would the Earl of Marchwood make up his mind to marry again?

The ability of society to ignore the subject of his first marriage when it came to invitations never ceased to amaze him. But that, of course, was what a title and money could do for you.

It was just past nine when he arrived at Lady Somersby's splendid house in Clarges Street. 'Dominic, my dear,' declared Her Ladyship. 'You are frightfully late!'

Actually he was making his appearance earlier than usual. 'I apologise.' He bowed over the middle-aged lady's hand. 'You look exquisite, as ever.'

'Wicked, wicked man,' she scolded, tapping his arm with her fan. 'There are several delightful girls longing to meet you. Why you have exiled yourself to Marchwood, heaven only knows!'

Indeed, the gathering that night was not short of fashionable society and, just as Lady Somersby had gleefully anticipated, there were plenty of blushing maidens being thrust in his direction.

'Lord Marchwood!' The redoubtable Countess of Allendale was already blocking his way. 'Pray, let me introduce you to my daughter, Lady Petronella. It will be her come-out very soon, you know!'

He bowed to the young heiress who was glancing at him with some trepidation from behind her fan. Dressed in a rich cream gown adorned with pearls, she'd doubt-less been trained to ensnare a rich man, but she didn't help her cause by looking downright scared of him. He led Petronella into the dance, making a silent guess as to which topic of conversation she might try to introduce. Something about a delightful evening, perhaps?

'My lord,' she said, 'I find this such a delightful evening. It is so thrilling to be at this party and dancing with you.'

She couldn't even meet his eyes. He said, heaving an inward sigh, 'Tell me, Lady Petronella. What do you do when you're not at a party? Or preparing for one?'

Watercolours, he guessed. *Piano.*

'My lord, I am most fond of painting watercolours. And I play the piano—just a little, but everyone is most kind about my efforts.'

He forced a smile. 'I'm sure they are,' he said. Especially since Lady Petronella came with a dowry of ten thousand pounds. Somehow he found himself thinking of someone else—someone who had travelled from distant Ireland, living and working in a caravan. He was imagining just for one mad moment that he was dancing with Merryn, moving to the rhythm of the music with her, his body only inches from hers and his senses heightened by the rose petal scent of her skin.

He imagined himself asking her, 'And what are your interests, Miss Hythe?'

'Survival,' he guessed she would answer. 'And making sure that my brother gets everything that should be his.'

He misplaced a turn and almost trod on Lady Petronella's toes. 'Please accept my sincere apologies,' he said.

For being here. For dancing with you and scaring you witless, because I know you see me as the man who supposedly drove his young wife to her death.

At which point the dance finally, thank God, came to an end.

He returned to Castle Marchwood after an absence of three days and arrived at six in the evening, which gave Inchberry plenty of time to fuss over him before dinner and show his jealousy of the fact that Hinxton and not he had accompanied Dominic to London. Cook was eager to serve him a tasty repast of cold meats and salads, and since there was no sign of Felix, Dominic ate alone.

After the meal he decided to go for a ride, since it was a fine evening. He liked afterwards to pretend it was by chance that he went in the direction of Hythe Farm; he assured himself that he most certainly hadn't meant to go anywhere near the house itself. But as he approached the boundary wall where the two estates met, he could see that lights shone from the building in the distance and he could hear music. Music and the sounds of merrymaking.

What the deuce was going on? Was Miss Hythe holding a party?

She would tell him it was none of his business. But it was, thought Dominic grimly, because she was still, in the eyes of the law, nothing but a usurper. Although dusk was already falling and he should be heading home, he altered direction and rode towards the farmhouse, slowing his pace as he drew near. There were crowds of people milling around.

Just then, a lad who was coming along the track arm in arm with a girl saw him approaching and pulled up in amazement. 'My lord!'

Dominic recognised Gabe's young brother. 'What's going on here, Dickon? Is there some kind of party?'

Dickon looked nervous and the girl positively cowered at his side. 'It—it was Miss Hythe's idea, my lord!' said Dickon at last. 'She'll explain!'

'She better had,' muttered Dominic, heading on towards the sounds of revelry. Winslade was right—he'd been a fool to let her stay here. She must have deliberately decided to ignore his specific command!

Reaching the courtyard, he realised that the lanterns strung from the eaves of the farmhouse illuminated a festive scene indeed. Several couples were dancing to the music of two fiddlers and some of them were clad in outlandish costumes. Already, he could see a jester, a medieval knight and—most peculiar of all—someone dressed as a dragon. The others appeared to be local farmers and their wives and in their midst was Gabe, the shepherd, partnering Miss Hythe's friend Cassie.

Then Dominic had another shock. Felix was there, standing at the edge of the crowd and inevitably close to Miss Hythe, who was watching the dancers with Liam at her side. Her thick brown hair was hanging in loose curls to her shoulders and…good God, she was wearing a farmer's smock and breeches!

For a moment he could hardly breathe and when he did, he felt raw physical desire punch him in the gut.

Damn it, she looked absolutely riveting. His opinion was shared clearly by Felix, who was watching her with a look of foolish adoration on his face. A moment later Dominic's thoughts grew even darker because Felix was hauling Miss Hythe into the midst of the dancing. She protested a little, but was laughing, too. No one had noticed Dominic yet because he was in the shadows, but as he watched, countless thoughts poured through his mind.

Who exactly *was* Merryn Hythe? She danced extremely well, with every movement fluid and graceful; certainly it was quite clear to him that unlike the others here, she'd had expert tuition. He was reminded of their first meeting in her caravan, when he'd realised that she must be well born and well educated; yet here she was, fresh from a fairground way of life and presumably penniless.

What was her real story? Whatever it might be, she was attracting a dangerous amount of attention from all the men there, and as for Felix, the young idiot looked besotted.

Just then the music stopped and the object of his gaze drew apart from the others, clapping her hands for attention. 'Time for refreshments!' she called out. He saw that three farmers' wives were already emerging from the house bearing huge iron cooking pots that they placed on the big trestle table. Merryn smiled round at everyone. 'Shall we pretend we're dining in some nobleman's mansion?'

'Yes!' they all roared out.

'Shall I be the host?'

'Yes!' Another shout of approval.

She nodded. Putting her finger to her lips, she frowned in mock concentration. Then she began, laughingly, to point at each offering in turn. 'Here, my friends, we have a dish called *cuisseau de porc*. Over here, *ragout de lapin*. And last but not least, we have *poussin fricassée*.'

She beamed round at them all. 'Of course, we ordinary folk would prefer to call these delicious savouries exactly what they are. Pork casserole, rabbit stew and fried chicken—all prepared by my very good friend Cassie and her assistants. Please help yourselves. There's plenty for all!'

Her audience cheered while Dominic felt yet another stab of astonishment. She was reciting the menu in French and her command of the language was perfect. During that dinner party at the castle, she'd been deliberately making a fool of all of them. Especially him.

It was at that moment that someone spotted him and a murmur of excitement ran round the crowd. 'The Earl is here! The Earl!'

Miss Hythe hesitated just a fraction, then walked towards him almost proudly.

'My lord,' she said. 'How very unexpected to see you here.' There was no denying the spark of challenge in her eyes. 'We thought you were in town for another few days at least. Was London not to your taste? Or did you perhaps wonder what mischief I might be getting up to?'

He looked around. 'You've been involved in quite a lot of mischief already, I gather.' His gaze fixed on his brother, who'd come up also. 'Felix,' he said, 'please go home.'

'Dash it, Dom, no! I was enjoying myself—'

'Go home,' repeated Dominic curtly. Then he turned to Miss Hythe. 'I've returned from London as you see and we need to talk, you and I. Shall we find somewhere more private?'

She raised her eyebrows.

'To talk, I said,' he rasped out.

'Of course,' she echoed sweetly. Then she turned to the watching crowd. 'Do carry on, please! I need to speak with the Earl. But maybe His Lordship will feel in need of some refreshments afterwards!'

They all watched, silenced perhaps by the expression on Dominic's face. Miss Merryn Hythe smiled on as she led Dominic behind one of the barns until they were well away from the courtyard, but the instant they stopped he saw that her smile had completely vanished. She said, 'Well, my lord? What did you wish to say to me?'

'I'd like to know,' he replied, 'what exactly is going on. I thought we'd agreed that you and the boy could live here quietly while my investigations proceeded. I thought we'd agreed, too, that your stay was temporary and that the Hythe estate remains officially under my care. Yet I come home to find you have defied my instructions completely!'

'My brother's name,' she said softly, 'is Liam, not *the boy*. And in what manner, pray, have I broken our agreement?'

'Do I have to spell it out? You've taken advantage of

my generosity almost instantly by deciding to throw a free-for-all party in my absence!'

She jutted that determined little chin of hers. 'I was informed that a troupe of travelling actors from London always visit the area at this time of the year. Tonight they performed the story of St George and the Dragon— and very good it was, too! After that, they suggested music and dancing, which apparently is customary. My lord, if you had taken any true interest in the neighbour-hood, you would know this already.'

He inhaled sharply. 'But is it appropriate for *you* to host such a party, Miss Hythe?'

'Because I'm a woman, you mean? Or because I'm only here thanks to your so-called generosity?'

'Yes! Yes, I mean both! Furthermore, is it right for you to be dancing so freely with my brother, who is known for his foolish infatuations? Is that the right ex-ample to set to the neighbourhood? As for your attire, words fail me.'

Just for one moment, he saw such a flash of anger in her expression that he wondered if she was maybe going to walk away. But then—then, she sighed. 'Oh, dear. I imagine it's not how your high-class London ladies would behave, is it? Dancing in a courtyard amid such lowly folk. Goodness, I imagine the very idea would send them into a swoon. I suppose I must apologise for my attire, but I've been helping to set up the tables and prepare the food and I could hardly wear a delicate mus-lin gown for that, could I?

'You see, I'm not a high-class London lady. I've lived with a travelling show. As for those men and women you clearly dismiss as common, they have actually been up night after night helping the ewes to give birth—they've gone without sleep and without food out there in the fields and I thought they deserved something a little more than a curt "thank you". Liam and I might be here only with your permission, but I still have a duty to my neighbours!'

For a moment, Dominic was lost for words.

She went on cheerfully. 'Did you find yourself a nice, meek bride in London? Is she sweet and obedient—rich as well, presumably? Do tell, my lord!'

She gazed up at him and he would almost swear she was fluttering her eyelashes. He was furious with her because she must know how tantalising she looked, with her hair loose and her eyes sparkling with outright defiance. As for that smock and tight breeches, ridiculous though they were, they heightened her femininity in a way that would cause any red-blooded man to find his brain—and other more obvious parts of his body—positively seething with lustful imaginations.

Not him, though. Never him.

He snapped, 'What I get up to in London is none of your business.'

She sighed. 'Sometimes, you know, I wish I actually did have magical powers to foresee the future. Your future, for example. You must be one of the most eligible bachelors in the country, and surely you're not going to pretend you'll stay single for ever?'

She didn't know, he thought. She hadn't heard yet about Teresa. 'I went to a couple of parties,' he grated out. 'But the Season, as it happens, hasn't officially commenced. Anyway, my sole aim in going there was to talk to my lawyer, about you and your brother.'

She nodded. 'Come to think of it, you told me as much. To see your lawyer—oh, my! Is that supposed to frighten me?'

'Only if you've done wrong. And my lawyer can as yet find no decisive proof one way or the other as to whether your brother's claim to the estate is valid.'

He'd noted the flash of disappointment in her eyes. 'Did you show him the letter?'

'I did. But he said that the lawyer who wrote it is now dead. He also pointed out that it could be a clever forgery.'

The colour flared in her cheeks. 'And I've no doubt you assured him that was all too likely.'

'As I said,' Dominic answered steadily, 'I've been accustomed all of my life to tricksters. I trust *no one*.'

There was a sudden flurry of movement and her friend Cassie was at their side. 'Beg pardon for interrupting, Your Lordship.' She bobbed a nervous curtsy to Dominic, then turned to Miss Hythe. 'Merryn, love, it's Liam. Could you talk to him? It's late and you know how tired he gets. But he absolutely refuses to go to bed.'

Miss Hythe's expression had changed instantly. 'Has something upset him?'

'I took him for one last look at those two tiny lambs we're keeping by the fire in the kitchen. And Liam just will not leave them. The smallest lamb won't feed, you see, and Liam's anxious.'

Miss Hythe turned to Dominic. 'I must go to my

brother, my lord. But in the meantime, the party will continue because I am not sending everyone home at a whim of yours. If the company offends you, then I suggest you return to Castle Marchwood.'

She turned to go, but he caught her by the shoulder. She whirled round, almost in shock, he thought, then stared at his hand until he took it away.

He said, 'I take it your brother has a tender heart? That can be a drawback when living in the country.'

She still looked rather pale. At last she said in a voice that was very quiet, 'One of the ewes died this afternoon in giving birth, so Gabe suggested we bring her two lambs into our kitchen to feed them and keep them warm. Liam is caring for them, and yes, their plight upsets him. Of course they are only farm animals and I apologise if he's not behaving as an aristocrat would. I also apologise, if you wish it, for my eleven-year-old brother's *feelings*. Now please excuse me. I need to go to him, straight away.'

She turned her back on him and headed swiftly for the house.

Chapter Ten

Dominic knew exactly what he should do. He ought to banish all these guests from the property, then he should go straight home and write to his lawyer: *She has deliberately broken the terms of our verbal agreement and I will take immediate action to remove her.*

Instead, he ignored the revellers in the courtyard and followed her into the house, where he saw Liam kneeling on the hearthrug before the fire, offering a feeding bottle to one of two newborn lambs nestled in a wicker basket. Merryn was kneeling also and murmuring something, but when she saw Dominic she rose slowly to her feet and just for a moment he saw uncertainty again in her usually bold gaze. Liam, still holding the bottle, stood, too, after glancing swiftly at his sister.

Dominic said to Merryn, 'With your permission, I've come to see if I can help in any way.'

The boy regarded him with wide, clear eyes. His sister said, 'My lord, there's absolutely no need for you to concern yourself with these lambs. But, no—I'm wrong, aren't I?' He saw that bright smile of hers again. 'Of course, you must regard all livestock as your property, as well as the farm.'

He said, speaking to Liam, not her, 'I hear that one of the lambs is not feeding properly.'

'N-no, sir,' said the boy, stumbling slightly over the words.

'May I try?' He reached for the bottle, then he stooped over the lambs and nudged the teat gently but repeatedly against the mouth of the smaller one. At first the lamb resisted. But suddenly, it fastened its mouth to the teat and began to suck.

The boy gasped. 'Merryn! The lamb is feeding!'

Merryn said nothing, but her expression was intent. Dominic handed over the bottle to Liam. 'It's a trick I learned when I was a boy,' he said. 'You try it. If he refuses the bottle again, just stroke the teat against his mouth, ever so gently.'

'I will, sir! I will!' Liam had already taken the bottle and was eagerly offering it to the lamb.

'Liam,' his sister said, 'it's "my lord", not "sir".'

Dominic shook his head swiftly. 'No matter.' He turned back to Liam. 'Once both lambs have had their fill, they'll sleep for hours in the warmth of the fire, so be sure to get some sleep yourself, won't you, Liam? They will know you're still close by. Keeping them safe.'

Liam met his gaze resolutely. 'I shall look after them. All day and every day, sir!' He pointed to a finely carved shepherd's crook resting against the wall. 'Gabe gave me that. He said I shall make a fine shepherd.'

'I think he may have been right,' said Dominic.

All the time he was aware of Merryn watching him. He repeated to Liam, 'So. Bedtime now for you, young man?'

Liam nodded. 'Yes, sir. And thank you!'

'I'll be up to see you in a few minutes,' Merryn told him, and Liam, after casting one last look at the lambs, headed for the stairs.

Dominic stood there in the silence that followed, wondering what had come over him. But really, he knew it was the sight of a young boy looking lost and alone. A boy who had so far had one hell of a lot of bad luck—and he, Dominic, was doing little enough to help. He headed for the door, intending to leave. But before he could reach it, Merryn had caught up with him.

She said, 'A moment, my lord.'

He waited, unsure of himself, unsure of everything. He was the Earl of Marchwood. He was a cold, emotionless widower who was thought by many to have driven his wife away. Yet here he was in this farmhouse kitchen, having his heart strangely shaken by a young woman from a travelling show who wore a smock and breeches and whose only adornment was a cheap little locket.

'Well?' he said to her. *Cold and arrogant*, he reminded himself. That was him. 'What's your complaint now, Miss Hythe?'

'I have no complaint this time, my lord.' She looked up at him, her green eyes with their golden highlights so clear and so damned beautiful that he felt his pulse thud dangerously again. She went on, 'It's just that I wish to thank you for your kindness just then to Liam. His life has not been easy.'

He saw then that she was trembling a little. Unable to help himself he moved closer, thinking again what a heavy burden she bore for one so young. He said quietly, 'Your life has not been easy either. You've certainly faced considerable challenges.'

She'd drawn away instantly, as if his movement towards her had terrified her. He saw a sudden pulse leap in her throat and it was a moment or two before she lifted her chin and said almost defiantly, 'Perhaps. But I wouldn't change my life for the world, you know! I've seen so many different places. Met so many marvellous people—'

'Stop it,' said Dominic. 'Stop it. Just for a minute, will you?'

She stopped and he noticed that she was extremely pale.

'I'm not going to argue,' Dominic went on, 'that your life hasn't been colourful because I've no doubt it has. But you've also had to care for a young boy who badly misses his parents, which accounts, I imagine, for your determination to claim what you believe to be his rightful inheritance.'

Oh, that fired her up all right. There was no trace of fear now. 'This *is* his rightful inheritance! I know that the letter I gave you is genuine—my father would never have lied about such a thing!'

She looked all around the room before focusing on the shepherd's crook Liam had been so proud of. She said steadily, 'A farmhouse and some sheep may mean nothing to you, my lord, but I can see that all this is exactly what Liam needs. I know him, you see. He's intelligent and kind, but he would never want to take on the responsibilities of a rich man like you. Clearly you think little of this place, but I believe it will give him everything he wants.'

'And you?'

'Me?' She looked surprised at his question. 'I shall be here for as long as he needs me.'

His eyebrows lifted in query. 'Won't you miss your old way of life?'

She glanced at him coldly. 'I can guess exactly what you're thinking after tonight's events. You're worried, aren't you, that I'll bring some of my brazen ways here? Maybe even invite some of my fairground friends to stay and taint the neighbourhood of Castle Marchwood?'

His eyes narrowed. 'You can't do that,' he said.

'Oh, can't I?' she challenged. '*Can't* I? We could have such fun,' she went on wickedly, 'with dancers and tumblers, sideshows and games. We could charge the public and even have fencing matches.' Before he could blink she'd taken up that shepherd's crook and made a deft feint that missed him only by inches. '*En garde*, my lord,' she challenged softly.

Dominic stepped aside. He knew how to fence and his blood was thrumming at the elegance with which she moved. He said, 'Who taught you *that*?'

She put the crook back against the wall and was silent.

He pressed on. 'Was it someone from the fair?'

She shook her head then. 'My father.'

'Your father was an expert fencer?'

'He had many talents,' she replied tonelessly.

He was sure, now, that there was a great deal more she wasn't telling him. And that locket. That little locket, set with fragments of green glass…

He was looking at it again and his throat had gone a little dry. 'I think,' he said, 'that you have many other hidden talents. For example, I heard you speaking French earlier this evening, fluently. I believe you were laughing secretly at us all that night at the castle when those fancy dishes were put on the table.'

She shrugged. 'I may have been laughing at your sister. It's hard not to.'

He had to agree there. 'You've been well educated, haven't you? Your brother, too, I'm sure. And that locket of yours.' He pointed. 'I thought it was a cheap trinket, but it's made from gold and what I thought were bits of glass are tiny emeralds. Was your family once wealthy?'

She looked for a moment as if she almost hated him. Certainly, she hated this intrusion into her privacy. But she did answer him at last.

'My father lost his money months before he died,' she said. 'He'd made poor investments and everything had to go, except this locket. It was my mother's. And damn you for your intrusion into what is none of your business.'

She was trying to push the locket back under the neckline of that smock, but the fabric slipped slightly from her shoulder and he saw just beneath her collarbone a raised white scar. Where the scar finished, there was a tiny inked design that he couldn't decipher.

He caught her wrist. 'That scar is from a knife,' he grated out. Some strange emotion was welling up inside him. Something that hurt, almost. Surely not tenderness. It couldn't be tenderness! But her wrist, trapped in his big hand, was so slender and the skin of her throat so delicate that the cruel white scar wrenched him in a way he had never, ever experienced.

And suddenly she was fighting him. She'd gone very still when he grasped her wrist, but now she was struggling to drag herself away and she was, he guessed, about to lash out at him. Her eyes were wide with fear.

He dropped her wrist and raised both his hands in a gesture of peace. 'I'm sorry,' he said. 'I shouldn't have touched you. But how did that happen?' He pointed to the scar.

She pulled at her smock so it covered the scar again. He noticed that she was still trembling. Then she said without expression, 'I was careless. About my own safety.'

Dominic frowned. He wanted to know more, much more, but clearly she wasn't going to tell him. She'd perhaps been attacked by robbers somewhere, a while ago. 'And the tattoo?'

'I had it done by a sailor in Dublin. It's an ancient Gaelic symbol that means *Harm me and you will pay for it.*'

Yes, he thought. Robbers. He said, 'A warning for me, then?'

She stood there in that damnably enticing outfit of

smock and breeches and said, 'I don't think you intend me actual harm. But I am not giving up on my brother's right to inheritance.'

Her voice was steady again, but she must have realised then that her long, thick hair was tumbling freely from its ribbons because she raised her hands to push it back. It was done, he felt convinced, without a hint of vanity, yet the way she lifted her arms showed the pouting of her small but rounded breasts beneath her clothing and Dominic realised he'd not felt so disturbed by a woman's mere presence for a long, long time, if ever.

Maybe because she makes no secret of the fact that she detests you, he reminded himself harshly.

He hardened his voice accordingly and said, 'I've warned you. Legally, you have no right to stay here. The Hythe estate is mine until the case is proved.'

Merryn said casually, 'You're quite sure about that, are you? Because I, too, have spoken to a lawyer.'

'What?'

'While you were in London, I visited a lawyer in Weybridge. He was extremely helpful. He pointed out that you gave Liam and me permission to move in here—which means, he said, that you won't find it easy to get rid of me.'

Dominic inhaled deeply.

This woman. Tonight she'd dragged him through the full gamut of emotions and it was damned dangerous. He said, 'If necessary, Miss Hythe, I will pay you an appropriate sum to abandon your claim.'

Another mistake and of course she spotted his error immediately. 'Really?' She tilted her head to one side.

'Doesn't this offer—this bribe, I should say—indicate that you realise you are in the wrong? You cannot buy your way out of everything, you know.'

'Enough,' he said.

He marched towards the door, but turned one last time. 'Your brother must have missed out on his schooling during your travels. There are some books and games in the castle that belonged to Felix and myself, years ago. I'll send some of them over for him.'

Then, before she could say a word, he left.

Merryn didn't move until she heard the clatter of his horse's hooves fading into the distance. Then she put her hands to her cheeks and whispered, 'Oh, my goodness. What is happening to me?'

When she was a girl, she'd loved to ride horses or drive their small gig and she'd found that breeches were the only sensible attire to wear. Today, while she was helping Gabe clear out the main barn for the players, she'd put on the smock and breeches she'd found in a chest upstairs and wore them with a renewed sense of the freedom that she'd known long ago.

I don't care what you think of me, this outfit said. *I dress to please myself and nobody else.*

The Earl of Marchwood's reaction to the way she was dressed tonight had shattered her confidence completely. Of course, she must have shocked him; after all, he wouldn't be expecting to see her dressed like a farm lad, with her hair hanging loose and her face warm from the dancing.

But shock, she guessed, wasn't the foremost of his

emotions, for his dark eyes had gleamed silvery with speculation and the way he held his tautly muscled body had expressed what she knew from bitter experience could only be lust. He'd actually gazed at her as if she were a fine banquet and he wanted to eat her all up. And she hated it.

She knew too well that a look like that meant danger. Like the knife scar, the memory of the bailiff's attack would never leave her. It was impossible to forget the way that treacherous man's supposed kindness had turned to anger, then violence; impossible to forget the way he'd blamed her afterwards.

'Your fault,' he'd said as he turned to go. *'Your fault for leading me on, you stupid little hussy.'*

Merryn realised she was shaking. No doubt the Earl, having felt himself drawn to her tonight, was already condemning her for the way she'd dressed tonight and danced so freely. He was dangerous, she reminded herself. He was playing his own dark game, trying to beat her down not only with lawyers, but with his determination to prove her a wanton slut, with his brother and with everyone. He was seeking to humiliate her at every turn.

She wanted to see him stripped of his pride. She wanted to see him in thrall to her and begging for...

For what? Her kisses? *No.* Never! The trouble was that since that very first night at the fair, she just could not get him out of her mind.

Oh, goodness. Her cheeks were warm again and her pulse was fluttering strangely. Trying to shake some sense into her head, she went to damp down the fire and stroke the woolly heads of the two orphaned lambs.

Then she sat cross-legged on the sofa and tried to concentrate on really important things, such as her visit that afternoon to Mr Percival, the lawyer in Weybridge.

She had lied to the Earl about the result. The meeting had, in fact, not gone well. 'You have no real proof of a claim to the Hythe estate,' the lawyer had said.

She'd replied, 'There is a letter!' But then she had to tell him that the Earl had taken it.

Mr Percival had frowned at her once more. 'Fighting him will be difficult, I fear.'

As if she didn't already know it.

Unable to bear the thought of going to bed and lying awake brooding over her troubles, she went outside and saw how the full moon was still shining down on the courtyard, with only a child's mitten lying on the cobbles to remind her of the festivities earlier. Suddenly, though, there were footsteps and Cassie appeared from the shadows beyond the small garden. She was heading swiftly for the door of the farmhouse, but she pulled up when she saw Merryn.

Merryn was startled. 'Cassie! I thought you were upstairs in your room. Where have you been?'

Her friend looked guilty. 'I've been keeping Gabe company in his cottage. I hope you don't mind?'

'Not at all,' said Merryn heartily. 'Gabe is a wonderful help to us here and he seems very kind.' She hesitated. 'But, Cassie—he's not exactly your usual type, is he?'

To both her surprise and dismay, Cassie burst into tears. 'No. He's not, Merryn—and that's the trouble. I'm just not good enough for him!'

Merryn guided her to the stone bench by the front door and sat beside her. 'Darling. Of *course* you are!'

'But if he knew, about when I was younger and all those men...'

Merryn hugged her. 'Listen to me. All that is behind you. You're kind and loving and extremely pretty, and besides, your past was *not* your fault!'

She offered Cassie her handkerchief. Cassie sniffed and tried to smile. 'As for you, Merryn Hythe,' she declared, 'you'll catch a chill for sure, out here after dark without a shawl. And talking about men, what did His Lordship have to say? I suppose he wasn't happy about the play and the dancing?'

Merryn shrugged. 'He is extremely unhappy about us being here at all. But he's going to have to resign himself to the inevitable.'

'He's really got it in for us, hasn't he? What did he actually say?'

'Oh,' said Merryn lightly, 'he thinks me guilty of deceiving him and considers me a fraud. But the trouble is, Cassie, he was very kind to Liam tonight and Liam likes him. My brother trusts so few people that I find it unsettling. In fact, I find everything about him unsettling. It's as well that I also find him easy to detest.'

Cassie suddenly sat upright. 'Merryn. I heard some news about the Earl tonight.'

Merryn looked at her quickly. 'From Gabe?'

'No, Gabe's not one for tattle. But I was chatting to two farmers' wives earlier and they were gossiping like mad. They said the Earl's had beautiful mistresses in London, which is only to be expected since you can't really look at the man without thinking deliciously wicked thoughts, can you? I can't, anyway.'

Merryn suddenly felt a little faint. 'That's tattle, Cassie,' she reminded her, pulling herself together. 'Have you learned yet why he isn't married?'

'Ah, now here's the thing. Apparently he did marry around seven years ago, and he chose exactly the kind of bride you would expect—a beautiful young heiress. But apparently she left him after only a year!'

Merryn's heart thumped to a stop. 'Why? What on earth happened?'

'Nobody knows for sure. But the talk was that she ran because he was very cruel to her and she died abroad, in poverty. No one in the Earl's household is allowed to talk about it or the butler will find out and they'll be dismissed.'

Merryn felt herself freeze in shock. A man who could drive his young wife away was a formidable enemy indeed. The night air might still be warm, but she was shivering.

Men are dangerous, she'd realised on the night she was attacked. She'd vowed then and there that she didn't need one in her life ever and never had she felt the least temptation to break her vow. But, back there in the farmhouse kitchen, when the Earl stood so close that she couldn't help but be aware of his perfect, powerful body, the thought of his arms around her and his lips on hers had made her yearn to throw her caution to the wind…

Never. She'd been right to mistrust him, right to fear him from the very beginning. But she remembered his kindness to Liam tonight—to her as well, however briefly—and something that was close to physical pain squeezed at her heart, shaking her to her core. Oh, who was the fool now?

The next morning at breakfast, Felix informed Dominic that he intended to become a farmer. Dominic's reply was a stunned *'What?'*

His brother, who was normally an avid follower of the *ton*'s latest fashions and could spend literally hours preparing himself for a night out, wanted to live in the countryside for good? As a *farmer*?

Felix shoved aside his half-finished food. 'You're always nagging me to find myself a career, aren't you? So let me manage one of your estates, Dom! With all the clever new methods coming in, it's becoming quite gentlemanly to take an interest in agriculture.'

'Has this sudden interest in rural living got anything to do with Miss Hythe?'

Felix coloured. 'Whether it is or not is nothing to do with you!'

'It certainly is when we're discussing my property.'

Felix didn't reply. Dominic sighed and gazed around the breakfast room, which, like most rooms in Castle Marchwood, had a lofty ceiling and dark-panelled walls. A fire had been lit in the stone fireplace, but the air was still chilly.

Dominic felt decidedly low. He was tired, that was all, he told himself. The ride back from London yesterday followed by the contretemps with Miss Hythe had tested his patience to the limit. If he was honest, she tested more than his patience; in fact, she'd disturbed his sleep last night considerably.

Those breeches. That knife scar. 'I was careless about my own safety,' she'd said lightly. But he'd seen there was still a lingering fear in her eyes and, yes, she was afraid of *him*. Which was hardly surprising, considering the way he'd treated her.

He realised his brother was talking again. 'What was that you said, Felix?'

'While you were in London,' Felix repeated, picking up a piece of toast and buttering it, 'I looked around the Marchwood estate and talked to some local farmers. There's a lot of excitement about the new methods, new inventions, too, like seed drills and threshing machines. Amazing! And I realised, Dom, that I could be interested in that kind of thing. I'm becoming more mature, like you told me to be. Seeing wider possibilities ahead.'

Dominic shook his head, incredulous. 'But you've always told me you detest the countryside!'

'I can see the attractions of rural life,' said Felix obstinately.

'Rubbish. You've always said it's nothing but mud, rain and utter boredom. Are you hoping to impress Miss Hythe into becoming your mistress? Take my word for it, brother. That young woman isn't interested in what you can offer her.'

Felix fired up. 'That just shows how shallow you are, Dom. Merryn is not after money! Do you know, I'm really starting to wonder if you've taken a fancy to her yourself?'

'Don't be ridiculous,' said Dominic. 'Do you want more coffee?'

Felix struggled for a final, cutting word, failed to find it, then marched from the room.

Dominic shook his head. Was falling out with his brother really necessary? He tried to analyse why he felt so extremely irritated. Merryn Hythe, he reminded himself, was an intruder who pretended her one desire was to run a small farm and meanwhile she was deliberately luring his brother into her net. The image of her dancing with Felix was burned on his mind.

And that was the entire trouble. Last night her startling garb had stirred his basic instincts considerably more than he'd wanted, though what really confounded him was that there were moments when her mocking bravado all but vanished and he saw beneath it a vulnerable young woman who'd been scarred both physically and mentally by her life. How did she manage to carry on? Her courage was extraordinary.

She was also too alluring for his peace of mind. Gritting his teeth against yet another unwanted and disturbing sense of arousal, he looked once more around this gloomy room hung with portraits of his ancestors, then remembered the cosy kitchen of Hythe Farm last night. Not only had there been a glowing fire, but it was also warmed by the presence of a vibrant, loving household.

It had reminded him too much of the emptiness in his own bleak heart. An emptiness that would probably never be filled and nor did it deserve to be.

Chapter Eleven

A week later, Merryn was busy replenishing the supply of oats in George's stable. The morning had brought more glorious sunshine, but it had also encouraged the wildlife to emerge and she sympathised with the old horse heartily as he flicked his tail against the buzzing of insects.

'They're a pest,' she murmured to him as she wafted her straw sunhat around his ears. 'Aren't they, George? Just like the Earl.'

She said it lightly, but the lack of any further news from the castle troubled her sorely. Every day, the sun shone. Every day, she and Liam and Cassie rose at dawn with a fresh list of jobs to be done: potatoes and herbs to plant in the vegetable garden, old straw to be swept from the barns and young lambs to be moved out in the fields under Gabe's supervision. Gabe and his young brother, Dickon, were unfailingly good to Liam, giving him jobs that made him feel useful and built up his confidence. Merryn had never seen him so happy.

The Earl had the power to ruin this idyll, she knew that. When one day a box of games and books had arrived for Liam, just as he'd promised, it troubled Merryn more than she could say because it was an act of kindness and she wanted to think of him as her enemy. She *had* to think of him as her enemy, because truth to tell, she was thinking of him far too much anyway.

Her own weakness appalled her and she had to overcome it.

Each day, though, she felt more and more that this was her true home. Her face was golden from the sun, she felt fit and lithe, and unless she remembered the Earl, she was happy. Cassie felt the same, she knew. Cassie had taken on the role of chief cook, using her Irish recipes to make delicious meals that they ate every evening in the big kitchen together with Gabe and Dickon.

Gabe was clearly attracted to Cassie. Merryn had been anxious at first that Cassie's teasing ways might worry the quiet shepherd, but on the contrary Gabe seemed delighted with her banter. His presence was of huge value to them all because Gabe wasn't merely a shepherd, but knew all the practicalities of running a farm. He repaired the broken harrow and mended George's harness so they could plough a long-neglected field for wheat. He hired local men to repair the roof and climbed up there to fix it with them, while Merryn and Cassie put strawberry plants in the little garden to the side of the house and Liam fed the hens Gabe had brought over for them.

This would be Liam's home for good; Merryn silently vowed it. But what did she want from her own life?

Not a man, she told herself. Never a man. But there was something about the Earl's hard, almost harsh features that stopped her breathing whenever he was close. He'd driven his young wife away and she'd died abroad in poverty, Cassie had said. But the gentle way he'd shown Liam how to feed the lamb that night had almost brought a lump to her throat. Surely, she thought, he would love to have children of his own?

She'd finished grooming George and was bedding in more strawberry plants when Cassie came out with several mugs of tea on a tray. 'For the workers,' Cassie pronounced as she handed Merryn hers. 'Penny for your thoughts, Merryn love. You look miles away.'

Merryn smiled as she took her mug. 'I'm not really thinking of anything, to be honest.'

Cassie's eyes sparkled with mischief. 'You're quite sure? I guessed your thoughts might be very much taken up with a tall, dark stranger who just happens to be an earl!'

'What nonsense,' said Merryn calmly. Putting her mug aside, she bent down to pat the last little strawberry plant into its place.

Yes, she repeated to herself. Absolute nonsense.

That was the moment when she heard the rumble of a big cart coming along the drive. Rising to her feet, she watched in astonishment as the cart, pulled by two horses, came to a halt in the courtyard and the driver and his companion jumped down.

Merryn walked towards them, frowning. Both men

had gone to the rear of the cart and were trying to heave down a large contraption that she couldn't identify. Though they were clearly strong men, they were struggling to deal with its weight.

'What on earth,' demanded Merryn, 'is this? And who has sent it?'

By now the perspiring men had succeeded in lowering the mysterious object to the ground. Built of metal and wood, it rose almost to their shoulders. One of them said to her, 'It's for Hythe Farm. We're obeying orders. That's all.'

They climbed back up on their cart and off they went.

It was a mystery to all of them, even the everknowledgeable Gabe, who came to examine it a few moments later. 'I'd guess it's some kind of farm machinery,' he said, 'but I'm blowed if I know what it's for.' He was scratching his head as he wandered around it. 'It has sharp blades and they're turned by this handle, do you see? Could be it's meant for chopping up wood, since there's this funnel on top for feeding in. And it's on rollers, which makes it a bit easier to shift. But beyond that, I'm at a loss.'

Merryn reached out warily to touch it. Might it be from the Earl? If it was intended for the farm, then could it be that he'd decided to accept Liam's claim to the land?

She shook her head. Yes, and pigs might fly.

It continued to sit there as an object of mystification.

Then, an hour later, when Gabe was back up his ladder mending some guttering and Merryn was tending the garden, she heard the sound of a rider coming swiftly their way.

The Earl? For one wild moment Merryn thought, *I cannot let him see me like this. I am in a horrid old gown. My hair is wild and I have splashes of mud on my cheeks...*

It wasn't the Earl, though. It was Felix, on a fine bay mare. Merryn blinked as he dismounted, because he was dressed not like a young gentleman of fashion, but like a farmer. Yes, a farmer, in a serge jacket, corduroy breeches and stout boots. Gabe, who'd come to her side, suppressed a snort of amusement.

'Miss Hythe!' Felix swung himself out of the saddle. 'I thought I'd ride over to see how you're getting on.'

'We are fine, thank you,' she answered politely. She was aware of Liam, who'd drawn close to her, gazing at Felix's attire with wide eyes.

Felix was pointing to the large machine on rollers and saying, 'What do you think of *that*, Miss Hythe?'

'I find it difficult to pass judgement,' she answered, 'since I have no idea what it is.'

'It's a threshing machine!' he announced triumphantly. 'In fact, it's absolutely the latest thing, invented by a Scottish fellow called Meikle. You see, I happen to have become extremely interested in agriculture. Dom keeps telling me I need to enter a profession like the army or the church, but I've realised that farming is the way to make our country more prosperous. There'll be no need for revolutions, like that ghastly French business, if everyone's well fed!'

Merryn said, a little faintly, 'I see. And when exactly did you take up this interest in agriculture?'

'About two weeks ago, I'd say,' murmured Gabe at her side.

Thankfully Felix didn't hear because he was still gazing at the machine. 'So,' he was saying, 'all you have to do with this is simply turn the handle and the blades inside separate the wheat from the chaff. Much better than using old-fashioned flails or whatever. Don't you think it's a wonderful idea?'

'It impresses me very much,' Merryn replied pleasantly. 'But when it arrived, neither Gabe nor I had any idea what to do with it.'

'Then allow me to give you a demonstration.' He looked round. 'Have you a sheaf of wheat handy?'

Merryn heard Gabe stifle a chuckle. She said, 'I'm afraid not. Actually, I believe wheat isn't harvested until the summer.'

Felix looked taken aback, but Gabe, recovering, said, 'We could perhaps try it with a bundle of straw?'

'Capital idea.' Felix nodded.

So Gabe fetched some straw from one of the barns, Felix tipped it into the funnel on top of the machine and he began to turn the big handle. Merryn watched as chopped-up straw began to gather in the open cavity near the base.

Felix stood back with his hands on his hips, looking extremely pleased with himself. 'If you need anything else, just let me know, won't you, Miss Hythe? And a word of advice: don't take any notice of my brother. He's a sound enough fellow in his way, but he takes life far too seriously. Power, that's what he enjoys. That's why he's being so mean to you, accusing you of taking land he'd assumed was his.

'You deserve this estate and if I can help you in any way at all, just let me know! I've decided I quite fancy becoming an inventor of farm machines myself. This fellow Meikle has apparently done pretty well out of it.' He looked all around. 'I'll call again in a day or so, to see how you're getting on. But before I go, I'll just move the machine a little nearer to the barn and out of your way for now, shall I?'

'Thank you,' Merryn said swiftly. 'But I'm sure Gabe and I can deal with it perfectly well…'

Her voice faded, because Felix had already gone over to the thresher and was pulling at a lever that looked like some kind of brake. Indeed it was, but he'd underestimated the weight of the machine, and thanks to those rollers, it began to move by itself.

The cobbled courtyard was on a slight slope here, to allow for rainwater to run off into a gulley. As the machine gathered pace Gabe and Merryn rushed to stop it, but were too late to prevent it crashing into the corner of the nearest stone barn. The entire building quaked.

Felix frowned and walked over to inspect it. 'I say,' he called back to her. 'This old barn needs a bit of repair in places, doesn't it?'

Merryn wanted to cry out, 'It certainly does now!' Instead she said, 'Just leave it alone, *please*!'

This was a heartfelt plea, because Felix was already heaving the thresher aside and she thought she saw the building shake once more. But Felix was satisfied. 'There!' He stood back and rubbed his hands together. 'Absolutely no harm done.'

'Yes,' said Merryn rather faintly. It was difficult to see if his statement was true, due to the cloud of dust the collision had caused.

Felix, meanwhile, was looking at her admiringly. 'Did I ever tell you how I actually went to look for you when that fair of yours came to Weybridge? My friends had told me about you, and I must say I expected... Well, some men do talk nonsense, we all know that. As for myself, Miss Hythe, I must say that I find you to be intelligent and strong-minded and, in a word, I admire you greatly. Besides, there's a great deal to be said for leading a simple way of life. Surely those who work the land should be valued just as highly as those born to wealth!'

Merryn answered, 'Perhaps you'd better not let your brother hear you say that. I imagine he would cut off your allowance and tip you out of Castle Marchwood on the spot.'

She saw Felix flinch at the thought of such a disaster. He glanced at the barn. 'I say. You won't tell Dom about this little incident, will you? He's cross enough with me as it is.'

'Of course I won't tell him. I haven't seen him for days.'

Felix nodded. 'Dom's trying his hardest, you know, to get you and your brother out of what's rightfully yours. There are lawyers' letters arriving daily at the castle and he's combing the files in his library for details of Hythe's history. But you stick it out—and remember, I'm on your side!'

With that, he rode off on his magnificent horse while Merryn stood on the spot for quite a few moments, absolutely speechless.

Was she supposed to be flattered by this foolish young man's compliments? At least his older brother made no secret of his determination to get her out of his life—which according to Felix had not abated one bit.

Lawyers' letters. Combing the files in his library for details of Hythe's history.

And there was she, stupidly beginning to hope the Earl's opposition to her was fading. All of a sudden she felt very low.

Meanwhile Gabe was hauling the machine well out of the way. 'I don't think we'll have much need of this for a while yet' was his only comment. Liam was looking anxious, but Gabe suggested that he take his dog, Nell, and go to see how the lambs were faring in the nearest field. Merryn watched her brother happily obey. She'd loved her father very much, but again she found herself wondering why he hadn't realised that Charles Hythe had died childless and that this farm ought to be his.

She rebuked herself silently for her disloyalty, since her father had faced many tragedies in life.

But she felt low in spirits for the rest of the day, even experienced a sense of foreboding—and indeed at around nine that evening, when she was up in her room folding away some clothes and Liam was asleep in the next bedroom, she heard Cassie calling frantically to her from the bottom of the stairs.

'It's one of the barns, Merryn! Oh, my goodness— part of a wall has collapsed and there are ewes trapped inside. Gabe and Dickon are trying their best to get them out.'

Dear heaven. Merryn rushed downstairs and followed Cassie to the barn where, by the light of a lantern, she saw that one corner of the structure had fallen in, leaving the heavy beam that supported the roof dangerously insecure. Gabe was up a ladder struggling to secure it, while Dickon steadied the ladder from below and watched him anxiously.

Merryn called up to Gabe, 'How can I help?'

Gabe glanced down at her, his face streaked with grime and sweat. 'It's all because of that fancy machine of young Felix's. It's done a fair bit of harm. We need another strong man, maybe even two to hold this great beam while Dickon and I wedge in the stones beneath it. We'll have to send to the castle for help.'

Merryn's heart was sinking as she realised the full extent of the damage. Fallen stones from the walls littered the barn's floor and she could see now that some ewes were trapped in one corner and bleating in distress. Yet to have to send to the Earl for help after she'd declared how well she would manage on her own—the mere idea was disastrous.

Cassie was at her side, wringing her hands. Gabe was calling out again, 'Those ewes are going to panic and get badly hurt unless we get them out soon. Dickon, get old George saddled up and ride over to the castle, right away!'

* * *

Dominic gazed at the ancient suit of armour that stood in one corner of the castle's vaulted dining room and thought, just for a moment, that he saw a grim warrior's face staring back at him. Good God, he thought. This place was affecting his senses. It needed a complete overhaul as, perhaps, did he.

Over this evening's meal he'd had an argument with Felix, yet again—Felix, who exasperated him mightily but of whom he was mighty fond. But Felix a farmer? How long would it take for the young fool to grow out of that absurd idea? He walked to the far end of the room and was about to pour himself a stiff drink from the array of bottles on the sideboard when Inchberry appeared, looking anxious.

'My lord, Dickon has ridden over from Hythe Farm. He says one of the barns is damaged and there are sheep trapped inside. Shepherd Gabe asks if you can send someone to help.'

Instantly Dominic was on full alert. 'Tell a groom to get my horse ready,' he answered curtly. 'I shall ride over there myself.'

'But, my lord—'

'Inchberry, you're a good fellow, but sometimes you argue too much. You heard what I said.'

Chapter Twelve

As soon as Dominic arrived at the farmhouse, he saw that several lanterns had been set up around the yard and they shone on something that astonished him—for there sat a large piece of machinery, brand new from the looks of it.

How the devil did that thing get here? As he strode into the main barn, more lanterns enabled him to see that a huge roof beam was looking dangerously unstable. The floor of the barn was covered in rubble and large stones, while beyond the mess there were at least a dozen ewes milling restlessly.

Heaven help those creatures if they did start to panic. They would be stumbling against the wreckage and quite probably breaking their legs. Then he realised there were three people at work in there: Gabe, Miss Hythe and young Dickon, who must have returned here just before him. All three were labouring to shift the fallen stones.

Gabe was first to see him, exclaiming, 'My lord!'

Miss Hythe's expression was one of surprise and

dismay, but that quickly changed to defiance. 'Lord Marchwood,' she said, stepping forward. 'We were not expecting you yourself to come.'

'It seemed easier than calling out my staff,' he answered. 'And I'm as strong as any of my men.'

She hesitated, then nodded. 'We certainly need help,' she said, 'as you can see. Gabe suggested that if we can shift a few more of these stones, then we can maybe wedge up the fallen end of the beam and make a clear passageway for those poor sheep to leave the barn.'

She shouldn't be doing this, he thought.

His sudden anger surprised him. She looked almost fragile next to the sturdy shepherd and her faded print dress was so unsuitable for this work as to be almost laughable. But he didn't laugh. Instead, he felt some inexplicable emotion tugging at his heart.

All he said aloud was 'That's a good plan.' He inspected the scene again. 'But how has this happened?'

She hesitated a little too long. 'It was an accident. This afternoon.'

He thought instantly of that big machine in the courtyard, all shiny and new. He rapped out, 'My brother's been here, hasn't he? Did you ask *him* for that monstrous machine out there?'

'I most certainly did not!' This time she looked furious. 'I had no desire for that ridiculous contraption! Your brother was demonstrating it and it rolled into the corner of the barn. I didn't realise it had weakened the structure so badly, but I should have done.'

Dominic was already removing his coat and rolling up his shirt sleeves, but he glanced at her again. Clearly she had been labouring hard. Her hair had fallen loose from its ribbons, her face was warm with exertion and it suddenly struck him like a punch to the gut that she looked utterly, amazingly desirable.

Stop that. You utter fool.

He laboured with them in silence and very soon, Gabe and Dominic between them were able to lift up the fallen end of the beam high enough to wedge it in again safely. Then the last few fallen stones were removed, the ladder was hauled back to its usual place and Gabe said, 'Thank you, my lord, for coming to our aid.'

Dominic nodded. 'No trouble at all. It's a good job you were around, Gabe.' Then he went outside. Dickon, he could see, had moved the sheep into another barn and was fastening the door. 'That's it for now,' Dickon said to the Earl. 'I'll bid you goodnight, my lord.'

'Goodnight, Dickon. You've done well.'

'Thank you, my lord.' Dickon went to join his brother and together the two of them headed off to Gabe's nearby cottage. All was still. All was silent. Dominic looked around and saw that Miss Hythe was standing alone at the far end of the yard, gazing out into the night.

Once again he felt a wrench at his gut. This woman was not born to live with a travelling show—not born to be a sheep farmer either. She hadn't noticed him yet so he was able to drink his fill of the queenly elegance of her in the moonlight—the trim line of her bosom and tiny waist, the tempting swell of her hips. And he felt suddenly alive again, as if his hunger for living, extinguished by the failure of his marriage, had somehow been reborn. Desire burned, making him yearn not simply for an hour or two of pleasure, but for much more from this brave and lovely woman. His blood thudded and heat surged to dangerous places.

It wasn't only Felix who was at risk here.

He cleared his throat to attract her attention and said, 'Miss Hythe. That was an unwelcome incident for you, I fear.'

She whipped round, looking defensive. 'Maybe,' she answered in a low voice. 'But how easy I've made it for you, my lord, to accuse me of not being able to look after this place.'

'No,' he said. 'You've got it all wrong. You see—' and he took another step closer '—this was actually my fault.'

'But how? It was Felix who—'

He interrupted her. 'Indeed, my brother may have prompted the incident, but Gabe warned my steward months ago that after the winter storms, there'd been some weakening in that barn's structure. I should have sent workmen over to fix the beam far sooner. Felix's foolish gift merely hastened an incident that was bound to occur, so this was my fault and I apologise.' He looked over at the machine. 'Is that contraption actually of any use? What is it?'

She walked over to it and he followed. 'It's a threshing machine,' she said. He was glad to see a glimmer of a smile on her face. 'And of use? I doubt it very much, since Gabe and Dickon have only planted half an acre of wheat and Gabe assured me that can be easily threshed using the old methods. This thing takes two strong men to move it safely, let alone operate it. And the handle itself requires strength.'

As if to demonstrate, she put her right hand to the wooden cranking handle but immediately snatched it away and nursed that hand with her left. *'Ouch,'* he heard her whisper. 'Damn it…'

He saw a trace of fresh blood on the handle. He caught her by her shoulders and didn't let her go. 'Are you all right, Miss Hythe?'

She looked very shaken. Very white. 'Of course I am! I'd forgotten that I scratched my hand earlier while shifting that rubble in the barn, but it's nothing.'

She pulled away from him. She'd drawn a clean white handkerchief from her pocket and was about to press it against her right palm when he saw that an ugly cut there marred her delicate skin.

It seemed an abomination to him, this injury. He felt more real anger than he had for a long, long time.

This should not be happening to her. She should not be living like this, with no one to take care of her. No one to cherish her.

She'd bound her handkerchief around it before he could examine it further but he said, probably too harshly, 'You must bathe it. You must make absolutely sure there's no dirt in that wound.'

She stood there, very still and very pale. 'Yes,' she said. 'Thank you, my lord. And now, I think you had better go.'

He took a step closer. He said, 'I don't want to go, Merryn. I don't want to leave you alone.'

* * *

At his words, Merryn felt such a pull at her insides, such a melting and yearning, that she could hardly breathe. *'I don't want to leave you alone,'* he'd said.

Why? Whatever he meant, it was wrong, she knew that. It was dangerous—but something in her expression must have given her away, because he reached out to cup her face with his big, strong hands and she found herself in the grip of what had to be a brief madness. For she'd risen to stand on tiptoe, with both her hands spread flat across his chest, and his shirt's fabric was so thin that she felt the power of his muscles beneath it as if he was naked. She'd expected to feel fear, revulsion even, but somehow her lips parted to the caress of his tongue and his kiss was sweet and tender, stripping away the last of her defences.

She should be hating this. She should be hating him for weakening her so.

But out here in the courtyard, as the stars sparkled in the night sky overhead, she felt that her beliefs had been rocked to their foundations. She'd thought she could never be tempted to give way to this kind of vulnerability but his kiss was irresistible and, heaven help her, she wanted more, much more. She leaned into his strong body until she felt the unmissable hardness of his arousal, while all the time his tongue was plundering her mouth, sending darts of delicious torment to her breasts, her abdomen, to the secret place between her thighs.

She realised she had forgotten to be afraid. She had forgotten the mind-numbing terror she felt if any other man even drew near.

But this was crazy. This was madness, both for him and for her. How could this in any way strengthen her battle with him for Hythe Farm? He was a rich and powerful man who was said to have driven his wife away with his cruelty. Did she believe it? She wasn't sure, but the thought chilled her and it was as if he had sensed it because that was the moment he drew away, his face expressionless.

He said, 'If I went beyond the bounds of acceptable behaviour just then, I apologise.'

She shrugged, pulling her loose hair back into its ribbon. 'I assure you, my lord, there is no need to apologise. What just happened was my fault as much as yours.'

'Fault?' Dominic spoke too sharply, he knew. 'You speak,' he said, 'as if what happened then was something to be heartily regretted on both sides.'

'It was far from what you intended, I'm quite sure. What a scandal it would be for you if news of these last few moments spread around the neighbourhood!'

Dominic felt the impact of every one of her words. What a *fresh* scandal for you, she might as well have said. She knew, he realised. She knew about his first wife; he should have guessed it, yet he still hadn't been able to keep his hands off her. He caught sight again of the makeshift bandage round her hand and saw tiny spots of blood on it.

You brute. You kissed her, knowing she was hurt and vulnerable.

But his loins still throbbed urgently.

He said, in the gravelly voice he always used to hide his emotions, 'I should have been in control of myself. I wasn't.'

'Don't worry. I could have stopped you if I'd wanted. I know how.'

If it hadn't been for the slight break in her voice, he'd almost have thought the entire episode meant nothing at all to her.

Suddenly the door to the house swung open and her brother emerged. Liam had clearly flung on his clothes in a hurry—a half-buttoned jacket, some trousers and a pair of shoes that weren't properly laced—but he walked towards them both without hesitation. 'My lord,' he said. 'Merryn. I woke up and Cassie told me the sheep were trapped in the barn. They weren't hurt, were they?' He glanced at Dominic as if for reassurance.

'They are all fine, Liam.' Merryn was soothing. 'The Earl came to help. Come. Let me take you back inside.' She started to guide him towards the house.

Dominic heard Liam say, 'I'm glad the Earl came to help. Are we staying here for good?'

Merryn said, 'If I have anything to do with it, then yes, we're staying. For good.'

Time to go, Dominic told himself and set off towards his horse. He'd done enough damage for one night. He'd known she was afraid of him, yet still he'd taken her in his arms—only to comfort her, he'd told himself, liar that he was. But it had turned into a kiss that had enchanted him and he was sure, yes, he would swear she had felt the same because he'd felt her entire body tremble.

It was against her will, he reminded himself. She didn't *want* that kiss.

And now—he'd probably made an enemy of her for good.

On reaching Castle Marchwood he left his horse in the care of a groom and found Felix playing yet another solitary game of billiards in the large games room. Dominic entered and closed the door. 'Felix,' he said flatly. 'Your efforts to win Miss Hythe's approval are proving positively dangerous.'

Felix backed away, but swiftly retaliated, 'Dangerous? Deuce take it, Dom, what are you talking about?'

So Dominic told him about the threshing machine and the damaged barn, and as he listened Felix grew rather pale. 'Is she all right? Merryn, I mean?'

Dominic thought of the cut on her hand. 'She is, but no thanks to you.'

'I'm sorry,' Felix said at last. 'I really am.' Then his look became more challenging. 'But like I said earlier, I'm beginning to wonder if you need to be careful yourself.'

'What, exactly, do you mean?'

Felix was looking agitated now. 'Well, why did you go over there yourself to help her out, instead of sending a couple of our men? Maybe it's you, not me, who's starting to show rather too much concern for her!'

'Felix, don't be—'

He broke off because Felix was already marching out of the room. Dominic rested both his hands on the edge of the billiard table and gazed down at the green baize. Felix was right. He was starting to care, far too much.

The door opened and he whirled round, only to see the ever-dutiful Inchberry.

'My lord,' his butler said. 'A courier arrived in your absence, with a letter from London.'

He handed it over, then departed with a bow, and Dominic opened it immediately. It was from his lawyer.

My Lord,
I have made an important discovery which I believe will very much help your case.

I intend to make the journey to Marchwood tomorrow to see you in person, since the matter is urgent.

He put down the letter and rubbed the back of his neck in an attempt to ease the tension there. His lawyer sounded confident of success. He should be mighty pleased. Why, then, did he feel as if an impossible burden lay on his shoulders?

Merryn lay awake in her bed, turning restlessly from side to side. It was that hour of the night when all was blackness, all was silence and she knew she needed to sleep, but she was too hot. She longed for water and her right hand was throbbing mercilessly. She realised she must have a fever because faces were looming out of the darkness of her room: first her mother, trying to reach out for her, and then her father urging, 'You must fight. Fight them all, Merryn.' She tried to speak, but couldn't because her throat ached so and her forehead was burning.

Then she was crying out despite her pain, because the Earl was at her bedside saying, in a voice she'd never heard before, *'Listen to me. I want you out of here and out of my life.'*

The Earl. The man with the dark eyes and damaged soul. She'd thought she was finished with men for ever, but, oh, God, she wanted him to kiss her again. To hold her in his arms, to caress her lips and make her think of things she knew she shouldn't…

Someone was shaking her frantically. 'Merryn, darling. Oh, Merryn—what is it?'

She opened her eyes, recognising Cassie's anxious voice. Her friend reached to touch her forehead. 'You're so hot,' she whispered. 'My goodness, Merryn, you're truly ill.'

'No,' Merryn tried to say. 'I just need to sleep. That's all.'

'Nonsense.' Cassie was already heading for the door. 'I must send for help.'

Chapter Thirteen

When Merryn opened her eyes again she was lying in a four-poster bed in the middle of a large room. Sunlight streaming through the windows showed her that all around were pieces of heavy oak furniture, while a crystal chandelier hung from the lofty ceiling.

Was she dreaming again?

Her hand still throbbed and she felt slightly sick. She realised she was wearing a nightdress that wasn't her own, made of crisp white cotton with lace trimmings. A young housemaid in a black gown with a white apron and cap was sitting sewing in a chair by the window, but as soon as Merryn tried to raise herself, the maid put her sewing aside and hurried to her.

'Miss? Are you all right?'

'Where am I?' whispered Merryn. But she was starting to guess.

'You're at Castle Marchwood,' said the girl. She had, Merryn realised, a sweet face and kind eyes. 'My name is Agatha. You were ill, miss, so the Earl's doctor said you must be brought here to be looked after.'

'The Earl's doctor?'

'Yes, miss. Your friends at Hythe Farm asked His Lordship for help last night. So he sent his carriage for you and summoned his doctor.'

Indeed, vague memories were coming back now of anxious faces peering down at her, of being wrapped in blankets, then carried in a jolting carriage to the castle, where the Earl had waited at the big doorway, his face dark with concern.

Concern? It couldn't be.

'I'm ill?' she whispered at last through dry lips. 'What with?'

'It was that cut, miss. On your hand. It turned nasty, got all swollen up. And the doctor who came said you were worn out. You had no energy to fight it.'

Merryn closed her eyes.

Agatha was fussing, checking the bandage that she now saw swathed half her hand.

Then a footman arrived, bearing a tray on which were a jug and a glass. 'Cook thought you might like some of her chilled elderflower cordial, Miss Hythe,' he said.

Merryn burst out, 'No. This is ridiculous. All this fuss!'

Agatha was indignant. 'Certainly not, miss. The Earl insists you must be treated as a guest.'

Merryn was silent, but as soon as the footman had gone she turned again to Agatha. 'My brother,' she whispered. 'He'll be missing me badly.'

'No need to worry,' Agatha assured her. 'The Earl knew you'd be anxious so he said to remind you that your friend Cassie is there with him. How old is he?'

'He's eleven. He is clever and thoughtful, but he is very shy.'

'Ah, bless. He'll be fine with your friend, I'm sure. You just rest now. But, miss…'

Merryn could see Agatha was hesitating. 'Yes? What is it?'

'When I was changing you into that nightgown, I noticed you had a scar. Just here.' Agatha touched her own collarbone. 'Did someone hurt you?'

'No.' Merryn had no hesitation in lying. 'No, it was an accident. That was all.'

Agatha had left after that and Merryn had lain back on those soft pillows and must have slept because when she next woke an elderly man in a brown coat was sitting at her side.

'Miss Hythe,' he said, 'I'm the Earl's doctor. You are on the road to recovery, but you still have a fever and you must be free of it before you are fit to return home. I've left some medicine for you and do try to eat a little when you feel like it. Please don't worry, though. You should be completely well within a few days.'

'A few days?' Merryn was horrified. 'As long as that?'

'I fear so.'

He left, with Agatha at his heels. Merryn realised that if she turned her head she could gaze out through the window at the stately trees of the Earl's parkland, beyond which lay Hythe Farm. She missed Liam horribly.

She was also afraid for herself. Something had happened to her when the Earl kissed her and she didn't understand quite what. But his kiss—just one kiss, from a man who was said to have driven away his first wife—had left her reeling with desire.

Dominic escorted the doctor to his carriage, while Felix hovered anxiously nearby, then moved closer as the carriage rattled out of the courtyard. 'Will she be all right?' he asked Dominic. He looked as crestfallen as a scolded puppy.

'Yes,' Dominic replied. 'It will take a few days, the doctor said, for Miss Hythe to recover. But there's really no need to worry.' He forced a smile, but he felt utterly wretched. Yes, Felix was to blame for that infernal machine, but Dominic himself should have realised that the injury to Merryn's hand needed urgent attention.

Instead, what had he done? He'd damn well kissed her—and villain that he was, his body had clamoured for more. Whatever next? Was there no end to the punishments he was inflicting on her?

Felix said, 'I've already arranged for that threshing machine to be taken away. And, Dom, don't forget that you're hosting a ball here in a few days. Can I take over any of the arrangements?'

Now, if Dominic hadn't been secretly dreading the event as it drew closer, he might have managed a genuine smile at Felix's offer. Yes, there was to be a ball—but to let his brother take charge? That really would be a recipe for disaster. Aloud he said, 'Perhaps you could check with the grooms that they'll be fully prepared for all the carriages and horses arriving on the night.'

'Of course. I'll speak to them now.' Felix hurried off and Dominic returned inside.

This ball at Castle Marchwood loomed up at the same time every year. It was the first in a series of local events known as the Surrey Stakes, hosted by himself and his neighbours as a precursor to the forthcoming Season when all the nobility would be moving to their London mansions.

In the meantime, however, he had more urgent matters on his mind. Winslade had said he would arrive that morning.

When he duly turned up at around eleven, he delivered his news with even more eagerness than usual.

'My lord,' Winslade announced as he settled himself in Dominic's study, 'you'll be pleased to hear I've found evidence that leads me to believe the marriage of Miss Hythe's grandfather Hugo—Charles Hythe's younger brother—was not legal.'

'What?' For once, Dominic was completely floored.

'The marriage was not legal,' Winslade repeated. 'The woman that Hugo Hythe thought he was marrying was already married to someone still living at the time. Therefore the union was bigamous, which means that Miss Hythe's father was illegitimate. To put it bluntly, he was a bastard, so neither he nor his son, Miss Hythe's brother, Liam, have any right to Hythe Farm whatsoever. But as I said to you in London, I'm afraid it was unwise of you to let her stay there. She could still make some sort of claim and though it's unlikely to succeed, I do advise you to evict her and her brother as a matter of urgency.'

* * *

When Dominic went up to Merryn she was sitting in an armchair by the window of her bedchamber, clad in a long blue nightrobe that she wrapped even more tightly around herself when he knocked and entered.

Dominic saw there was a fresh bandage encasing her right hand. She didn't speak, but from the look in her eyes, he guessed she could see he was the bearer of bad news. This, he thought, was perhaps one of the worst moments of his life.

He said at last, 'Miss Hythe. I sent a groom over to the farmhouse this morning to check everything is all right there.' He hesitated, then went on, 'My groom took one of our ponies with him.'

'I don't understand.' She shook her head. 'Why?'

'The pony is for Liam. She's called Dolly and I thought she would provide a pleasant distraction for your brother.'

She said at last, 'Indeed, there's nothing my brother would like better. I am obliged for your kindness. But you have something else to say, I think?'

She always showed such damned bravery, he thought. Always. Once again Dominic felt that the armour that he'd built up around his soul for so very long was losing its iron grip. Well, now it was time to tell her the truth and make her hate him properly.

He sat on a chair—not too close, or he might inhale the rose petal scent of her—and he told her his lawyer's news. He told her that her father was the son of an illegitimate marriage and so neither he nor Liam had ever been entitled to the Hythe legacy.

She said nothing. Gave no sign of reaction whatsoever.

'However,' he blundered on. 'This is not the end. I've been thinking, you see, of various ways in which it might be possible for you and Liam to stay on at Hythe Farm, maybe as tenants—'

She suddenly said, 'Stop.'

He stopped. And Merryn needed his silence, because it gave her time to remember now all the half-forgotten pieces of her life that hadn't made sense before.

She said at last, 'My lord. It would be quite wrong of me to fight on, or to stay at Hythe Farm in any capacity whatsoever. You see...'

Her voice trailed away.

'What?' he asked. He sat down in another chair to face her, though not too close. 'Merryn. What is it?'

'I think,' she said very quietly, 'that perhaps I've always known my mother was for some reason estranged from her own family.' Her voice shook a little, but she forced herself into steadiness. 'There was a time when I was small, four or five, I think, that she took me to visit them. They had a large house in Dublin—I remember that—and my mother told me that often they spent time in England, too. They refused to see her, or me. A servant told us to go away.'

She paused as the memories engulfed her. She remembered that it was the only time she'd ever seen her mother cry. 'They wanted nothing to do,' she continued, 'with my mother and her family. They didn't even come to her funeral and I couldn't understand why. But now I realise that they knew what I didn't—that my father was illegitimate.

'I think my father and my mother must have been fully aware of the fact, but when it came to the Hythe inheritance, my father perhaps deluded himself. He was probably growing desperate by then. I told you he had money troubles towards the end of his life and he cannot, I fear, have given enough vital evidence to that lawyer who wrote to confirm his claim.' She paused a moment. 'I was foolish not to have guessed the truth. I apologise for my opposition to you. I am to blame as much as my father.'

She had always known that her Hythe grandfather came from England, but there had never been any communication from relatives there. The news just over a year ago that Liam was entitled to a Surrey farm had come as a complete shock to her, but she'd believed it with all her heart because she'd badly wanted it to be true.

Now, in this bedroom with the Earl gravely watching her, she imagined her poor father trying to convince himself, in his final illness, that it might be possible for Liam to claim it, because by then he was probably close to bankruptcy. In the past their little family had lived comfortably on the small estate; her father, she knew, had investments. But that was the time when his investments began to fail and Merryn would find her father staying up late into the night, trying to calculate how he would pay his bills, what else he could sell, who he could borrow from.

Then came a final blow, for the news arrived that

their lease was coming to an end and would not be re-newed. Yes, her father must have been in despair and seeking any way out for his children, even if it involved lies.

Feeling unutterably weary, she spoke to the Earl at last. 'We will move out of Hythe Farm as soon as pos-sible,' she said. She tried to raise herself from the chair. 'In fact, I wish to leave now and return to my brother.'

'No!' He stood and put out a hand to stop her, look-ing almost angry. 'I told you, the doctor insists you stay until you are completely better. He told me your wound was infected and could have been dangerous. He also said you must have been in a state of near exhaustion when this happened and he absolutely insists on four days of rest.'

'But what am I supposed to do with myself?' she cried. 'I'm feeling much better. I refuse to lie in bed for four days!'

He shook his head and spoke more softly. 'It's dif-ficult for you, I know. But once you are strong enough, you could perhaps walk in the gardens—one of the maids would accompany you. And if the weather is poor, you can help yourself to any book you please from my library.'

She said nothing. For a moment he looked as if he was about to speak again, but then he changed his mind and left.

Merryn bowed her head. She had told him she was getting better, but in truth she felt as shaky as a new-born lamb. Her dream for Liam and his future had been destroyed. What was almost worse was the fact that she'd betrayed herself last night by not only allowing this man's caresses, but also responding to them in a way she'd not thought possible.

His kiss had rocked her world. Why had he done it? It was obvious. It was because she'd dressed and acted shamelessly, provocatively even—she, who'd guarded herself from men so carefully—and now the man was being kind to her. Feeling sorry for her. It wrung her heart—because she was beginning to realise that pity wasn't what she wanted from him, not at all.

By the next day Merryn was able to go for a walk in the gardens with Agatha, the maid, who was delighted to escape the routine of housework. Merryn also borrowed some books from the Earl's library, but she read hardly a word and time lay heavy on her hands. She saw nothing at all of the Earl. To her surprise, she found that the staff were actually inclined to like her, perhaps because of Agatha's good reports. Even Mr Inchberry showed signs of softening towards her when she thanked him for the servants' care of her. Each day Dickon rode over from Hythe Farm with a letter from Liam, which normally she would have received with gladness—except that he wrote all about his new pony, Dolly, and his adventures with her, which reminded Merryn that soon all this would come to an end. However was she going to tell him so?

There was also a single, hasty note from Cassie. 'Merryn, you'll never guess. Gabe has told me he wants us to be married! And he's such a love!'

All of this added fresh soreness to Merryn's aching

heart. This meant Cassie would be moving into Gabe's cottage, of course, so she would be staying. But Hythe Farm could never be Liam's home now.

The doctor visited twice a day and told her she was improving steadily. Felix, she heard, had gone to London—maybe to learn more about threshing machines? She truly hoped not, for everyone's safety. Still she didn't see the Earl, but she guessed he was busy making arrangements for the grand ball that was to be held here.

'His Lordship's a worry to us all,' sighed Agatha as she brushed Merryn's hair on the day before the ball. 'What lovely thick hair you've got, miss! Such a pretty face, too. You could have gentlemen at your feet, you know.'

Merryn's laugh was a little hollow. 'I really don't think so, Agatha. But why did you say the Earl is a worry to you?'

'Because the poor man's all alone!' exclaimed Agatha. 'And he shouldn't be. It doesn't do him any good.'

Merryn spoke carefully. 'I know, of course, that he was once married. Did you ever see his wife, I wonder?'

'Lady Teresa? No, miss.' Agatha shook her head firmly. 'That was long before my time here.'

'But you must have heard something about her?'

'Not I. Besides, it's none of my business, that's for sure.'

The staff here liked the Earl, she realised, and it didn't come from a mere sense of duty; no, it was as if they were defending him, guarding him from the vicious words of gossips.

'Now,' Agatha was saying, 'will you let me put up your hair? Oh, if only you could be at the ball tomorrow night. You're so much prettier than all those fine ladies in their fancy gowns and jewels!'

'Will there be many guests, do you think?'

'Indeed. It's the start of what they call the Surrey Stakes, when every year there are fancy parties for the rich folk all around the district—and it starts here, with the Earl's ball. All of us servants enjoy seeing the castle lived in. But it doesn't half make extra work!'

After Agatha had gone Merryn thought of the Earl's wife, Lady Teresa. She pictured her, beautiful and vivacious, descending the main staircase in a gorgeous gown, then dancing in the ballroom with her husband, all eyes upon them.

She'd left him, though. She'd fled the country to get away from him. What kind of man was he, to make his young wife so desperate?

The man who'd been unbelievably kind to Liam. The man who'd kissed her—and with that kiss had awoken thoughts and desires she'd tried to bury for good.

The ball was tomorrow night and it would be unbearable for her to still be here, alone in her room amid all the rich guests. She absolutely had to leave the castle before then. She asked Agatha to bring her paper, pen and ink and wrote a note to the Earl.

My Lord,
I hear you are holding a ball tomorrow evening,
so I wish to return to Hythe Farm before then.
Once there, I will begin my preparations to leave.

Half an hour later came the written reply.

Miss Hythe,
I am afraid I must insist on delaying your depar-
ture until the morning after the ball. The doctor
was specific that you remain here until then and
I do not wish to be responsible for any deteriora-
tion in your health.

The next day Felix returned from London. He'd arrived while Merryn was out walking in the garden with
Agatha and when Merryn entered the house he was
heading for the stairs, but he stopped the minute he
saw her.

'Miss Hythe!' he exclaimed, striding towards her.
'My brother's just told me about your grandfather's marriage not being legal. But this can't be true. And I swear
I'll help you to get what is rightly yours. Dominic must
do something about this situation, immediately!'

'Felix,' she said wearily. 'It is true, unfortunately.
And don't you think it's time you grew up a little? Thank
you for your concern, but I don't think there's anything
your brother can do. Now if you don't mind, I'd like to
be alone.'

He backed off in astonishment and she walked
steadily up the grand staircase to her room.

Her mother had come from a wealthy family, she had
no doubt of that, and her father had been a gentleman.
But society was harsh indeed on those who broke its
rules and now Liam, on account of his father's birth,

would never get the inheritance which would have transformed his life.

As she gazed out of her window she became gradually aware of a flurry of activity down below in the main courtyard, where already there were carriages arriving, bringing the elite of local society to Castle Marchwood's grand ball. She, of course, would stay in her room tonight. It was the way of things, but she'd had such dreams.

Dominic was in his bedchamber dressing for the ball when he heard those first carriages arrive. He checked his image in the cheval glass, noting that Hinxton had done his usual immaculate job in selecting his evening clothes, then he braced himself to go downstairs and greet his guests.

But he was haunted by thoughts of Merryn. Of her scent, her hair, her voice—perhaps most of all by her bravery. By kissing her at Hythe Farm, he'd betrayed her trust; in fact, that kiss had perhaps been even more fatal for both of them than his discovery that her father was illegitimate.

No doubt during her stay at Castle Marchwood she'd heard the rumours about his marriage, hence her determination to move on. He couldn't blame her. She was wiser than he was.

Just at that moment Hinxton coughed behind him. 'My lord. Your guests…'

'Yes,' he said. 'I know. Thank you, Hinxton.' Already he could hear the excited chatter of the arrivals down in the hallway and as he descended the staircase he saw that Sarah and her husband were there, so he greeted them and all his guests with mannered courtesy. Most were old friends, but others were new to the neighbourhood and he noted how their eyes gleamed as they took in their surroundings, especially those who had daughters about to make their debut.

They, he knew, couldn't have cared less about the whispers surrounding his dead wife. They were thinking only of his title and wealth and towards them he felt utter indifference, for he wanted the one woman who surely wouldn't have him if he went down on bended knee.

It was justice, after all. Life had its own ways of serving retribution.

Chapter Fourteen

Merryn was in her room upstairs, attempting to finish a book she'd borrowed from the Earl's library earlier. But by eight o'clock she was completely distracted by all the goings-on out in the courtyard, where grooms and footmen scurried to attend to both coaches and people.

Agatha had told her that Inchberry had been in his element all day as he and the housekeeper organised furniture, flowers and the lighting of candelabra, and Merryn couldn't help but be fascinated by the way that music, laughter and the light cast by hundreds of wax candles were utterly transforming this grim old building.

'As for Cook,' Agatha had told her eagerly when she brought up some tea and biscuits, 'poor Mrs Butterworth has been working so hard she'll hardly be able to move from her bed tomorrow! But she loves it all. Like Mr Inchberry, she's always thrilled to bits when the Earl has guests. Of course there'll be parties at other grand houses in the district over the next few days, but this is the best and biggest.'

'The Surrey Stakes, you told me,' said Merryn.

'That's right, miss! Tomorrow there's a ball at the Duke of Witham's house, then there's a party at the home of Viscount Garfield near Epsom. Finally they all end up here again for an entire weekend, with lots of grand folk staying. But I'm afraid the Earl—' and Agatha looked suddenly sad '—doesn't enjoy it greatly. In fact, we servants believe he doesn't like being at Castle Marchwood one bit.'

Because of his wife? Merryn longed to ask. But Agatha had already hurried off to prepare yet another bedroom for an unexpected guest.

Merryn bowed her head. She was aware that all around the castle, guests were congregating in laughing, happy groups, but she felt almost overwhelmed by despair. She'd thought at first it was the prospect of losing Hythe Farm that had plunged her into the depths but now, though it was selfish and abominable of her, she was finding that the thought of never seeing the Earl again was unbearable. Yes, unbearable, whatever the rumours were about him.

She tried to read another chapter of her book and failed abysmally. Exactly how long she sat there she didn't know, but she almost jumped from her seat when there was a light tap at her door and Agatha peeped in again, looking excited.

'Miss? Do you want to come and watch the dancing?'

'Agatha! That's ridiculous. I don't really see how…'

But Agatha had already grabbed her hand and was leading the way along narrow corridors to the gallery that overlooked the ballroom, from where they could look down on the dancing without being noticed. Agatha's face was alight.

'Oh, look, miss,' cried the young maid. 'The gowns! The jewels! Some of the dresses are ever so daring, aren't they? And there's plenty of fine gents down there, but the Earl is the one who's a real treat for the eyes.' Agatha sighed in appreciation. 'Do you know, just the other day he smiled at me when I took some tea and scones to his study? It was a good thing I'd already put down the tray on his desk, because I went weak at the knees!'

Merryn could see the Earl only too well. He was standing talking to some men in a shadowed alcove and the contrast of light and dark made his starkly sculpted features all the more breathtaking. She felt an aching sense of loss, as if this part of her life was already over.

Agatha was watching her with a little smile on her face. 'You're staring at him, too, aren't you? Bless me if you're not just as bad as me!'

'Nonsense.' Merryn tried to laugh.

Just then she saw that two women were approaching the Earl, one young and pretty, the other somewhat older—mother and daughter, Merryn guessed. The mother was speaking to the Earl effusively while the younger one fluttered her fan.

'Here we go,' sighed Agatha. 'They're all after him, the young ladies. It's a wonder he's fought them off for so long. He'll have to give in soon.'

'Agatha,' began Merryn, 'about his first wife—'

Agatha cut in almost immediately. 'Sorry, miss. I

told you, I don't know nothing about that— Oh, my saints. Look out!'

Without another word Agatha went shooting off towards the servants' stairs and Merryn realised why, for none other than Lady Challoner was heading along the gallery, her full-skirted grey ball gown giving her the air of a ship in full sail.

'Miss Hythe!' she called out. 'What on earth do you think you're doing up here? Are you *spying* on the Earl and his guests?' She put her hands on her hips. 'This is quite shameful. You have weaselled your way into Castle Marchwood and you are chasing after my brother. Ever since you arrived, I've known it!'

Merryn was so angry that she briefly imagined tipping the woman over the balcony. 'You are completely wrong,' she replied. 'I travelled here solely in order to—'

She broke off abruptly. *To claim my brother's rightful inheritance*, she'd been going to say. But she'd been wrong all along and Sarah wasn't going to leave that silence unfilled.

'I warned Dominic,' she declared, 'that it was fatal to let a fairground girl move into Hythe Farm. It was even more foolish of him to let you stay here in the castle. I've told him what I think of you and your ill-natured brother.'

'Liam is not ill-natured!' she cried out.

'Do not raise your voice to me, young woman! Your brother is a menace and he will get what's good for him. I've actually told him so.'

'You've told him? When? What are you talking

about?' Despite the heat of the ballroom, Merryn was suddenly cold.

'Wilfred and I,' announced Lady Challoner, 'happened to come upon your brother the other day. And we told him that there's a remedy for boys like him.'

'A remedy? I still don't understand. You must explain—'

But Lady Challoner had already bustled off.

What had happened? What had Sarah said to Liam? Merryn was desperate now to get back to Hythe Farm, but there was no way she could do so till tomorrow. Feeling almost sick with anxiety, she went back to her room, but couldn't settle. She made huge efforts to console herself.

You know that Cassie and Gabe will be looking after Liam. Be patient.

It was easier said than done. Still agitated, she decided to return her book to the library and perhaps read there for a while, since it was in a distant wing of the house where she wouldn't be taunted by the sounds of the ball. Once there she wandered around the large room, studying the tall shelves, picking up one book after another, but all the time wondering what her future held.

Maybe she could find another small farm in another part of the country, though how could she afford the rent? Perhaps she could re-join the fair—Ashley would have her back any time, he'd told her so. But that would mean Liam would spend his entire youth travelling from place to place, with no friends and no chance of proper schooling.

She put her hands to her cheeks. She was trying to be positive, truly she was. But always her thoughts came back to the Earl.

Cassie had heard that his coldness had driven his first wife away. Merryn, so wary of men anyway, should have been able to close her heart to him easily. But when he'd kissed her, there had been a moment when she had felt an almost unbearable yearning to be his, in every way.

Impossible. How could she have let this happen?

Glancing through the French windows, she realised that lanterns had been strung out all along the garden paths and on impulse she opened the tall windows to step out into an enchanted world of illuminated walkways and terraces. Night-scented stock perfumed the warm air and in the distance a fountain threw out showers of sparkling water, while towering yew hedges, tightly clipped, marched in formation alongside perfect lawns.

Faint music from the ballroom drifted to her ears and she wondered if Dominic was dancing with yet another beautiful girl. She stopped in her tracks as a fresh onslaught of emotion—of loss, even—left her trembling. She didn't know what was happening to her, but whatever it was, how it hurt.

She headed in the direction of the summer house, where sometimes she'd spent a quiet hour or so sitting with Agatha during their afternoon walks. The interior was shadowy, so it was only when she opened the door that she realised someone was already in here.

Dominic.

Yes, it was Dominic as she'd never seen him before, seated on one of the chairs with his coat flung aside, his cravat undone and his face etched with nothing less than despair.

Merryn felt her pulse rate hitch violently. 'My lord,' she said at last. 'I'm truly sorry to disturb you. I thought you would be at your party! I'm intruding. I should leave—'

'Stay,' he commanded. He rose to his feet, towering over her so she was even more aware of the strength of that muscular body which no elegant clothes could ever disguise. 'Yes,' he went on, 'I should be with my guests. But I needed to get away for a while.'

She couldn't help but burst out, 'Why?'

He gave her a sudden, crooked smile. 'Because it was all utterly, damnably boring. Felix found it so as well—I believe he and his friends have sought refuge in the billiards room.'

'Oh, dear.' She tried her best to sound light-hearted. 'What would your guests have to say to that, I wonder?'

He poured himself brandy from a decanter on a side table and drank. 'I neither know,' he said, 'nor care.'

Merryn couldn't help but notice how his shirt clung in absolutely fascinating ways to his powerful shoulders as he moved. She moistened her dry throat. 'I had better leave you in the solitude you wished for,' she said at last.

He looked at her swiftly. 'I'm sorry. You wanted to go home today, didn't you?'

Home. That was the trouble—Hythe Farm wasn't her home and couldn't be, ever. 'I did, but your doctor's orders have to be obeyed,' she answered lightly. 'I just came out here for some fresh air.' She hesitated then said more quietly, 'Are you all right, my lord?'

'Perhaps I'm slightly drunk.' He lifted his glass. 'But not excessively so. I am, though, in a most peculiar state of mind.'

Oh, so was she. His presence—so near to her, so raw, so real—made her lungs ache with the need for air. At last she said, 'If my arrival in your life is at all responsible for that, then I am truly sorry. All I can say is this. Once I've made arrangements to leave the area, then of course you and I won't ever see one another again, which is surely for the best—'

She broke off because he'd put down his glass and reached her in two steps. 'Are you mad?'

'What?' She felt a little faint, because of something she saw etched in his taut features. Despair. Hunger. *Desire.*

'I said, are you mad, or maybe blind, Merryn? Don't you see that what's driving me crazy is *you*? Oh, not the stupid legal business—as far as I'm concerned, all the lawyers can go to hell in a handcart. I want *you*. Though God knows I've tried to fight it.'

His eyes were dark with intent. Merryn felt as if she was inhaling air that was suddenly crackling with danger and her uneven breathing was reflected in her trembling hands.

Suddenly he reached out to put one finger on her cheek and stroked downwards until he was softly caressing her neck. She didn't flinch, though her heart was pounding and her resistance was melting yet again.

I want you, he'd said. She felt her world spinning.

He said, very quietly, 'Did you know I was once married?'

This, she had not expected. 'I had heard,' she said. 'I'm sorry.' She couldn't think of anything else to say, because surely it was forbidden territory.

'My marriage,' he went on, 'was a disaster. I'm surprised you've not learned about it already.'

'I haven't,' she said.

'Not even from my brother?'

She shook her head. 'No! Felix hasn't said a word.'

'Well,' he said, 'at least he has a tiny element of loyalty still.'

'I'm sure he has, my lord. I believe that he thinks the world of you.'

He gave a short 'Ha!' Then he pointed to a couch set against the wall. 'Please sit,' he said.

She sat down. He settled beside her, but the warnings that should have screamed from every pore of her body were silent because she couldn't leave. Not now.

He drank from his glass again, then he started to speak.

'When I met Teresa,' he began, 'I was twenty-two and she was nineteen, the only child of rich and ambitious parents. She was entrancingly pretty and knew it. My father told me it was my duty to marry as soon as possible since I was the heir to the earldom, so we had an extremely grand wedding and after that we travelled to Paris, Rome, Venice—all the finest cities in Europe.'

He shook his head slightly, not looking at Merryn now. He was in another world, she realised. A world of memories he hated to revisit.

'I got to know her then,' he said. 'As I've told you, she was an only child and the world had always revolved around her. I tried at first to indulge her every wish, for I really did want the marriage to work. I knew my parents' marriage wasn't particularly happy and I stupidly thought I could do better. But Teresa was difficult to please. She hated Castle Marchwood and adored London life, which didn't help her many problems since she drank and she had dangerous friends. I tried to help her by finding good doctors for her, but she rejected them and then me, declaring herself bored with me and what she called my rigid sense of responsibility. Then she began to accuse me of having secret mistresses.' This time he looked straight at Merryn. 'I didn't. I tried my best to make her happy, but her doting parents blamed me—and still do—for everything that happened after that.'

Merryn said quietly, 'What did happen?'

'She ran away,' he answered after a long silence. 'She went with some rogue of an army officer to Brussels, where she became addicted to laudanum. I went there myself to plead with her to return, but she refused. Months later she died, after taking a fatal concoction of laudanum and sleeping powders. After her funeral, I went abroad for four years. Then my father died and I had to return.'

He picked up his glass, but on realising it was empty he put it down again. 'Since then,' he went on, 'I've done what's expected of me. But part of my duty is to provide an heir which, of course, means marrying again—and I have not been able to bring myself to repeat that episode of my life. Perhaps I'm not fit to be a husband and father.'

Merryn felt herself hurting almost unbearably for this proud, seemingly unreachable man. 'Surely,' she said, 'you cannot still blame yourself for your wife's troubles?'

He looked at her in some surprise. 'Of course. Who else should I blame? Isn't it obvious I made her unhappy?'

'I don't quite see it that way. Not from what you've just told me.'

He shrugged. 'Maybe I should have found better doctors for her. Maybe I should have tried to understand her better from the start.'

Merryn hesitated. 'I presume—and I don't mean to pry—that you've had relationships with other women since. Have any of them complained?'

A faint smile twisted his mouth. 'That's a bold question, but it's an obvious one. I've had associations with women who've enjoyed my company and I theirs. But I failed poor, weak Teresa.'

'My lord, it's a tragic story. Though from what you've said and from what I know of you, your wife sounds as if no one could have pleased her. Tell me, do any of your friends blame you?'

'We hardly ever mention her. But, no, I don't think so.'

Merryn gazed at him. His dark hair was rumpled, his cravat was dangling loose and on his face was an expression of haunting sadness. Proud. Noble. Broken. The distant music from the ball seemed to mock his despair.

'You've carried this guilt with you, for all of this time,' she said softly. 'Has it struck you that in trying to care for her as you described, you perhaps did more for her than anyone else would ever have done?'

'I was her husband!' he cried bitterly. 'I should have been able to save her from such a dreadful end!' He rose abruptly and went to the open door, as if seeking some respite from his cares, but finding none.

And Merryn couldn't bear it. She walked to join him, she put her hand on his arm and it was as if a spark had been struck because instantly he moved to grasp her by the shoulders and gazed down into her eyes. 'That first night we met, Merryn. You looked at the three cards I'd chosen—The Emperor. The Hermit. The Fool. Do you remember what you said?'

Her fear, she realised, her terror of being touched by any man had vanished. Because of *him*. The discovery made her tremble, but somehow she managed a smile.

'I remember,' she answered, 'how I told you that you were maybe a little too proud. But I also guessed you were loyal. Honourable. A fierce defender of the truth. Though as I keep telling you, my lord, I do not predict the future.'

'My name is Dominic, not *my lord*!' he exclaimed. He rubbed his forehead as if to ease an unbearable wound. 'And I wish to hell that you could see a happy future for me.'

She couldn't believe she had heard him aright. 'Surely,' she exclaimed, 'you have a life anyone would envy?'

He looked straight at her. 'No. I don't have everything I want. You, of all people, know that.'

Me? she thought. *Me?*

She couldn't say a word and then suddenly he was reaching out to touch the locket her mother had given her.

'There's an inscription on this,' he said. 'Isn't there? Is it a name?' He lifted it slightly on its slender chain.

'It says *Arvon*,' she told him as he let the locket fall. 'That was my mother's maiden name. It was all she had to remind her of her family. You see, despite their treatment of her, she didn't want to forget them entirely.'

He nodded. 'Is that why you've never thought of selling it?'

'That's right.' Then she closed her eyes briefly as his hand travelled on to touch her collarbone and the white scar left by the bailiff's knife as they'd struggled.

Keep your distance, she urged herself. *Keep away.*

Yet he stood there, not an earl but a man with a look in his eyes that spoke of raw need. And she felt her body melt in longing.

This man—this noble-hearted, badly damaged man— had shaken the foundations of her existence. He wanted her and she had to say no; indeed, she had to keep summoning the strength to say no. But slowly, inevitably, he was drawing her closer so she could feel his body heat and smell that pine soap he used, while at the opening of his loosened shirt she could glimpse the sculpted contours of his chest.

Desire flared in her and she lifted her face to his. Wordlessly he reached for her and she stepped right into his strong arms.

Who kissed whom first, she wasn't quite sure, but

her vow of *never again* vanished into thin air. This, she realised with a jolt, had been bound to happen. The anticipation of it had been quietly rolling through the air like an approaching storm for days. It was also everything she had expected—and more.

He tightened his arms around her and because he felt warm and strong, she nestled closer until her sensitive breasts were deliciously compressed against his iron-hard body. He was murmuring something under his breath and caressing her slender waist, then he let his hands slip down to her hips and fire surged through her veins.

He kissed her as if he owned her, with nothing hesitant or fumbling about it, and as her lips inevitably drifted open she was glad, yes, glad to surrender because it made such a glorious change from having to *fight* all of her damned life. She found that her hands were gripping the front of his shirt, not in protest but to draw his strong body into even closer contact with hers, until she realised with a strange thrill that his muscular thighs were pressing against her most secret parts. She was hot there, she was moist; she needed to get more of him, in any way she could.

Suddenly he lifted his hands, allowing them to run through her loose, long hair from which the ribbon had long since fallen, then he cupped her face to tilt it to exactly where he wanted it. An exquisite shiver tore through her as she felt the slide of his strong mouth, then the decadent thrust of his tongue tangling so erotically with hers.

On first meeting him her first instinct had been fear.

Of course it had. She'd almost been raped by a man who'd claimed to be her friend. Why wouldn't she do everything she could to fend off a man who openly declared himself her enemy? So, yes, she'd feared the Earl's power, his blatant masculinity, his apparent cynicism towards women and the world.

But now—now, she felt she understood the dark memories that haunted him, the guilt and the regret. She believed that he was a good and honourable man and, dear heaven, it wasn't because of fear that she allowed him to lead her back to that couch in the corner. No, it was the feeling that this was right, this was inevitable, because she realised she could *trust* this man.

He had broken through her defences because he had suffered, too, something she'd recognised from the start. Besides, her arms were already around his neck and she wasn't letting go.

She felt a rush of exhilaration as he lowered her to the couch and her hands were already running over his supple, sinewy torso. He was kissing her again and his tongue went deeper this time, thrusting against hers in a way that heated all those parts of her she didn't usually allow herself even to think about. His strong body was half over hers now and as their legs twined, she could once more feel the steely evidence of his arousal.

A fierce jolt of awareness was rippling through her from head to toe. She knew how hungry men could be for sex—she had that scar to remind her. But no one had warned her that when Dominic unbuttoned the bodice of her gown and reached to stroke her breast, she would feel an almost overwhelming surge of desire all the way down to that most intimate of places at the juncture of her thighs. His thumb was rasping first one sensitive nipple then the other and she was desperate for more of him, so desperate that she wrapped her hands round his back, revelling in his sheer strength, then she arched towards him, her breathing fast and shallow.

Already his hand had slid lower to reach behind and clasp her bottom. She felt the warm caress of his large hand through her flimsy dress and she cried out; what she said, she didn't know, but he let her go. Instantly.

'I'm sorry,' he said. 'I didn't mean to hurt you.'

She felt cold as he drew away.

No, she tried to say. *You didn't hurt me.* She also longed to whisper, *You did nothing at all that I didn't want you to do.*

But she didn't, because already he'd moved yet further away and was straightening his clothes, turning away from her as he did so, perhaps to conceal the all too clear evidence of his arousal. Merryn rose, too, and tried to pull her hair back into its ribbon, though it was a futile attempt, as futile as her efforts to rein in her overwhelming feelings for this man. She felt empty without his arms around her.

He regretted it, she guessed. Yes, he regretted this second lapse even more bitterly than the first because he was still raw from the wounds inflicted by his wife. Yet he must, she realised, have once loved her very much, for he was still protecting the woman by bearing all the blame himself for her tragic end. She ached with pity for him and felt hollow with yearning for what she could never have.

When Dominic turned to her again it was to say in an expressionless voice, 'I will find some way to let you keep Hythe Farm for your brother. Although the lawyers say it's legally mine, I could surely make a gift of it—'

'No,' she said. Swiftly. Stubbornly. 'I do not want your charity.' She'd composed herself somehow, for she knew that she had to be strong. She had already decided she could not carry on living so near to him. It would break her pride and her heart and, yes, tonight had reminded her that she was the one with everything to lose.

His strong features hardly shifted, but as she answered him she saw a bleakness in his expression that pierced her heart. 'Very well,' he said. 'This, after all, isn't the time or place to discuss your future. And I ought to return to the ballroom.'

She nodded. 'I shall return to your library once you've gone inside.' She knew it would be disastrous for him were he to be seen with her. 'Tomorrow I shall leave the castle, as we agreed.'

He looked about to speak again, but instead gave a curt bow. 'I shall see you in the morning. Goodnight, Miss Hythe.'

After he'd gone Merryn went to stand by the open door, breathing in the cool night air as if it could restore her sanity. She would have to start planning a new life for herself and Liam, but at the moment, all she could think about was the fact that she would soon be facing a future without the man who'd somehow captured her closely guarded heart.

She smoothed down her sorely rumpled gown with fingers that shook a little. 'Haven't you always prided yourself on your common sense?' she told herself. 'Then use it.'

But that common sense was no good at all, when all she wanted for herself—so badly that it hurt—was the man who had just left her.

Dominic had calculated that his guests at the ball wouldn't miss him for a while. Hopefully people would guess he'd gone with his friends to the card room, or maybe joined the men playing billiards. But his time was surely up and he knew there would be talk unless he re-joined his guests soon.

First, though, he went to his bedchamber and summoned his valet. 'A fresh shirt and cravat, please, Hinxton.'

In addition to the shirt and cravat, Hinxton provided a glass of brandy and soda, which Dominic gratefully downed, though what he really needed was an ice-cold bath and some solitude.

He was fully aware that rumours about his marriage still circulated everywhere. Probably many of the elite—yes, including those gathered here as his guests—secretly believed that Dominic's lovely young wife had been driven away by his coldness.

Merryn was different. She'd believed him without question when he'd told her his story and then she'd responded to his caresses with an ardour that had heightened his physical need to the point where his loins had pounded with the primitive longing to possess her entirely. Of course, he'd known lust often enough and knew how to control it, too. But this was something he had no power over, because it involved his heart.

And Merryn?

He remembered how after that kiss she'd looked dazed—vulnerable even. That was because it was the kiss of a man who had told her ever since he first met her that she had no right to her dream of a true home.

Since his marriage to Teresa he'd kept silent about her failings because he believed that he, too, must have made mistakes and been callous to her without realising it. Perhaps his very ardour for his young wife in the initial stages of their marriage had overwhelmed her or even repulsed her. Doubtless Merryn had been shaken also by his passion. But once more he found himself picturing Merryn's impossibly thick lashes framing those wonderful green eyes. Remembered the way she'd shivered, yet pressed herself even closer to him as he kissed her delicate cheekbones and wonderfully soft mouth...

Hinxton chose that moment to cough lightly. 'I suspect, my lord, that your guests will be missing you by now.'

Dominic realised he was staring into space. 'Yes. Of course.'

By now Merryn would have gone up to her own small room in the castle's east wing—but dear God, he would rather she was in his bed, so he could make love to her all night long.

Damn the ball. Damn his guests. With a glance of silent sympathy from Hinxton, Dominic straightened his cravat, then went downstairs, heading first to the billiards room to summon Felix from the company of his friends.

'You must come and dance with our guests, Felix. It's your duty.'

Felix lifted his eyebrows. 'Really, big brother? I gather you've been absent yourself for quite a while.'

'You're absolutely correct.' Dominic gave his brother a wry smile. 'A fine example I am.' He pointed in the direction of the ballroom. 'Come. Let's face battle together, shall we?' With that, Dominic led the way back to the ballroom while resolving that he was, most definitely, not going to let Merryn Hythe out of his life.

The next morning those guests who'd stayed overnight were served a late breakfast in their bedchambers. Dominic, by contrast, was up early—though the hot dishes on offer in the breakfast room offered little temptation, probably because he'd hardly slept.

As he drank his strong coffee he could see that out in the courtyard the grooms were already preparing the carriages to take his visitors away. Soon, too, Merryn would be returning to Hythe Farm and starting her plans to leave for good. No. *No.* He must find some way to stop her.

He was still wrestling with the problem when Inchberry came in a little hesitantly. 'My lord,' he said. 'A man has arrived from London. He says he has urgent business with you.'

A man. Not a gentleman. Inchberry's use of the word conveyed his butler's strong doubts about this particular visitor. Dominic rose and headed for the hall, where a fellow in a long black coat and shabby top hat bowed to him.

Dominic recognised him immediately. He was Frank Nugent, the private investigator from London whom he'd paid to look into Merryn and her past. He felt a prickling of disquiet. 'Good morning, Nugent. This visit is unexpected. I thought you would probably write if you had any news.'

He ushered him into his study, where Nugent began to speak with a certain amount of relish. 'My lord, you requested information about a certain female. Well, I've found it right enough and I thought it more useful to deliver the facts myself than put them in writing. You'll remember how you told me the woman in question travelled with some fairground folk?'

'Of course I remember,' Dominic rapped out. 'What else have you got for me?' He could see the fellow couldn't wait to share his news, whatever it was. His feeling of unease grew.

'The fact is,' went on Nugent, 'that Miss Hythe was good friends with a man called Ashley Wilmot, who's the owner of the fair.'

I know all that, Dominic wanted to say. *I told you that myself.*

'Here's the thing,' went on Nugent. 'I found out last week that this Wilmot fellow and his companions were setting up their stalls on the outskirts of St Alban's, so I went there to ask a few questions and I learned something very interesting.' He paused and wagged a finger for effect. 'You see, it turns out that your Miss Hythe was Ashley Wilmot's mistress—yes, indeed, his fancy piece—for many months as they travelled the length of the country.'

Dominic reeled.

'It's true,' added Nugent. 'Everyone knew it!'

Dominic said not a word. Instead, leaving the man standing there, he strode out of the room to find Inchberry. 'Is Miss Hythe still here?'

'Why, no, my lord. One of your grooms drove her to Hythe Farm an hour or so ago. I understood that was your wish.'

Dominic stood there, feeling his world once more crumbling about him.

As the Earl's carriage took her through Marchwood's parkland, Merryn took no interest whatsoever in the lush scenery. She didn't even glance out of the window, for she knew she wouldn't see a thing. All she could picture was Dominic's face last night just before he kissed her.

He desired her. There was no doubting it; she saw it in his eyes, in his mouth, in the tense set of his powerful body. Just as she desired him. For a while last night she'd believed she had seen something of the truth behind this powerful man's façade. She'd realised that behind his harsh exterior Dominic was vulnerable, even lonely, for he was a man who had built a hard shell around himself in order to protect his heart from any more of the deep hurt caused to him by his wife.

Merryn, too, had created barriers; indeed, she'd had to, to safeguard herself as a single woman in a harsh world. But in Dominic's arms, she'd risked losing that strength and her vulnerability had shaken her to her core. She couldn't help the way she felt when he was close, couldn't help the way her blood sang and her senses tingled at his nearness. It had been wonderful, miraculous even, but she'd also opened herself up to unbelievable pain.

Never again, she warned herself. *Never again.*

Suddenly she realised they were approaching the farmhouse. Already she could see the hens pecking contentedly in the yard and the sweet peas she'd planted climbing riotously up the garden wall. It looked like home—but not for much longer.

As the coach pulled to a halt, the driver came to open the door and help her down, but Merryn had already jumped out. 'Thank you,' she said to him. 'It's most kind of you.'

'A pleasure,' he told her, then climbed up to his seat again to return to the castle. Merryn stood there alone for a moment, expecting the front door to burst open and Cassie or Liam or maybe both to come rushing out to greet her, but there was no one and everywhere seemed strangely quiet.

She opened the front door calling, 'Hello? Liam? Cassie? Are you there?'

There was no reply so she went back outside—only to realise that Cassie was hurrying across the courtyard towards her.

'Merryn. You're back!' Cassie's hair was dishevelled and she looked as if she'd been crying.

Merryn stepped forward. 'Yes, I'm back.' Fresh anxiety was suddenly chilling her to the bone. 'Cassie. Is everything all right?'

'No. It's Liam. No one can find him. He's run away. Oh, Merryn, he's run away!'

Chapter Fifteen

The ball, everyone assured Dominic, had been a great success. As the morning wore on, the guests who'd stayed overnight at Castle Marchwood left amid a flurry of thanks to their host and eager promises to meet at the next event of the famed Surrey Stakes, the party tonight at the Duke of Witham's palatial home.

Dominic listened and made suitable replies as the congratulations poured in. 'A wonderful ball, Lord Marchwood! We're so happy we'll be seeing you again this evening at Witham Court!'

He watched them all climb into their fine carriages. This morning, he noticed that his female guests were dressed almost as grandly as they had been last night, clad in silk pelisses and hats so extravagant that they had to stoop low to get into their coaches.

He thought of a lone figure setting off earlier from the castle, doubtless without a backward glance because she'd guessed this was the end. Indeed it was as well she'd already gone, but the thought did nothing to heal his inner wretchedness at the news Nugent had brought. He was relieved when the last of his guests disappeared because it meant there was no need to smile any more. Retreating to his study, he opened the mail Inchberry presented to him on a silver salver and realised there was yet another letter from Winslade.

> *The illegitimate marriage of Miss Hythe's grand-father is proved beyond question.*
>
> *But, my lord, let me repeat that since you have allowed Miss Hythe and her brother to settle on the property, this dispute could take many months to reach judgement.*
>
> *You must evict both her and her brother without further delay...*

He flung it to the far side of the room. Damn Winslade. Damn Nugent.

The study door opened and he realised that not all his visitors had left, for Sarah and Wilfred entered, and amazingly, Sarah looked slightly nervous.

'Such a fine party, Dominic!' she said. 'I trust you enjoyed it, too?'

He said, 'It went well, I believe.'

She nodded and said with a false kind of brightness, 'I think I saw that woman leaving earlier?'

Of course, he knew exactly who she meant. 'That is correct.'

'My dear Dominic, I'm so glad to hear it! And I really must repeat my warning to you. There's bad blood there, truly bad blood—'

She stopped. Dominic had noticed Wilfred nudging her warningly. She said to her husband, 'We had best be off then, Wilfred. Dominic will, I'm sure, have plenty of other business to attend to.'

They were right, he did indeed have a good deal to attend to, but he couldn't think of anything or anyone, except Merryn and what Nugent had told him about her. Could it really be true? *'Everyone knew it,'* Nugent had said gloatingly.

It was perhaps as well that he was kept busy. Inchberry wished to consult him about the extra staff they'd had to hire for last night's event, Galbraith wished to show him the list of expenses and then, just when he thought he was alone at last, the door to his study opened to admit Felix, who immediately sprawled in the chair facing Dominic. His highly starched cravat was bright yellow while his coat was green and had a ridiculously high collar. So much, thought Dominic, for his brother's ambitions to be a farmer.

'Well, Dom?' said Felix. 'Did you spot any prospective brides last night?'

Dominic sighed. 'Really, Felix, that coat you're wearing is quite ridiculous. As for the ball, no, I did not find myself a prospective bride.'

Felix rose and went to pour himself some brandy. 'To be honest, it never crossed my mind that you would.' He took a gulp of his drink. 'How is Merryn this morning?'

'Miss Hythe has returned to Hythe Farm. And isn't it rather early for you to be drinking spirits?'

Felix looked at his glass and drank some more. 'I

suppose you're still trying to make Merryn suffer for the fact that her father happened to be base-born?'

Dominic briefly closed his eyes. 'Unfortunately,' he said, 'it's the law. Miss Hythe's father could never have inherited and neither can her brother.'

Felix paced the room impatiently then stopped to face his brother. 'Right. Then how's this for a suggestion? I'll marry her and we'll find somewhere to live. You could give me one of your smaller estates.'

'What?'

'You heard me, big brother. That manor house in Northamptonshire would be just fine, since I could still get up to London whenever I wanted. I'm sure you wouldn't miss it in the least.'

Dominic stared at him, stunned. At last he said, 'Felix, you're aware, I'm sure, that the entire Marchwood estate is entailed, which means I could certainly not start giving parts of it away piecemeal even if I wanted to. And—let me get this straight—are you really thinking of proposing marriage to Merryn Hythe?'

'Why not?' Felix was starting to look angry. 'I love her, Dom. I've told you. Though of course, you don't believe in love, do you? Not after Teresa played you for a fool.'

Dominic rose from his chair at that and Felix swiftly lifted a hand in apology. 'Sorry. Below the belt, that one. But I really do love Merryn, you know! And what she needs is a man around, to protect her against stupid rumours and nasty enemies—'

'Felix. Be quiet.'

'What?'

Dominic felt as weary as he'd ever done in his life.

'I'll have to tell you, I suppose. I'm afraid she's deceived us all.'

'I really don't know what you're talking about.'

Dominic sat down again and gazed at his brother. 'I'm afraid I have bad news for you. You know, of course, that she was with a travelling fair?'

'And so? What does that matter to me? I know some of these people have a doubtful reputation, but Merryn is different. She's honest, she's truthful, she's also exceedingly lovely. She's amazing, Dom! And—'

'Felix. Just listen, will you? I've recently been informed that Miss Hythe was the mistress of the man who owned the fair.'

For a moment Felix looked astonished. Then, to Dominic's amazement, he gave a shout of laughter. 'You're saying Merryn Hythe was Ashley Wilmot's *mistress*?'

'Indeed, I am.'

'Are you joking? But of course, you've never seen him, have you?'

'No.' Dominic was mystified. 'Does that matter?'

Felix nodded. 'Yes. Yes, it damn well does matter, you idiot. Because if you'd merely glimpsed the man, you would know he's not interested in women at all! Where on earth did you get the idea of him and Merryn being lovers? It's ridiculous!'

For a moment Dominic couldn't speak. His thoughts were racing furiously. If this was true, then why on God's earth had Frank Nugent told him the tale?

'Someone's been bamboozling you,' went on Felix. 'And it just goes to show that, quite honestly, you're sometimes a bigger idiot than me.'

Dominic stared into the abyss. Oh, God. Perhaps he was. *Definitely* he was.

Felix was watching him sympathetically. 'What have you done, big brother?' he softly asked.

Dominic met his gaze. 'I have,' he said at last, 'made a terrible mistake.'

But there might—just might—be some way to redeem himself. He suddenly realised Felix was still talking. 'There's something else, Dom,' Felix said. 'You really are going to have to sort out the Dragon. For instance, you'll never guess what our sister's done now.'

Dominic tried to regain control of his tumultuous brain. 'Sarah? What has she been up to?'

'She's only told the boy he's to be sent away to a school for reprobates.'

'What on *earth* are you talking about?'

'I overheard our sister speaking to one of her female cronies this morning, just before she left. Apparently a couple of days ago when Merryn was staying here, Sarah and her boys went out for a drive in that open barouche she's so proud of. They must have been close to Hythe land, because they came across Liam riding the pony you gave him—what was she called?'

'Dolly.'

'Yes, Dolly. Anyway, according to Sarah, the carriage halted near to the river to let the boys play there. Then—again, according to Sarah—Liam rode up, jumped off his pony and went for Marcus, punching and kicking him for no reason whatsoever. Or so our sister claimed. My guess is that Marcus probably shouted something rude to Liam, perhaps about Dolly—he might even have thrown things, the little wretch. Anyway, Sarah told Liam he would be sent to an institution for rascally boys where the schoolmasters would beat some sense into him. She really is a prime mischiefmaker! So, like I said, I've a good mind to marry Miss Hythe and look after her and Liam, take them off your hands so to speak. As for you, I hope you'll give our sister a good rollicking when you see her at the Duke of Witham's party tonight—'

He broke off because Dominic was already heading for the door. 'Where on earth are you going now, Dom?'

Dominic paused. 'I might be late to the party tonight.'

'What?'

'I said, I might be late. If I am, give the Duke and Duchess my apologies, will you?'

He left. Within minutes he'd had Meg saddled and was on his way to Hythe Farm. What had Sarah said? What had Sarah *done*? How much more punishment could he and his family inflict on Merryn and her brother? On approaching the farmhouse, his apprehension grew as he realised that a small crowd had gathered in the courtyard. Gabe was there with Dickon and there were several other men, some of whom he recognised as local farmers. Already Gabe was hurrying towards him as he dismounted. 'Gabe. What's going on?'

'It's the young lad, my lord.' The shepherd looked distressed. 'He's only gone and run away!'

Since learning that Liam was missing, Merryn had not rested for one minute. She'd told Gabe to ride round the local farms to ask for any sightings and he'd reported that all of the neighbours were searching their own land for him, while she'd gone out herself on foot with Dickon to hunt through the nearby woods. They'd all agreed to meet back at the farm at one and Merryn was there first, only for fresh fear to engulf her every time a group of people arrived with the same message.

No news.

She begged them to try again. Her voice, she hoped, was calm, but inside she was tormented by thoughts of her brother lost and maybe hurt. Her fault. Her fault, for not being here when he needed her.

When Dominic rode into the yard, all the men who'd gathered to help in the search murmured in astonishment before doffing their caps. Merryn tried desperately to compose herself as Gabe took the bridle of Dominic's big horse and Dominic strode towards her. 'Miss Hythe,' he said abruptly. 'I heard that the boy has gone.'

She nodded, at first unable to speak because all of a sudden a great lump had formed in her throat. 'Yes, my lord. He's run away and it must have been early this morning, but I don't understand it. I have no idea why...' Her voice broke.

He said, 'It was my sister's fault.'

She gazed up at him. 'Your sister? I don't understand.'

Swiftly he explained and at first she could hardly take it in. 'Oh,' she said at last, 'oh, how could she be so cruel?'

'I don't know,' said Dominic grimly. 'But I'm sure as hell going to sort this out.' He added quietly, so no one else could hear, 'Merryn. Are you all right?'

'I am, my lord.' Her voice was steady, but her heart was in turmoil, because he was too close and she so missed the way he'd held her in his arms last night. 'I should never have left Liam. I should have been here with him.'

He said, 'Listen to me. You had a fever and needed medical attention. You were in no state to look after anyone and might have delayed your recovery still more if you hadn't obeyed the doctor's orders and rested at the castle. Besides which, no one—*no one* could have been a better sister to Liam than you, do you hear me? And I've come to help you. We will find him. We will.'

Merryn didn't understand. He regretted last night, surely, so why was he being kind? Why was he even here? But already Dominic was speaking to the gathered men and she could hear him asking which areas of the countryside they'd already searched, whether they knew of disused barns or empty cottages or other likely hiding places.

As the men set off in groups, with those on horseback heading for the furthest destinations, Merryn came up to Dominic. 'I must look for him, too,' she said. 'I've been searching all the nearby fields, but I must try again—'

'No.' His voice was firm. 'Merryn, you've been ill. Leave this to me.'

'I'm fine!' she cried. 'And I cannot do nothing. I cannot sit inside, wondering where Liam is, or what might have happened to him!'

'I understand.' He spoke more gently now. 'But what if he decides to come back and no one is here at the farmhouse to welcome him? How will he feel then? Believe me, he needs to find *you* here.' He looked around and saw Cassie hovering anxiously. 'Cassie. Look after Miss Hythe, will you?'

Cassie bobbed a curtsy. 'Of course, my lord.' She gently took Merryn's arm. 'Come inside, my love. We'll make you comfortable and I'll bake some of Liam's favourite gingerbread men, so he'll have a treat waiting when he's home again.'

Home. Merryn said nothing to contradict her, but she knew this wouldn't be her home for much longer.

As long as Liam is found, she told herself, *that's all that matters. We can live anywhere if my brother is safe.*

As the afternoon wore on Merryn tried to keep busy, helping Cassie with the baking, then tending to the herb garden, but all the time she was waiting for news. At around five Cassie joined her out in the garden. 'You must rest,' Cassie urged. 'You *must.*'

So Merryn allowed Cassie to lead her inside and lay down on the old sofa near the fire Cassie had lit. She must have dozed off, for when she opened her eyes all the curtains were shut and candles flickered in the wall sconces. The fire had burned down to embers.

She sat up sharply and remembered that Liam was gone. Despair settled on her like a chill breeze. She looked at the clock and saw that, dear God, it was past eight now. If her brother had to spend the night outside, he would be cold and hungry and frightened. What if he'd decided to return but had lost his way in the dark? Were the searchers still looking? And where was

Cassie? That was when she heard the sound of horses, together with raised voices. Rushing outside, she saw that in the lantern-lit courtyard there was a group of riders with Dominic in their midst. And sitting in front of him, astride Dominic's big horse, was…

'Liam,' she called. 'Oh, Liam!'

Chapter Sixteen

An hour later Merryn stood in the small bedchamber where her brother lay fast asleep. The glow of a single lamp cast shimmering shadows across the room.

When Dominic brought Liam home he'd been cold and hungry, but first of all he'd wanted to see Dolly. Then he settled close to the fire in the kitchen with a supper of milk and gingerbread, but after he'd eaten Merryn sat by his side and said quietly, 'Liam. You didn't really think I would ever let you be sent away to school, did you?'

He hesitated. 'But that lady is the Earl's sister. And she said it was nothing to do with you.'

'It has *everything* to do with me,' Merryn answered fiercely, 'because you are the most important person in the world to me. Do you understand?'

He nodded but she could see he was still tense. 'Merryn,' he said at last, 'while you were away at the castle, Cassie said that soon we might have to leave here. That's not right, is it?'

She took his hand in hers. 'Don't let that worry you, my love. Just remember that we'll always be together, I promise.'

She hoped she'd comforted him a little, but she returned downstairs feeling low in spirits and acutely aware of the silence that had settled around the farmhouse. Of course all the searchers had gone home and Dominic must have left, too; Cassie, who seemed to know everything these days, had told Merryn he was due to attend a grand society party this evening at a neighbouring estate. Cassie had then asked her, almost shyly, if Merryn minded if she spent the night at Gabe's cottage. 'Dickon's away with friends,' she added. 'So...'

'So you two will have the cottage to yourselves? Of course I don't mind!' It was clear that the couple would soon be married and that Cassie's future, unlike her own, lay here. *Liam is safe*, she kept repeating to herself. That was all that mattered—Liam was safe. She said it again and again as she headed down the stairs, but her heart ached all the same.

The lighting was dim in the big kitchen so it took her a moment to realise that someone was standing by the fire. It was Dominic. Her hand flew to her throat. 'My lord. I thought you had gone home.'

He said, 'I wanted to know that Liam is all right.' Then he added, 'And you, also.'

Her pulse bumped unsteadily. She turned up the oil lamp close by and said, 'My brother is asleep now and he's fine. He said you were extremely kind to him.' She hesitated. 'I don't quite know how I can thank you enough for finding him.'

'It was no hardship. And I will be speaking to my sister about the harm she has done. Be sure of it.'

'My lord, there is no need…'

'My name is Dominic,' he almost growled, 'and there is every need.' He stepped closer. 'Sarah will offer a proper apology to you. As will I.'

She shook her head. 'I don't understand. Why should you need to apologise?'

'In the past,' he said, 'I've frightened you. Haven't I?'

She looked up into his dark, heartbreaking eyes. 'I told you, I think, that I've had good reason to fear certain kinds of men.'

'Men who desired you?' he asked abruptly.

She nodded, unable to speak.

'That scar,' he said. 'I thought it was maybe a robbery. But did someone try to force you, Merryn? Using a *knife*?'

'Yes.' She said it very quietly. 'He was a bailiff, in Ireland, working for the wealthy man who owned the lease on our house and land. He offered to help me. He said he would speak to the landlord on my behalf and maybe get our lease extended. He was pleasant, he was kind—or so I thought. Then one afternoon, when I was alone in the house, he tried to force himself on me. He threatened me with a knife. I fought him off, eventually.'

She looked up at Dominic, seeing…what? Incredulity at first. Then anger—a powerful anger that shook her to her very foundations.

He said at last, in a low voice, 'My God. I've been a brute to you. After all that you'd been through, you still had the courage to make the long journey from

Ireland to come to me, for your brother's sake—and I have treated you atrociously.'

'No!' she cried. 'No, Dominic. I've been afraid of other men, yes, but with you, once I saw how kind you were to Liam and to your own brother, once I realised how hurt you'd been by your wife's betrayal, I—' She broke off. 'I trusted you,' she finally said very quietly.

And more. Much more, she added to herself.

For a moment he didn't reply. Then he said, 'There's another apology I must make.'

And he told her how he'd set a private investigator to ask questions about her. 'He reported to me,' Dominic said, 'that there were rumours about you and the fairground's owner.'

'Ashley?' she cried. 'Ashley? Rumours about us being lovers? I know. Because it was me who started those rumours!'

She felt desperate, but then she saw he was nodding. 'Please,' he said very quietly. 'Will you tell me about it? I think I know the truth, but I would like to hear it from you.'

She sat down, and he did, too. 'As you know,' she began, 'I wished to get to England. But the fare from Dublin was expensive and I realised that Liam and I might be in danger travelling on our own. The truth is that Ashley is not interested in women at all. But you'll know that to be that kind of man is against the law of the land. You'll also know that men can be gaoled or even hanged for it.'

He nodded and she carried on. 'Soon after the fair reached England, I realised that hateful reports were spreading about Ashley, even though he'd led a solitary life for many years. So I suggested that if people wished to think I was his mistress, I would let them. Perhaps it was foolish of me—but he was my friend.'

She paused, remembering how it had been easy to convey the illusion in small ways, like spending the evening in his caravan chatting and laughing together or letting Ashley put his hand on her shoulder while she talked to him.

She looked at Dominic again. 'You said you learned this from an investigator you'd hired. Did you believe his story?'

For a moment he looked haunted. 'God help me,' he said in a low voice, 'for a moment I almost did, but someone—it doesn't matter who—told me the truth about your friend and I came to my senses. I think I knew anyway that it couldn't be true. You see, I only had to remember our kisses to be quite sure of it.'

Her mouth was dry. 'Why?'

He met her gaze steadily. 'For a while,' he said very quietly, 'last night in the summer house, you were mine. And your kisses were the sweetest and most innocent I have ever known. Merryn, I have treated you despicably.'

'No,' she cried. 'You were right from the beginning to tell me that Liam had no right to claim Hythe Farm!'

He reached out and put one hand on her shoulder. It was only a light touch, but somehow it burned through the fabric of her dress and all the way to her damned heart. Then he said softly, 'You are always thinking of your brother. I know I've asked you this before. But what about your dreams for yourself, Merryn?'

'I don't—' she began. She stopped. *I don't have any*, she was going to say.

But she knew differently now. She did have dreams. Of this man taking her in her arms again and kissing her and whispering his love. But dreams were for fools, everyone knew that.

She said, as lightly as she could, 'I think we've talked enough. I've heard you were supposed to be going out tonight, to some grand party.'

'Be damned to the party,' Dominic said almost cheerily. 'I hate them anyway.'

His laugh—yes, it was his laugh that undid her, because it was lovely. She dashed away the stupid tears that had suddenly formed in her eyes and he must have seen them because he said decisively, 'I'll make us some tea, shall I? Stay where you are.'

So Merryn sat on the sofa and watched as Dominic strode over to her ancient stove, placed the kettle on the hob, then fetched two mugs and a teapot from the shelf. Dressed in that loose shirt and breeches, he looked utterly irresistible doing such an ordinary task. 'A domesticated earl,' she murmured under her breath. Oh, goodness, she wanted to laugh, she wanted to cry—and most of all she wanted to be in his arms.

Had she given up her own wishes and dreams? No, but she knew she had to try. Because she'd realised ever since that kiss last night that her dreams would always be of Dominic.

Cassie had once warned her that men were like children. 'Desperate for one thing,' she'd scoffed. 'A few moments of pleasure, then it's all done. My advice, if you ever have the misfortune to fall for a man's smooth talk, is to make him wait until he does the right thing and marries you. Just remember that the last thing you want is a fatherless babe.'

But now Cassie had found happiness with Gabe, who was kind and decent. As for Merryn, she felt shaken with physical longing for the man who even now was carefully measuring out the leaves into the pot, then finding the jug of milk. It was true, he'd been endlessly kind to Liam. Kind to her.

But she didn't want his kindness. No, she wanted much, much more.

He came back and put the two mugs on the small oak table nearby. He sat on the sofa with her, but not too close. Like a friend, she thought hollowly, with whom she'd shared some spine-tingling kisses and more than a few secrets.

But he was an earl and she was a fairground fortune teller. What greater gulf could there be?

He handed her the tea and said, 'Is Liam all right now? Do you think he'll sleep well?'

Merryn took her mug, trying not to notice how strong his hands were, yet how elegant. 'Yes,' she replied. 'Thank you, he'll be fine.' She tried to sip her tea, but of course it was too hot and she almost dropped the mug. Oh, heavens, it was as if her brain had been tossed around in a winter gale and she felt quite dizzy as she tried to adjust to the feelings that all but overwhelmed her.

I have fallen desperately in love, she realised. *And it's impossible.*

He reached and took the mug from her, setting it

down on the table. Drawing closer, he put out his hand and gently tilted up her chin so their eyes locked. 'Listen,' he said quietly. 'I want to make a promise to you. If you will agree, I intend to make sure that Hythe Farm is Liam's for good.'

She felt herself shrink away, because the temptation to fall into his arms was almost too strong to resist. She shook her head. 'How *can* you? You told me yourself that no one can argue with the law! Liam is not legally entitled to the property, so I will make my plans and move on.'

'Merryn,' he said, 'I understand that my past and what you've learned about my wife must have frightened you. But I beg you to take your time. If you change your mind about leaving, you have only to tell me. Listen to me. No one could be a better sister than you have been, do you hear me? It strikes me that everything you've done for many years, every decision you've taken, has been for Liam. You have given up your own wishes and dreams for far too long. You've been through much unhappiness in your life—you've faced homelessness, danger and poverty. Aren't you ever to be allowed to have a life of your own?'

Dear heaven, she could see it again in his eyes. Passion, stark passion, for her. She found herself aching with the sense of something infinitely precious that she was about to lose for ever. But she shook her head obstinately. 'I have Liam. That is enough.'

Dominic sighed. He said at last, 'I know you've told me you don't ever try reading the cards for yourself. But if you did, I believe they might tell you that although you have many admirable qualities, you are also quite maddeningly stubborn, Miss Hythe.'

She was almost—*almost* laughing. 'Maybe. But thank you, Dominic. Thank you for coming here and helping me to find my brother, then for being so kind to him.'

She rose gracefully from the sofa. At least, she intended to rise gracefully from the sofa, but sheer fatigue made her stumble, only to find he was on his feet, too, and holding her. The air around them tingled with expectancy and Dominic's hands on her shoulders were drawing her nearer, nearer...

He was going to kiss her and it would be wonderful. She knew that. She had no power to resist.

His finger lightly touched her cheek, then slid down to her lips. 'So beautiful,' he whispered. 'So brave.'

His kiss was tender at first. Gentle. Coaxing. But she needed more and she let him know it, clasping her hands around the back of his neck and opening her lips to his.

He really, truly kissed her then. His lips were hungry and fierce, his tongue thrusting to tangle with hers and his hands around her back pulling her against him so that she could physically feel how much he wanted her when the ridge of his manhood pressed hot and hard against her hips.

She wanted him. This man made her weak with longing. He made her needful in a way she hadn't known existed. She closed her eyes tightly as she clung to him, aware of a multitude of sensations coursing through her veins. She was desperate for more, desperate for *him*, and had been since the night she first saw him in her tiny caravan. The kiss ended, but he still held her tightly. Time passed, she wasn't sure how much time, then he drew away, only a little, and said, 'I don't want to lose you.'

Oh, dear God. She realised now what she'd done— she'd opened her defences and she was lost. If he asked her to be his mistress, she would agree. She was blinded, mad with love.

Love, she realised, was a sign of a complete lack of control, not only over one's emotions but over one's entire body. Tonight, she believed she'd seen the actual truth behind this powerful man's façade. She believed she knew now that, behind his harsh exterior, Dominic was vulnerable, even lonely. He was a man who had built a hard shell around himself in order to protect his heart from any more of the deep hurt caused to him by his first wife.

Merryn, too, had created barriers, for she'd learned early on that a single woman had to be strong to survive in a harsh world. But in Dominic's arms, she'd risked losing that strength and her vulnerability had shaken her very existence.

'Well?' he was saying softly. His arms were still loosely around her waist. 'I mean it, Merryn. I don't want you to leave my life.'

Somehow she pulled herself away from the man who'd captured her heart. Away from the little things that she found irresistible, like the shadow of stubble on his strong jaw and that lock of dark hair that fell now across his forehead. Yes, she drew away, because they all weakened her.

She said steadily, 'It's no good, Dominic. We have to face the fact that I can have no real place in your life,

ever. Whatever you want me to be to you, I would make
you a laughing stock. I would pull you down among
those who are your equals and your friends.'

He, too, had drawn away and his expression had altered completely. Those barriers of his were up again
and she saw before her a man wounded to the heart by
life and its blows. He said, with his voice almost raw,
'Do you think I care, Merryn, what society says about
me? Do you think I give a damn about the sort of people
who came to my ball last night, the same people who
gossip and laugh behind my back about the disaster of
my marriage?'

She shook her head. 'You *must* care. Dominic, you
have to protect your position in society because many
people depend on you. You are in a position of power,
the power to do good. You have to marry suitably and
have children.'

'Merryn—'

'No,' she said softly. 'I will not be your mistress,
because it would break my heart when you find yourself a bride.'

'I did not ask you,' he said almost harshly, 'to be my
mistress. Did I? Who could I want for a bride if not you?'

She backed away then, feeling the blood draining
from her cheeks. 'No. No, you cannot be thinking of
marriage. With my family's history of illegitimacy and
bankruptcy and my months with a travelling fair? *No.*
I must leave Hythe Farm as soon as possible, for my
sake as much as yours!'

'And where the hell will you go?'

She said, 'When I got here this morning, there was a

letter waiting for me, from Ashley. He's written to tell me he's sold the show and is buying a house with some land close to the sea in Devon. That was always his dream.' She knew she was talking too quickly, rushing through every agonising word. 'He's also asked me to come and live with him there as his housekeeper. With Liam, of course.'

He nodded, but she saw devastation in his eyes. 'Very well,' he said at last. 'Very well. You did warn me after all about the cards I picked that night in your caravan. You pointed out that I'd marked myself as a fool and perhaps I was one, for dreaming the impossible.'

She was shivering inside, dying inside.

It's for the best, she told herself, *for both of us.*

'I told you,' she said, 'that it's up to my clients to make what they will of the cards they choose. Maybe it's time for you to leave and spare us both any more of this regret. I'll make arrangements to travel to Devon and I shall let you know the date of my departure as soon as I can confirm it.'

He nodded. He reached out and he lightly touched the little locket she wore, then Dominic, the Earl of Marchwood, walked through the door and out of her life.

Merryn stood there until the fire had died down, then at last she went upstairs and sat on her bed. Too much. All of it, too much.

She always tried to tell herself that she was strong and that she needed no one else in her life, or so she'd thought. But tonight, all her previous certainties had been demolished. Tonight, she'd realised that her feelings for Dominic had become crucial to her existence.

Of course, she found him devastatingly attractive. But there were all the other things, like his quiet acceptance of all blame for his wife's death and his concern for Liam. He'd trusted her with the tragic secret of his first marriage and it tore at her very soul. He felt he was maybe not fit to be a husband and father.

She'd wanted to cry out, *But look at Liam!* Look how tonight, the distraught boy had been calm in his firm hold! Liam trusted Dominic, for he'd realised long before Merryn did that Dominic was a man of integrity, a fact she had been afraid to acknowledge, maybe because she'd known she might let her heart be broken if she fell in love with him.

Which she had. But it was hopeless because it would ruin him—and her whole being hurt, more than she could have believed possible.

She had no need of a fortune teller's tricks to decide her next move. She was going to live with Ashley and forget Dominic and her dreams. But a little voice whispered, *You will never forget him. Never.*

Now, there was a prediction that she knew was as cruelly accurate as anything ever could be in this world.

The next morning Dominic was on his way to the stables to get his horse saddled up when he saw his sister's carriage arrive in the castle's courtyard. At least this saved him the trouble of riding over to her house, which had been his intention. For once Sarah had come on her own; there was no Wilfred cowering in the background.

'Dominic,' she began, 'I need to speak with you.'

'And I with you. Come inside.' He led the way into the morning room, where he firmly shut the door. 'Well, Sarah?' he said.

Sarah settled herself fussily on a chair and removed her bonnet. 'I have come to ask you,' she said, 'where on earth you were last night. The Duke of Witham was most put out that you didn't attend his party.'

'I sent a message over to Witham Court this morning with a full apology,' Dominic said. He didn't sit down. 'But I'm glad you came, Sarah. Because I have a matter of some importance to discuss.'

'Really?' His sister looked eager.

He wondered, with a fresh shaft of dislike, if maybe she was hoping he'd chosen himself a bride. 'What I wish to say,' he said, 'concerns the boy Liam Hythe.' He saw her stiffen. 'Let me make it quite clear, Sarah, that his welfare is absolutely none—I repeat none—of your business.'

He could tell Sarah was shaken, by the force of his words, though she quickly pulled herself together. 'I'm rather surprised,' she said, 'by your constant defence of that low-born woman and her ill-natured brother. Don't you realise she's nothing but a fortune hunter?'

Dominic felt his inner rage mounting. 'Let me tell you this. During my various meetings with Miss Hythe, I've realised that she is unambitious in terms of wealth. She is no fortune hunter, believe me.'

'Not a fortune hunter? But perhaps she's after something more…like a title.' She wagged her finger. 'Have you thought of that?'

Dominic's tone was truly harsh this time. 'Don't be ridiculous. Your sharp tongue is becoming tiresome. And you had no business warning Miss Hythe's brother he would be sent away to some barbaric boarding school.'

She went very still, but after Liam's recent ordeal he didn't regret his current mood one jot.

Just then the door to the morning room swung open and Felix—poor, unwitting Felix—wandered into what had become a very tense atmosphere.

'Good morning, Sarah,' he said. 'And hello, big brother. My goodness, Dom, you were missed at the Duke's party last night. You wouldn't believe the number of disappointed young ladies who were searching the ballroom for you. I hope you've remembered there's another party coming up at Viscount Garfield's? They'll be desperate to see if you turn up…'

His voice faded as he was met by stone-cold silence. He let out a low whistle. 'Oh, my. Are you two having a row?' He looked at his brother. 'Is it about you missing the party, Dom, and letting down all your admirers? You really do need to find yourself a wife. It'll put an end to all our sister's nagging, you know.'

Yes, thought Dominic. *I need a wife.* One with laughing green eyes, gorgeous brown hair and the loveliest face he'd ever seen.

There was an awkward silence, then Sarah rose and swept out of the room. Felix looked at Dominic and said, 'I shan't ask what that was about, since I'm not even sure I want to know. I just came to tell you I'm off to see Merryn, to check that she's all right after that nasty illness of hers.'

Dominic drew in a deep breath and said, 'Please don't, Felix. I wasn't at the ball last night because I was at Hythe Farm.'

'You were *where*?'

'Her brother had run away, thanks to our sister.' Briefly Dominic explained Sarah's threat. 'Both she and Liam are all right, but they need time alone, and right now, so do I. If you'll excuse me?' As he was leaving the room he realised that Felix was sinking rather dazedly into the nearest chair.

Dominic, meanwhile, went to his study and began to compose a letter to his lawyer.

I am coming to London today, Winslade, for a brief stay. I wish you to make urgent enquiries about an Irish family by the name of Arvon, who I believe might own property in London as well as Dublin.

If by any chance they are in town, please contact them. Tell them…

He paused a moment in thought. Then he dipped his pen in the ink again and completed his sentence.

…that the Earl of Marchwood wishes to make their acquaintance.

Chapter Seventeen

One week later

It was a warm spring afternoon, the kind to make your spirits sing. But Merryn took little joy in the sounds of birdsong or the scent of the blossom filling the hedgerows. She was making one last tour of the Hythe lands, for in two days' time she and her brother would be leaving here for good. She'd written to accept Ashley's offer of a home with him in Devon and Ashley had replied immediately. 'The sooner the better!' he'd said.

Of course, Cassie would not be coming with them. 'Gabe wants us to be married next month,' she'd said, her cheeks quite pink with joy, and Merryn had hugged her.

'Oh, Cassie. I'm so happy for you, darling!'

Merryn had told Liam about their forthcoming departure and he'd accepted the news bravely, but she knew that his heart was here. As was hers, for ever.

She had not been able to stop thinking about the time

she'd spent with Dominic after he'd found Liam. The secrets they'd shared, the kiss they'd shared when he'd not been a proud, haughty earl, but a very human man scarred by memories of a former love that had turned into a poisoned chalice. She guessed he'd quite probably meant it when he'd implied there could be a place in his life for her. But—marriage? She knew that for him, any open connection with her would bring ruin on him. No doubt he realised it, too, in the cold light of day, for she'd not heard from him since.

It was as well. Sensible, practical Merryn, that was her. So why—*why* did she feel as if her heart was cracking in two?

She had one final obligation to him. One final personal challenge: to demonstrate that during her brief stay here, she'd done as much as possible to ensure the farmhouse and its lands were in a better state than when she'd moved in.

She suddenly realised Gabe, who was accompanying her on her tour round the fields, was speaking to her. 'I'm sorry, Gabe,' she replied. 'What was that you said?'

They'd arrived at the western edge of the Hythe estate, where a fast-flowing stream marked the boundary with the Marchwood lands. Running along the top of the stream's far bank was a stone wall and beyond that, she knew, was a broad track leading to the castle.

Gabe was pointing down at the stream where a large birch tree lay uprooted in an untidy mess of mud and clinging turf. 'A recent gale must have toppled it,' Gabe told her. 'And it needs shifting. See how all those branches are blocking the flow of the stream? It'll cause flooding further back if we don't do something. I'll go and fetch Dickon to give me a hand.'

He was turning to go, but Merryn caught his arm. 'No,' she said. 'No, I can help.'

'But your clothes!'

She gestured at the smock and breeches she wore, as she always did now when doing any work in the fields. 'These can stand a bit of dirt.' She pulled off her old straw hat. 'Just tell me what to do.'

Hadn't she always insisted to Dominic that she was as capable of looking after the estate as any man? *Dominic.* Her heart ached again. She blinked hard and tried to concentrate on what Gabe was telling her.

'I think it's best,' he was saying, 'to grasp the tree's stoutest branches and haul it up on to the bank here.'

Unfortunately it was easier said than done. Together they heaved until Merryn's arms ached, but still the stubborn tree could not be dislodged. At last Gabe stood back and mopped his brow. 'It's no good,' he said. 'We need another man.'

'I'm sorry.' Merryn sat despondently on the grassy bank and put on her straw hat again. 'Clearly there are some jobs I can't do.'

Gabe looked at her in his honest, warm way. 'Aye, that may be true, miss,' he said, settling down beside her, 'but all of us have been glad to have you around, you can be sure of that.'

Oh, no. That brought another lump to her throat because of all her dreams for Liam, all her mad, foolish hopes for herself. Those hopes had ended, predictably, in disaster and in two days' time she was leaving. It was as well.

Suddenly Gabe was on his feet. 'I can hear horses coming along the track over there, miss. Carriages, too!'

Merryn stood up also. Gabe had waded across the stream in his heavy boots and climbed the far bank so he could see over the stone wall into Marchwood lands. 'Looks like the Earl is taking his guests on a tour of the estate,' he called back to her.

Oh, no. Her heart started beating heavily. 'Guests?'

'That's right. I believe he's got a number of fine folk staying at the castle and they're coming this way. Some are in open carriages and others are on horseback, ladies as well as gentlemen. They'll be enjoying the sunshine, no doubt. And His Lordship is leading the way on that big black mare of his.'

Merryn felt panic rising. 'Come back down here, Gabe. I don't want them to notice us!' She certainly didn't want Dominic or his aristocratic guests to see her in her muddied smock and boots with her hair all over the place—that would be the ultimate humiliation. Obediently Gabe scrambled down the bank and waded through the stream again to join her.

She prayed that the wall would screen them from view, but her prayers went unanswered. For just as the Earl's house party was passing by, that stubborn tree decided at last to shift of its own accord. Its roots groaned as they lifted themselves free from the clinging earth, then both trunk and branches settled with a resounding thud so they still blocked at least half of the stream. Merryn heard the squeals of the ladies in their carriages at the unexpected noise and saw the faces of those on horseback peering over the boundary wall. They were gazing down at the tree. Gazing also at her and Gabe.

Dominic, of course, was with them. Merryn, frozen with embarrassment, saw that his face registered no emotion when he saw them there, but instead he called to his guests, 'Carry on, please. I'll catch up with you in a few minutes.'

The next thing she knew, he'd called to one of his grooms to tether his horse close by, then he climbed over the wall and was coming down the far bank in his elegant grey riding coat, buff breeches and superbly polished boots. He said, 'You two look as if you need help.'

Already the sound of carriages and horses was fading away as his guests moved onwards. Merryn stood there in her muddy smock and battered straw hat and said, in a toneless voice, 'I'm sorry to have interrupted your outing, my lord. Gabe and I have been trying to unblock the stream and we'll get Dickon to help. Please, re-join your guests.'

But Dominic, who'd swiftly assessed the situation, stripped off his coat and said, 'You have a rope, I take it?'

Indeed, Gabe had brought a rope, along with a saw and a shovel. Merryn nodded. 'I'll fetch it.'

Hurrying back with the rope, she handed it to Dominic, then watched as Gabe coiled one end of the rope around the birch tree's trunk and Dominic began to haul on the other. At that point she almost stopped thinking rationally, because he'd pulled off his cravat and unbuttoned his shirt.

She felt sudden heat blaze through her veins as she watched him brace himself firmly on the bank, then pull at the tree with all the power of his strongly muscled arms. Only a few nights ago he'd kissed her. Only a few nights ago, he'd all but asked her to marry him. But it was over. It had to be over, for his sake, for wouldn't he soon regret it? Hadn't his first marriage been enough of a disaster for him?

Swiftly she forced her mind back to the present because Gabe, who'd been straining to shift the roots, called out, 'Nearly there, my lord!'

With fresh scatterings of earth and sprays of water, the tree came free and crashed on the bank, allowing the stream to rush on in full spate, free of obstruction at last. Dominic, though, had lost his balance as the tree toppled and he ended up on the grassy bank with Gabe sprawled next to him. After a moment the two men raised themselves, both of them laughing, then clasped hands in mutual congratulation.

Gabe thanked Dominic heartily for his assistance. 'But,' he added, 'if Your Lordship will excuse me, I'll be needed up at the sheepfold now. Dickon will have been expecting me this past hour.'

Merryn, once more conscious of her own ridiculous attire and feeling dizzy with the churning emotions of heartbreak, added, 'I'll come with you, Gabe.'

Dominic turned to her and shook his head. 'Stay here, Miss Hythe. Please.'

No. *No.* Gabe glanced at them both, then departed while Merryn stood there, shaking inside. He looked more desirable than ever with that damp, half-open shirt displaying his tanned chest. And he looked *sad* again.

She knew for certain now that she should have fled straight away with Gabe, but she was rooted to the spot. Her clothes might be damp, but by now the sun was blazing overhead and her limbs were heating with impossible desire. Oh, her stupid dreams. Then she went cold again when she heard the sound of horses approaching, this time on their side of the stream. She looked up and saw two female riders on beautiful horses trotting along the path towards them.

These elegant women in their expensive riding habits and stylish hats looked shocked out of their wits and really it was no wonder, since Dominic's damp shirt was clinging to his powerful torso. As for her, she knew she must look like someone completely beneath their notice. Dominic, however, hadn't forgotten his manners. Giving a slight bow, he said, 'Lady Smythdon. Miss Travis. I'm sorry I had to desert my guests, but a sudden emergency cropped up, I fear.'

The two women appeared desperately uncertain whether to drink their fill of the sight of his amazing figure or to swoon in ladylike shock. At last Lady Smythdon said, rather stiffly, 'I would have thought, Lord Marchwood, that you had menials to assist with that kind of work. We had to take a detour to get here, such was our concern for you. But...' she was looking now at Merryn '...good heavens. Is that creature a woman?'

Merryn couldn't resist it. She made a curtsy, but held her head high. 'That I am, Your Ladyship. But where I come from, we women learn to wield a shovel and clear ditches just as well as any man, I assure you!'

She caught sight of Dominic next to her smothering a smile.

Lady Smythdon and Miss Travis looked even more shocked. 'My lord. Really! For you to associate with such a slovenly creature!'

Suddenly Dominic's eyes were as cold as black slate. 'I suggest you ride back to the castle, ladies,' he said in an expressionless voice. 'I'll join you again as soon as my work here is done.'

As they went on their way, Dominic muttered, 'Bitches. Proud, cold-hearted bitches.'

Merryn forced herself to speak lightly again. 'Even so, my lord, you must tidy yourself up and re-join them. The fact that they've seen you here like this, with me, will soon spread all around the district. People will be shocked. You must go!'

He faced her squarely. He said, with a note in his voice that shook her to her core, 'I'm not going anywhere until I choose to.'

'But...'

'Sit down,' he said. 'Please, Merryn.'

A request from an earl. How could she disobey? She braced herself at the glimpse of fresh hurt to come, but as well to get it over with since she'd surely faced the worst. So she sat on the grass again, then he sat beside her and for a moment they both watched the tumbling water as the stream raced by.

He said, after a while, 'Well. This is better than riding around with those brainless ninnies.'

She was surprised. She was shaken. Was this some kind of trick or game? She was not going to show weakness now so she managed, somehow, to smile. 'Should I remind you they are your guests?'

Yes, she was pretending to be light-hearted, but this gorgeous man was too close, so that when he chuckled, that rich deep way she loved so much, the sound actually rippled right through her body and set up agonising reminders of the way he'd kissed her.

He said, 'Their looks of disapproval were something to behold. Lady Smythdon's expression would have put out a bonfire.'

Merryn nodded, clasping her hands around her knees. Yes. She had to pretend to be light-hearted. Pretend not to care. She managed to laugh and their gazes locked until once more she was conscious of that pull of desperate longing. His shirt was still open and she remembered the feel of his hard body against hers on that night they were together. *All* of her remembered, that was the trouble. And it was disastrous, because her common sense was dissolving into a haze of physical desire.

She said, in as steady a voice as she could manage, 'I think I should remind you that soon all your guests will be waiting for you back at the castle.' She attempted a smile. 'And from what I've heard, one of them might well be your future bride.'

He said, 'If it's Miss Travis, I'm not going back there ever.'

She wanted to laugh. She wanted to cry, because she loved this man but she knew there was no future for her in his life. As she watched him sitting there in the sun with his dark hair all tousled and his boots and breeches spattered with mud, she felt another desperate surge of longing.

She also knew she needed to get up and leave now, for her own safety. Her own sanity.

She began to rise, but he put out his hand to stop her.

'Merryn,' he said huskily. 'Oh, Merryn.'

Then he pulled her into his arms and kissed her until she thought she would die of it.

One last time, she whispered to herself. *One last time*.

He wanted this woman so very, very badly. The ladies of the *ton* were as nothing compared to her, for Merryn was real. She was brave, she was strong-willed—and she also looked entrancingly lovely in that smock and straw hat. There was not an ounce of vanity in her veins, she'd made no attempts to lure him and yet she made his heart sing.

There was no coy hesitation either in her response to his kiss. She opened her lips to him and kissed him back so their tongues mingled in urgent desire until, breathless, he eased away. But he was still holding her tightly. He reached to wipe a smudge of dirt from her delicious little nose and she said, 'I must look an absolute mess.'

She was trying to make light of it and yet there was something very different in her eyes. Hunger. Yearning, maybe, and again that hint of a deep sadness that he'd noted the very first time they met.

He wanted to kiss that sadness away for ever. He wanted to convince her she truly was worth ten, no, twenty of any of his foolish guests. He took her in his arms again and he kissed her once more, tasting her sweetness with his tongue. She was soft and yielding and his common sense was floating up into the clouds, way out of sight. The grassy bank they sat on was sunny and welcoming; the scent of flowers and the singing of birds made an entrancing backdrop. He kissed her again, and before he knew it, she was kissing him back ardently and running her fingers under his loose shirt, then round his back with a series of tantalising caresses that made his loins pound.

'Merryn.' His voice was hoarse with passion. 'Merryn. I need you.'

She eased herself away a little and for a moment he was afraid she was rejecting him. But then he saw that her gorgeous green eyes were lambent with desire. 'Dominic,' she whispered back. 'Don't you realise yet how very much I need *you*?'

Moments later his hands were round her waist, under that loose smock—and he realised that she wore absolutely nothing underneath it. He couldn't help himself; his hands travelled higher and she gasped as he reached her breasts. They were gorgeous, small but beautifully rounded, and when he cupped them and thumbed her nipples, she cried out and arched her body towards his.

Somehow he tugged down her breeches, then he reached for that sweet spot between her thighs and her whimpers of delight thrilled him as he began to stroke with his finger, steadily building the slick heat there. His self-control shook at the silent pleading of her body and his loins thudded anew, his fierce erection almost a torture to him.

Merryn was perfection. He'd never met anyone to match her and he knew now that he never would. Bracing himself to take his body weight on his forearms, he eased his hips between her thighs, then reached down to loosen the placket of his breeches before once more caressing the very heart of her.

She was ready, as was he, dear God. For a moment he gazed down to see that her face was flushed, her breathing rapid.

'Please,' she whispered. 'Dominic. *Now.*'

As he guided himself into her she moved with him, she was at one with him as he took her close to the peak of pleasure, then kept her hovering on the brink. Her hands were everywhere, on his hips, on his back, urging him on. He tried to keep her there, on that plateau of near bliss, until—

'Merryn.' He gave one final, powerful thrust and felt her convulsing beneath him. Her hands were raking his back, her fingernails sharp, but he didn't care because she was sobbing out his name and he was at last able to join her in that final, cataclysmic explosion of rapture.

Merryn had no idea how long they lay there while the birds chattered in the hedgerows and the sun shone down from an azure sky. She wished it could be for ever, so she could be to the man she adored and remember it all.

She'd heard other women warn there was often pain when a man made love to you for your first time, but his sweet kisses drove away her physical fear and it was not pain that she felt, oh, no. Somehow, though she wouldn't have believed it was possible, his manhood had probed deeper and deeper into the place where she was softest and most vulnerable until there was only him and he was filling her, filling her world, his strength enveloping her, his silken-smooth manhood possessing her while his hand had reached to both soothe and arouse her taut, aching breasts.

'Merryn,' he'd grated out. It could have been harsh, the way he said her name, but it wasn't and, instead, it was somehow the tenderest sound in the world. The sound of a man who needed her.

She'd responded with all her being, until he reached down to once more tease at the heart of her sex and began to move harder within her until she'd clenched herself around him, crying out his name. She remembered how her world had fallen away as if there was nothing to existence except that glorious cascade of sensation rolling through her. Had it been a mistake? Yes, without a doubt, but it was a memory she would always hold till the end of her days.

She was the one who pulled away at last. Sitting up carefully, she donned her smock and breeches, then rose to her feet and pulled on her boots, stout farmer's boots that reminded her exactly who she was. A woman of no wealth and very little importance. He cared for her, she knew that, but she would damage his life just as badly as his first wife had. Make him a laughing stock, as those women on horseback had clearly demonstrated.

'I think,' she said as lightly as she could, 'that it's time we both went back to our duties. I have a meal to prepare back at the farmhouse, while you, I suggest, really should be returning to your guests to assure them that you've not completely lost your mind and abandoned them for good.'

He rose to his feet also. He said quietly, 'Is that how you would describe what just happened between us? Do you truly think I've lost my mind?'

He didn't look like one of the highest aristocrats in the land any more. No, his hair was tousled and his dark eyes still burned with passion, while his finely sculpted mouth couldn't help but remind her of his delicious kisses.

Fresh longing, fresh loss surged through her. She knew she would have to fight to resist the longing for more and the only sure way to succeed was to leave his life for ever.

'I don't think you've lost your mind,' she said quietly. 'But you must know, as I do, that this is impossible. We have to say goodbye.'

She bent to pick up her hat, but as she straightened Dominic drew closer, gathered her into his arms and bowed his head to press his forehead against hers. She could almost hear how his heartbeat still thudded from their lovemaking.

'Merryn,' he said. 'I'm going to find a solution, somehow. I'm not going to let you go, you know.'

She said, as lightly as she could, 'Dominic. You know this cannot work. Some day, surely, you will find someone suitable to love.'

The man who had stolen her heart looked at her and said, 'What if I've already fallen in love with you?'

This time her strength failed her and she couldn't speak.

He drew away a little, though his hands still rested lightly on her shoulders. Then he lightly touched her small locket—why it fascinated him so, she had no idea. 'I've been in London,' he said, 'for the last few days, on business that is important for both of us. I'm not giving up on you yet, Merryn, be sure of it. You see, I—'

But what he was about to tell her she never knew, because at that very moment they heard the sound of voices coming in their direction. Quickly they moved apart.

It was Gabe, with Dickon at his side. Would either of them guess what had just happened? Merryn thought not, since it was so preposterous that the Earl and she should make love out in the open that it couldn't possibly occur to them. Besides, Gabe was more interested in the fallen tree and the damage caused to the stream's bank.

'Dickon and I will get this sorted, my lord,' he said. 'We'll clear away the tree and repair the bank.'

Dominic nodded. 'My thanks, Gabe. And now, I must be on my way.' He looked at Merryn. 'Miss Hythe. I'll be in touch.' With that, he went back to his waiting horse to return to where he belonged. She extinguished any sense of growing hope, because she knew it could be crueller than anything she'd yet endured.

On reaching Hythe Farm she swiftly changed into a plain print gown, then went to clean her clothes in the laundry room. That was where Cassie found her.

'Goodness,' Cassie said, looking at what she was doing. 'Have you been rolling around in a mud bath?'

Merryn forced a smile. 'That's a pretty accurate description. Gabe's probably told you he and I were clearing out a blocked stream.'

Cassie lifted an eyebrow. 'He did. He also told me that the Earl happened to be passing by as you were doing it, with his guests. But he abandoned them and stopped to help you. I wonder—did he get muddy, too?'

Merryn felt a flicker of panic. Had Gabe or Cassie guessed what had happened? But she laughed dismissively. 'He did, yes. It was generous of him. But I'm sure he'll be quite immaculate again by now and his guests will have forgiven him completely. Where is Liam?'

'He's out riding that pony of his.' Cassie hesitated. 'I'm afraid he's not taking it well that the two of you are leaving.'

Merryn nodded. Her brother's silent bravery tore at her heart.

She needed, badly, to distract herself so she went to work on the notes she'd kept since arriving here of the number of lambs that had been added to the flock, the crops planted in the fields and the stores of hay and animal feed left in the barns. But after a few moments she pushed her notes aside and closed her eyes.

All she could see was Dominic's face as he'd said, *'I'm not going to let you go, you know.'*

Impossible.

She suddenly realised Cassie had come in to hand her a note. 'It's from the castle,' she announced. She looked excited. 'One of the grooms has just ridden over with it.'

Merryn opened it and felt rather dizzy. 'This is a message from the Earl. He wants me to go there this evening.'

'This evening?' Cassie was astonished.

So was Merryn; in fact, she felt panic. 'Yes. So he says. He's sending a carriage for me at eight. But why?'

Cassie frowned. 'Perhaps he wants to go over the arrangements for when you leave?'

Merryn was shaking her head. 'He still has guests, so he won't have time for that.' She was truly dismayed, because if she went to the castle tonight, some of his guests might recognise her as the farm girl who'd been scrambling about in a muddy stream this afternoon.

'Well,' said Cassie, 'it's my opinion you have no choice.'

So Merryn dined at six with Liam and Cassie and she couldn't help but notice that her brother was quieter than ever. 'We'll be with Ashley,' she tried to console him. 'By the sea. And we'll have some wonderful adventures there.'

'I'd rather stay here,' he'd said.

And so would she. Oh, so would she.

As for tonight, she had no choice indeed since the Earl's carriage arrived at precisely eight o'clock to take her to Castle Marchwood. As she stepped out into the castle's courtyard, she saw candlelight spilling from the windows and heard music playing somewhere inside.

Of course. He still had guests.

Enter here if you dare had been her thought on first seeing this vast and daunting façade.

She remembered all too well how her courage had failed within her on first going through the great door and now it almost failed her again. Why did Dominic want to see her? To express his regret at what had happened? Or, most hateful thought of all, to pay her for services rendered?

She realised then that from the courtyard where she stood she could see through some ground-floor windows into the brightly lit ballroom where the Earl's guests were gathered. Her heart started to thud unevenly then, because she realised that most of them were clad in strange attire. Some ladies wore hooped skirts resembling the fashions of long ago; others were dressed in more daring styles that would have looked at home on the London stage. As for the men, most of them wore dashing silk-lined capes and every guest, male or female, wore a black mask to conceal their features.

The Earl was hosting a masquerade. Everyone was in costume. She had no place here and all of this must be a dreadful mistake. She stood there, frozen with uncertainty, when the huge front doors swung open and the butler, Mr Inchberry, stood there with his wig slightly askew as usual, but his smile surprisingly warm. 'Miss Hythe,' he said. 'I have instructions to take you to Agatha, who will make sure you have everything you need for tonight.'

Little Agatha was already rushing along the hall towards her. 'Oh, miss, it's lovely to see you again!' She looked Merryn up and down. 'You're looking as pretty as ever. But come, let me make you *really* beautiful!'

Chapter Eighteen

Dominic had spoken to no one after returning from the encounter with Merryn, and instead of joining his house guests, he'd gone straight to his room to change his muddy clothes, knowing that everyone would be relaxing in the various rooms of the castle or enjoying a leisurely wander round the gardens before preparing for tonight's ball.

As usual, Hinxton had made no comment whatsoever about the state of his attire, but calmly took his garments away to be seen to. After leaving Dominic in peace for a while, he returned bearing the formal evening clothes he was to wear for tonight's event.

'My lord,' Hinxton said. 'Your guests will be gathering in the ballroom shortly.'

'I know,' Dominic said. 'I know.'

He was almost ready to go down and had his mask in his hand when Felix burst in.

Dominic blinked. Somehow Felix had got hold of a gold-and-blue brocade coat of the kind that was fashionable at least fifty years ago, but he wore no mask yet, which enabled Dominic to see that his brother was rather angry.

'I hear,' Felix began, 'that you engaged in a bit of agricultural labour this afternoon, Dom. Clearing a blocked ditch, with a mystery female wearing a muddy smock and breeches.'

Dominic took a deep breath. Exactly how much more had his brother heard? Hinxton had already tactfully retreated from the scene. Dominic poured out two glasses from the opened champagne bottle on the dressing table and said, 'News travels fast.'

Felix shook his head. 'Of course it does. Your house guests were full of the story when they returned from their tour of the estate this afternoon. Was it Merryn?'

'It was Merryn, yes. Have some champagne.'

Felix gazed at him, astonished. 'Damn it all,' he said slowly. 'You're in love with her, aren't you? I thought I might try making an offer for her, but if you're going to step in and make her your mistress, then I've no chance. And I must say I object strongly to you treating her as a woman you can pay for!'

Dominic's expression altered immediately; indeed, anger blazed in his eyes. 'Let me make it absolutely clear, Felix. I have not asked her to be my mistress.'

'What? But if you want her—'

'I intend,' said Dominic, 'to ask her to marry me.'

This time his voice was clear and calm. Felix's eyes widened in surprise. 'But you as good as told me that marriage to her is impossible, even for me as a younger son, because she's poor and besides, her father was base-born.'

'Is that Merryn's fault?'

'No. No, of course it isn't! But, Dom, you know the rules of upper-class society just as well as anyone!'

Dominic was silent a moment. 'Do you know, Felix,' he said at last, 'sometimes I loathe the society we live in, that can make paragons out of women merely because they are rich.'

Felix nodded. 'Like Teresa.'

'Like Teresa.' Dominic bowed his head briefly.

Felix went over and put his hand on his brother's shoulder. 'Listen. I know how unhappy Teresa made you. I saw for myself how awful she was to you, messing with other men and all the rest of it. But after her death, when people blamed you for what happened to her, you never said a word in your own defence. You accepted everything your enemies threw at you.'

Felix sighed. 'So all in all, you're a damned good fellow and you deserve someone who will make you truly happy. Someone like Merryn—though if she really is going to be yours, I'm extremely jealous!' Felix gave a rueful grin. 'But with you around I never stood a chance, did I? So go for it, brother. Marry her and be damned to society!'

Dominic smiled. 'I haven't asked her yet.'

'Then get on with it. As soon as possible. You're not nervous, are you?'

Yes. He was nervous as hell, in fact. But he said, 'I will get on with it. And I do believe she will be arriving here, any minute.'

Felix's jaw dropped. 'She's coming to the ball?'

'Indeed. As an honoured guest.'

Felix shrugged and lifted his glass of champagne in a toast. 'Now, *that* should put the Dragon's nose completely out of joint. But start as you mean to go on, that's the spirit!'

'Exactly,' said Dominic. He, too, raised his glass and drank. 'Cheers.'

Agatha had taken Merryn to the room she'd occupied when she'd been ill and there the excited maid helped her into an exquisite gown of cream-and-green damask, with long sleeves and a neckline adorned with lace. Then Agatha pinned up her hair to the crown of her head, leaving a few soft curls to trail down her neck.

'I've not finished yet!' warned Agatha, who was clearly enjoying herself. 'I have orders to use some powder and rouge—just a little, miss—so you'll look like a grand lady out of history, just like the others down there tonight. Only you'll be so very much prettier!'

Merryn touched the gold locket nestling against the lace trimming of the gown. 'Agatha,' she asked very quietly, 'who gave you these orders?'

'Why, the Earl himself, of course! Now, here's your black mask. You hold it up on its little stick, close to your face—you see?—and you'll be a mystery to everyone!'

As far as Merryn was concerned, the whole evening was a mystery. She did not understand why she was here and she grew more and more anxious as Agatha led her to the crowded ballroom, where the guests circled in their costumes and masks. When Agatha prepared to abandon her, Merryn caught her hand.

'Don't go. Please! I don't know anyone.'

Agatha looked a little worried, too. 'I can't stay here. The Earl did say he would be here for you, miss.'

'But I don't see him! This must be a mistake. Where is he?'

Then a voice behind her—a rich, familiar voice—said quietly, 'He's right here, Merryn.'

She whirled round. Agatha was suddenly nowhere in sight and a tall, masked figure, dressed in black evening clothes and a black shoulder cape, stood there. *Dominic.* The unfamiliar garb did nothing to reduce his allure; in fact, it was quite the opposite. He looked amazing.

Merryn felt the familiar heat of desire for this man melting her insides. She said, as steadily as she could, 'Dominic. I don't quite understand all this. I hope it isn't some kind of joke?'

He moved closer and took her hand. 'No joke. I swear it. And I'm not surprised you don't understand. I've been rather confused myself. I've also been extremely stupid.'

She didn't know what to say and besides, she didn't think she could have uttered a word anyway.

All she could think was, *I don't want to leave this man. My life will be empty without him.*

Because of the mask it was hard to discern his expression, but his words were clear enough. 'Merryn,' he said. 'I love you.'

She knew she ought to make some kind of reply. Express incredulity perhaps, or even laugh. He must have sensed her disbelief because he shook his head and said, 'I'm going to marry you.'

She spoke clearly enough then. 'I've told you. You can't!'

'I can,' he said calmly. 'I can do whatever I like. You know that I don't give a fig for London society anyway and I do have some real friends, the ones who stood by me when my marriage ended in disaster. They will be happy for me—and they'll positively adore *you.*'

She was still shaking her head. 'Dominic. You know you don't have to marry me because of what happened this afternoon.'

'I've told you,' he said patiently. 'I don't *have* to do anything. That's one of the advantages of my title and my wealth. Now listen, because I have something important to tell you. Will you come with me, to a room where we can be alone?'

She hesitated and he saw it. 'Please,' he added quietly, 'trust me.'

She lowered her head in agreement and he led her by the hand through the masked crowds of the ballroom to a dimly lit conservatory further along the corridor. 'No one,' he said, 'will notice our absence. Privately I consider these masked balls tiresome, but they do have the advantage of anonymity.'

He motioned her to a sofa. Carefully she sat, holding her mask in her lap now, and he sat there also, but turned so he could look straight at her.

'I have news for you,' he said. 'I told you I'd been to London and I went there because I'd asked my solicitor to make some enquiries.'

Lawyers—again. She felt herself shrink away and he must have noticed because he put his hand on hers to reassure her. 'Hear me out,' he said. 'I've learned, you see, that your mother's parents were in town. Lord and Lady Arvon. They are aristocrats, Merryn. Didn't you ever realise that?'

His hand was still on hers, warm and strong, but she felt unsteady. No, she didn't know that at all. She hadn't realised. She tried to gather her thoughts but found it difficult, since her memories of her mother's parents were bitter indeed. She said at last in a low voice, 'All I remember of them is what I told you: that when I was small, my mother took me to visit them in Dublin. But they ordered a servant to shut the door on us. After that I never wanted to know anything further, since they had been so hateful to my mother.

'But you did know that they were wealthy?'

'I suppose I guessed it. For example, I'd heard my mother telling my father her parents were often in London, where they had a house, I presumed. But my mother had nothing to show for it except this locket, which they gave to her, she told me, when she was very young.'

She bowed her head briefly. 'When my mother was dying, my poor father wrote to them begging them to visit her. They refused and wrote back to say that my mother had disgraced their family by marrying him. I never understood why at the time, but of course I know now it was because he was illegitimate. When my father read that letter, it was the only time I saw him weeping.' She gazed at him. 'You didn't actually meet these people when you were in London, did you?'

He was still lightly caressing her wrist. He hesitated

before speaking, but said at last, 'I arranged to meet them, yes. They were delighted to make the acquaintance of the Earl of Marchwood and made great efforts to impress me.' His expression hardened. 'I informed them that I'd met their granddaughter. I pretended at first to be quite ignorant of the way they'd treated your mother. Then—*then*, I told them I intended to ask her to marry me.'

Merryn felt her world shake to its foundations. 'Dominic. I've told you, it's impossible—'

He put one finger lightly to her lips to silence her. 'I don't believe it's impossible,' he said. 'Not for one minute. Hear me out, will you? I've told you that I love you. I've realised you're convinced that your background is a barrier to our marriage and that was why I wanted to discover the truth about your grandparents. I did it in order to show you that you have no need to worry about letting me down by becoming my wife, since your mother was the child of aristocrats. So now, I'm asking you again.'

He clasped both her hands tenderly in his. He looked uncertain, she realised—vulnerable even. 'Merryn,' he said very quietly. 'Will you marry me? I realise I've made many mistakes since our first meeting. I know I've given you reason often enough to almost hate me.'

She shook her head almost fiercely. 'Never,' she said. 'Never have I felt hatred for you. At first I was upset and afraid for Liam's future, but since then I've learned all kinds of things. I've learned how you've borne the burden of your wife's betrayal with what can only be called true nobility. Everywhere I go, I see how patient and considerate you are, with your staff and with your brother.'

'Felix?' He was laughing now. 'Not always. He's a young idiot.'

She smiled, but then her voice was serious again. 'I haven't finished,' she persisted. 'You've always been kind to Liam. Somehow he knew from the start that he could trust you.'

'And you, Merryn?' He still spoke lightly, but in his face she saw a lingering sadness that wrung her heart. 'What's your opinion of me? Dare I ask?'

'I love you,' she said softly. 'I think I fell in love with you the night they brought you to my caravan. Actually—' now she tilted her head to one side and spoke with a hint of mischief '—you were fairly rude to me, but, yes, I fell in love. Which is something I thought I wasn't capable of.'

His face darkened. 'Because of that man who attacked you? The bailiff?'

'Yes. And because of my family's problems.' Somehow she was in his arms now. He was still listening, but holding her close. 'But, Dominic, you've helped me realise these cruel memories can be overcome. We've both been badly hurt by events in our lives, haven't we? But maybe what we've endured makes us even stronger.'

'Together,' he said. 'Stronger together.'

He kissed her. It was a tender kiss, but Merryn knew that behind it lay all the passion in this man's strong, noble heart. When they drew apart at last he cupped her face and gazed into her eyes.

'I can tell,' he said, 'that you're still worried, aren't you?'

'Just a little,' she confessed. 'I know you say you don't care, but I am wondering what people will say.'

He was smiling again now. 'Oh, darling Merryn,' he said, 'haven't I told you that problem is solved? Lord and Lady Arvon cannot wait to acknowledge you as their granddaughter, now that I've introduced myself to them! At first I could see they were rather anxious you might have told me about their despicable behaviour to your mother. But they soon recovered from that and they fawned over me like the worst pair of toad-eaters I have ever met. Incidentally,' he added, 'I would have married you even if your mother's parents were farm labourers. Come to think of it, I much prefer most farm labourers to them.' He gathered her in his arms. 'I love you, Merryn Hythe,' he whispered against her cheek. 'I don't want to live another day of my life without you. I want to spend every night in your arms.' He added, 'Preferably in a bed. Not on the bank of a stream, de-lightful though this afternoon turned out to be.'

Merryn didn't know whether to laugh or cry, she was so happy. She did a bit of both until he murmured more words of love to her, then they kissed and it was all wonderful until he said, 'Merryn.'

She broke away, knowing that her cheeks were flushed and her heart was racing. 'What?'

'You haven't answered my question yet. Will you be my wife? If you have any more objections, I warn you that I shall kiss them all away one by one until you say yes.'

'Dominic,' she answered, 'I love you so very, very much. Of course I'll marry you. But I have one urgent request.' Her eyes gleamed with determination. 'I do not want my mother's parents at the wedding.'

'That, I believe, can easily be arranged,' he said. Then he glanced at the wall clock 'Damn it, I'm supposed to be hosting a masquerade party.' He drew her to her feet and grinned. 'Darling Merryn, you're going to be a truly delightful countess. I believe it's time to show the world so.'

Perhaps masked balls weren't such a dreadful ordeal after all, thought Dominic afterwards as he lay sleepily in his bed with Merryn at his side. This particular event would doubtless feature in all society's gossip sheets for weeks to come.

The splendid surroundings, the gorgeous costumes and the superb refreshments had all been much appreciated by the guests, naturally, but the highlight had surely been the appearance of an unknown masked lady—a young woman in a beautiful gown of cream-and-green damask, whom the Earl kept close to his side always.

Masks were traditionally worn until midnight, so for a while the guests were kept in suspense as to the female's identity. But as that time approached, there was a display of fireworks in the garden and afterwards everyone went inside, where, as the clock struck twelve, the unmasking began to take place. As usual everyone enjoyed pretending that they'd truly had no idea who they'd been gossiping or flirting with, but really they were all waiting for the Earl of Marchwood to unmask his companion.

The ballroom sank into utter silence as Dominic, aware of all eyes upon the two of them, drew Merryn close and took her mask away. He heard the murmurs, even the exclamations. His guests had been stunned, he knew, by Merryn's grace and her beauty.

Now, two hours later, she was half asleep in his bed, in his arms. Softly he kissed her cheek, remembering how he'd smiled reassuringly down at her before turning back to face his audience. 'Friends and guests,' he'd announced, 'I wish to present to you Miss Merryn Hythe, the woman I am going to marry.'

Yes. As simple as that. He'd been anxious at first that she might find it overwhelming, but she was his wonderful Merryn and after that she danced with him and talked with his guests, accepting their congratulations with such modesty and intelligence that all of those there—well, most of them anyway—were absolutely charmed.

He loved her, his fortune teller from the fair. He had thought he could never trust himself to love again, but now his heart was healed and full of happiness, for Merryn was to be his wife, his lover, his lifelong companion and nothing else mattered.

There had been another hour of the ball to endure, of course, but every so often she had looked at him as if to say, *I love you. And very soon we shall be alone together.*

Once Dominic had seen off his guests, Merryn agreed to stay the night at the castle in his bedchamber, which was as well since he couldn't have borne to be parted from her. A message was sent to Hythe Farm that she would be home in the morning. 'And then you can tell your brother that the estate will be his now. For good,' he promised her. 'You cannot refuse my offer now. I'll get my lawyer to arrange it all.'

When they retired upstairs he had summoned neither his valet nor a maid, because they didn't need them. Instead, they tenderly undressed one another and he made love to her, though perhaps it was truer to say that this time, she made love to *him*. 'My turn,' she whispered, after he'd all but covered her naked body with kisses. Her eyes were mischievous. 'Lie down, Dominic. On your back—yes, that's right.'

He shivered with anticipation and did exactly what he was told.

Then—dear God—this woman of his heart coaxed him into groans of exquisite torment as her lips and tongue trailed their way down his chest and even lower, down to the very core of him where his manhood was straining almost painfully. He wanted her so much. The way her tongue tantalisingly stroked his rigid shaft was sheer heaven, but it was too early to succumb to the utter delight of it so instead he drew her into his arms.

He realised she looked uncertain. Anxious, even. 'Was that not right?' she whispered. 'Did I do something wrong?'

'It was wonderful,' he told her. He smiled. 'But I need to give you pleasure, too.'

Kissing her tenderly on the lips, he rose above her and eased himself into her. Her gasps of ecstasy aroused him almost beyond control, but he steadied himself, determined to make it last, for her. At last her hips shuddered against his, then she cried out his name and he, too, reached his pulsating climax, then fell to her side, still holding her tightly. She was all his.

After a while he raised himself on one arm to kiss her tenderly. 'How do you feel?' he asked.

'Very much in love,' she murmured. She reached to caress his lips with one fingertip. 'I haven't dreamed all this, have I?'

He drew her even closer. 'I hope not. Because that's how I feel, too. I never realised that I could be so...'

'That you could be so happy?' she suggested softly.

'More than happy,' he said. 'Oh, far more than happy, believe me.' A little smile lightened his strong features. 'Do you know, I think we should get married as soon as possible. Don't you?' He saw her hesitate and he felt his spirits fall. 'Merryn?'

She laughed, that lovely laugh that had made him believe his life could be worth living again. 'Absolutely as soon as possible,' she said, 'but can we have a small wedding, please? Here, rather than in London, with just Liam and Gabe and Cassie and some of your close friends as guests? Oh, and Felix, too, of course.'

He gave a mock groan. 'Felix? *Really?*'

'Really,' she said seriously. 'After all, he is your brother.'

'Sarah is my sister,' he replied. 'But she's not coming.'

'I understand. Of course I do. But, Dominic, maybe—'

'Yes,' he sighed. 'Maybe it would be just too awful not to invite her.' He kissed her. 'I love you. Have I said that too often?'

There was a moment's silence, then the woman of his heart quietly said, 'You can never say it too often.

You are the man I think I always dreamed of, without even realising it. You are the man who makes me feel beautiful and desired and complete. You are the man who has taught me passion—and love.'

He kissed her and she kissed him back, for both of them knew no more words were needed.

Love was enough.

Epilogue

One year later, April

The activity in and around Castle Marchwood that afternoon was extraordinary, with maids and footmen scurrying in all directions in preparation for the ball tonight. Merryn had been upstairs in her private rooms, trying on the new gown made specially for the occasion. Agatha had been her enthusiastic helper and the young maid was thrilled about the forthcoming event that would, as usual, mark the beginning of the annual round of parties known as the Surrey Stakes.

Merryn was about to descend for a meeting with the housekeeper, but she paused a moment at the top of the great staircase with her hand on the freshly polished oak balustrade and recollected how her life had changed since last spring, when she feared she had gambled and lost everything in bringing her brother here to claim his inheritance.

Her reverie was interrupted when someone called out, 'Lady Marchwood!'

Looking down, she realised that Inchberry was climbing the stairs towards her. The elderly butler was extremely slow now, but he was as determined as ever to do his duty. 'My lady,' he said, 'the Earl requests that you join him out in the courtyard as soon as you can. He has, I believe, an outing planned for you.'

'An outing? But what about the ball, Inchberry?'

'I did mention that to him, my lady.' Inchberry nodded, then became aware that the action had caused his wig to slip and he hastily adjusted it. 'Believe me, though, we have everything here under control.'

Merryn stifled her amusement at his air of profound dignity. 'I believe you, Inchberry. I'm sure all the staff are doing an excellent job.'

'Thank you, my lady.' With that, the butler turned to go.

Merryn had realised, months ago, that Inchberry had actually become fond of her; his initial coldness, she guessed, had been entirely out of concern for his master and a desire to protect him from potential enemies. Her husband deserved such devotion, without a doubt.

She returned quickly then to her dressing room, wondering now what this outing could be that Dominic had in mind. Her husband, once so serious and conscious of his duty, had become positively frivolous since their marriage. Hiding a smile, she swiftly put on a blue pelisse and blue-ribboned bonnet without calling for Agatha's help. Even though she was a countess now, she would never, she'd decided, get completely used to being waited on hand and foot and hoped she never would. Then she went outside, revelling in the spring sunshine, but her heart lifted even higher when she saw Dominic there, standing by his barouche.

The driver was already up on his seat and he tipped his hat to her as she approached. Dominic smiled his usual warm smile when he saw her and came towards her, making her heart, as ever when she saw her husband, warm with happiness. Liam was seated in the open carriage, clearly looking forward to the journey, wherever it took them. He, too, had changed during the past year; indeed, he was hardly recognisable as the silent and apprehensive boy who'd arrived with her at Castle Marchwood last year. Now, he was happy and brown from the outdoor life he loved.

As for Dominic, his face was tanned, too, from the time he spent here at Marchwood; indeed, the tension that had once made his features harsh had almost vanished. He and Merryn had married quietly last summer in the local church and since then they had spent their time between Mayfair and Surrey, as was expected of a man of his rank.

But Merryn knew where he was happiest. Here, with her—or to be specific, in her bedchamber, where he spent most nights. Although lately...

She touched her stomach. Lately he'd become more protective, ever since she'd told him about the baby that was due in the autumn; although she'd reassured him, in the most loving way possible, that she was most definitely not forbidding him her bed or her caresses. 'Not ever,' she'd emphasised, kissing him to prove her point.

Whenever the Earl and Merryn went to London, Liam stayed with Cassie and Gabe at Hythe Farm. Dominic had arranged for the estate to be legally Liam's when he came of age, but until then he'd suggested that it would be ideal for the couple to occupy the old house. 'I thought it best,' he explained to Merryn, 'for it to be lived in.'

And who better than Cassie and Gabe to care for it? They had a baby themselves now and Liam spent many happy afternoons there, helping Gabe and Dickon care for the sheep and the horses. Liam had a finely bred horse to ride now, but Dolly was still a favourite. Merryn guessed that although Liam sometimes came with them to London, the city would never tempt him away from the countryside.

As her husband helped her into the barouche, she peeked up at him from under the wide brim of her bonnet. 'Now, are you going to tell me where we are going, my lord? I thought tonight's ball would take all your attention today!'

He took her hand and pressed it to his lips, sending shivers of delight up and down her spine. 'Don't *my lord* me.' He grinned. 'The ball can be left to our servants, as you very well know. Liam and I have a surprise for you. Liam?'

On hearing his name spoken Liam dragged his eyes away from the lively chestnuts harnessed to the barouche. 'Those horses are beautifully matched,' he said to Dominic. 'And they really are ready to go. Oh, yes! A surprise! And it's a good one, Merryn. You see, we're going to a—'

'Hush!' Dominic put his fingers to his lips.

Liam grinned. 'Sorry.' Then he turned to his sister. 'You'll find out soon enough,' he said mysteriously.

Merryn didn't really care where they were going, for Liam was happy, Dominic was happy and that was all that mattered. She sat beside her husband just close enough for his strong thigh to nestle against hers. It was true that London society had been startled by the sudden announcement of their marriage, but as Felix pointed out, the Earl of Marchwood had always been rather a dark horse, doing things in his own way without caring overmuch what people thought.

There were probably still whispers among some about his first marriage, though the obvious happiness of the Earl and his new Countess was enough to prove to all those with any sense that the whispers were unfounded and unjust. Lady Challoner was resigned to the situation. She had to accept, of course, that Merryn was now her superior in rank and she was civil—just— whenever family occasions brought them together. That was probably the best one could say of her.

As for Lord and Lady Arvon, Merryn had met them at Dominic's London house soon after the announcement of their betrothal. Her grandparents' eager greetings had astonished her.

'So you are our daughter's child!' Lord Arvon had said, stepping forward as if to embrace her. 'What a wonderful reunion this is.'

Dominic had put his arm round Merryn's waist to draw her close. 'Lord Arvon,' he said coldly, 'I believe you forfeited the right to a fond reunion with my bride-to-be long, long ago. We invited you here only to say that while Merryn acknowledges her relationship to you, she would prefer not to see you and your wife again. You won't be offended, I trust, if I suggest that you find yourselves unable to attend our wedding.'

That wedding had been everything Merryn had hoped it would be. It was a small affair for an earl, the gossip sheets reported with some disappointment. But Cassie and Gabe were there, Liam and Felix, too, of course, and Dominic's true friends from London, who showed obvious delight that Dominic was happy at last. Ashley came, too, all the way from Devon—dear Ashley, who'd been such a trusty ally.

Now, as the barouche rolled along between sunlit fields, Merryn was lost in thought, only vaguely aware that Liam was eagerly discussing various breeds of horses with Dominic. Suddenly, though, she was alert because she thought she could hear music. Yes, most certainly she could. Someone was playing a hurdygurdy; there was also a fiddle or two and the sound was faint, but growing louder.

She sat up and looked all around. They were in open countryside, but in the distance she could see Weybridge Heath and between patches of woodland she glimpsed some brightly coloured tents and caravans. She realised then that Dominic and Liam were looking at her, waiting for her to speak.

'It's a fair!' she exclaimed.

Liam nodded happily. 'We thought you'd like it, Merryn,' he said. 'It won't be as good as Ashley's fair, of course. But there'll be stalls and acrobats and all sorts!'

He turned to gaze out of the barouche as it drew closer, eagerly drinking in the sights.

Merryn nestled closer to her husband. 'What a truly lovely surprise. I want to see everything.'

'Really?' He put one finger under her chin and gently tilted her face towards his. 'Even the fortune teller?'

The barouche had stopped in the field next to the fair and Liam was already jumping down. 'Perhaps not the fortune teller,' Merryn said to Dominic. Then she smiled, a radiant smile that came from deep inside. 'I have no need of imaginary hopes and dreams—because I know exactly where my home is and where my heart is. With you.'

'For ever,' he said and tenderly kissed her.

* * * * *

If you enjoyed this story, be sure to pick up
Lucy Ashford's other great reads

The Viscount's New Housekeeper
The Widow's Scandalous Affair
Unbuttoning Miss Matilda
The Master of Calverly Hall
The Captain and His Innocent

Get 4 FREE REWARDS!

We'll send you 2 FREE Books plus 2 FREE Mystery Gifts.

FREE
Value Over
$20

Both the **Harlequin®** Historical and **Harlequin®** Romance series feature
compelling novels filled with emotion and simmering romance.

Get 4 FREE REWARDS!

We'll send you 2 FREE Books <u>plus</u> 2 FREE Mystery Gifts.

FREE Value Over $20

Both the **Harlequin® Desire** and **Harlequin Presents®** series feature compelling novels filled with passion, sensuality and intriguing scandals.

Get 4 FREE REWARDS!

We'll send you 2 FREE Books plus 2 FREE Mystery Gifts.

FREE
Value Over
$20

Both the **Romance** and **Suspense** collections feature compelling novels written by many of today's bestselling authors.

YES! Please send me 2 FREE novels from the Essential Romance or Essential Suspense Collection and my 2 FREE gifts (gifts are worth about $10 retail). After receiving them, if I don't wish to receive any more books, I can return the shipping statement marked "cancel." If I don't cancel, I will receive 4 brand-new novels every month and be billed just $7.49 each in the U.S. or $7.74 each in Canada. That's a savings of at least 17% off the cover price. It's quite a bargain! Shipping and handling is just 50¢ per book in the U.S. and $1.25 per book in Canada.* I understand that accepting the 2 free books and gifts places me under no obligation to buy anything. I can always return a shipment and cancel at any time by calling the number below. The free books and gifts are mine to keep no matter what I decide.

Choose one: ☐ **Essential Romance**   ☐ **Essential Suspense**
                      (194/394 MDN GRHV)   (191/391 MDN GRHV)

Name (please print)

Address   Apt. #

City   State/Province   Zip/Postal Code

Email: Please check this box ☐ if you would like to receive newsletters and promotional emails from Harlequin Enterprises ULC and its affiliates. You can unsubscribe anytime.

Mail to the **Harlequin Reader Service:**
IN U.S.A.: P.O. Box 1341, Buffalo, NY 14240-8531
IN CANADA: P.O. Box 603, Fort Erie, Ontario L2A 5X3

Want to try 2 free books from another series! Call I-800-873-8635 or visit www.ReaderService.com.

STRS22R3

HARLEQUIN
PLUS

Announcing a **BRAND-NEW**
multimedia subscription service
for romance fans like you!

Read, Watch and Play.

Experience the easiest way to get
the romance content you crave.

Start your **FREE 7 DAY TRIAL** at
www.harlequinplus.com/freetrial.